Three Ages of Woman

Sarah Willis

PIATKUS

ਉਹ *Visit the Piatkus website!*

Piatkus publishes a wide range of best-selling fiction and non-fiction, including books on health, mind, body & spirit, sex, self-help, cookery, biography and the paranormal.

If you want to:
- read descriptions of our popular titles
- buy our books over the Internet
- take advantage of our special offers
- enter our monthly competition
- learn more about your favourite Piatkus authors

VISIT OUR WEBSITE AT: **www.piatkus.co.uk**

A portion of *Three Ages of Woman* previously appeared as a short story titled 'Plaster and Bones' in the May/June 2000 issue of *BOOK* magazine.

Copyright © 2004 by Sarah Willis

First published in the United States in 2004 by
The Berkley Publishing Group
A division of Penguin Group USA

First published in Great Britain in 2004 by
Piatkus Books Ltd of
5 Windmill Street, London W1T 2JA
email: info@piatkus.co.uk

The moral right of the author has been asserted

A catalogue record for this book is available from the British Library

ISBN 0 7499 3451 4

Printed and bound in Denmark by
Nørhaven Paperback A/S, Viborg

Also by Sarah Willis

Some Things That Stay
The Rehearsal

For my mother
(who had the smarts to know I write fiction)

Reality is not so much something against which memories can be checked as something established by those memories themselves.

The Remembering Self

Prologue

Rose carries *Look* magazine over to the couch, ready to relax for a few minutes before Michael gets home. The apartment's clean, boxes unpacked, meat loaf in the oven. But wait a minute. Something's wrong. This is the gray couch from the last apartment, and what's that over there? Her father's rolltop desk? How did it get here? And why is she wearing this yellow dress that she threw out years ago, the one she'd worn in the photograph for her high school yearbook?

The magazine slips off her lap as she stands up. That chair, over there. She's never seen it before. Her mouth goes dry and she can feel goose bumps rise on her arms. She goes to the kitchen for some water.

The kitchen wavers like a mirage and Rose holds on to the counter, trying to catch her breath. When the room forms again, it's a bright, airy kitchen with all new appliances, like the ads in magazines for Frigidaires. "No," she says very firmly to the room. *No.* And then it's her kitchen again, the one in the apartment they have lived in for three days. Really, she must be more exhausted than she thought.

Rose opens the freezer door to get ice, but it's empty except for a carton of strawberry ice cream. She hates strawberry ice cream. Now she's getting mad. Who the hell put strawberry ice cream in her freezer?

She blinks, and finds she's sitting in a lounge chair in the backyard of her home in Cleveland Heights, some ten years later. She must have fallen asleep and just dreamt about that old apartment. That must be it.

Looking around, she sees that the garden along the back fence is beautiful, but there are iris, black-eyed Susans, and mums, all blooming at the same time as if they have no regard for the seasons. She'll have to ask Michael what he thinks of all this.

Michael's dead, someone says to her. *He's been dead for years.* "But he's not," she says back. Then she wonders who she's talking to.

Someone *is* talking to her though, as if she's a small, stupid child, telling her some simple fable in a kind, patronizing voice. The story, what is it—*Snow White? Cinderella?* No. She shakes her head. It's her story! *It's hers.* She hears the words "spudding a well" and "Roxboro Rocket." But what's this baloney about naming ducks? What ducks? *Stop this*, she tries to say, but her throat is too dry.

She opens her eyes.

She's lying in a bed with rails. A stranger sits in a chair

nearby. The person with the smooth, crafty voice. *I don't like this at all*, she thinks.

Rose closes her eyes. She'll go back to that apartment. That was a nice time. No matter what, she won't wake up again.

Chapter One

When my mother moved in with us two months ago, she pounded on my arms with her fists like a little kid. "Who the hell are you? What are you doing to me?" Alzheimer's. It played silly games with her memory for a while, then got mean quick, draining her thoughts and personality like a pool unplugged, until she was dry and dangerous.

Those first weeks she lived with us, I spent hours calming her down, hours calming me down. There was so much to do: meals, medicines, showers, putting on her makeup, combing her hair, the multitude of coercions to take her outside for a walk around the block, the interminable fight to get her to come back inside. "I don't live there! Where are you taking me?" Now that it's late October, we hardly go out. I frequently ask her if she wants to take a nap. She knows that it is I who needs a rest.

"No! Gin rummy!" She has forgotten me, but remembered how to play gin rummy. I hate gin rummy.

Before she moved in with us, she lived in her own home with an ever-changing cast of home-care providers until that was no longer possible, and it was suggested by everyone that she be placed in a nursing home. Advice my sister and brother agreed to, advice I couldn't take. Almost one year ago, while driving my mother back to her house after a doctor's appointment, she made me promise to never put her into a nursing home. I promised. I work in a hospital. I know what those places can be like. But really I agreed because I was trying hard to be the good daughter after spending most of my life as the black sheep of the family. So when she could no longer live alone, or even with a home-care provider, I said she should come live with us. My sister, Betsy, said, "I think she needs professional care, but do whatever you want. You will anyway." Betsy has never forgiven me, and she doesn't have Alzheimer's. Yet. She's probably secretly thrilled Mother is staying with me, proper payback for all the things I'd done. I'd call it Karma, but Betsy's not the sort to believe in Karma.

My mother doesn't remember the promise I made; she would never know if I broke it. But I have a thing about keeping promises. I've been so good at it.

And I have an ulterior motive.

I need her to get better so she can forgive me. After all that happened, we never spoke of it. During the years before she got Alzheimer's there was a delicate balance to our friendship that neither one of us wanted to disrupt by bringing up the past. I believed she would see that I was sorry by my actions, if not my words. I was waiting for the right time to speak, when I felt we could talk openly without hurting each other. The Alzheimer's came first, along with doctors and medications and visits from my brother and sister. Before I knew it, I had lost my opportunity. She had forgotten what happened to us—she has even forgotten me, although part of me doesn't believe that. How could she forget me?

I have to remind her. She still has moments of grace, when she can speak clearly for an hour or so, missing only a few words. Last week she told me a story about her father selling Bibles. It's a story I can use. But those times are rare and even then she is timeless, living in the present of her past. I wait for those moments of grace to ask her questions, to fill in my picture of who she was, so I can recreate her fairly, then give her life back to her, like a gift in a box.

If it wasn't for me, she wouldn't be alone now.

Still, most of the time she is only a great deal of trouble.

She's living here, in my house, that is not really mine. It's my husband's. I have been married to Todd for only three years.

He insists this is my home, too, but I know better. Before we even met, he sanded and stained the hardwood floors, installed new plumbing, refurbished the bathrooms. He works at one thing at a time, ignoring the rest, so although the floors are sanded, the ceilings have holes and the walls need to be repaired—but he says he has to rewire the house before he repairs the walls, and he has to repair the walls before he fixes the ceiling. If I offer help, he says he'll do it, thanks. He wants to do it right. He was just about to start on the rewiring, and moving a few windows, when my mother moved in, but now he can't because it would be too dangerous for her. My mother living with us has stopped Todd from working on his house, and made it not his house. The doorways and stairways have gates. The bathroom is labeled BATHROOM, with red marker on white poster board. All the colorful braided rugs have been rolled up and stored in the basement since my mother's shuffling feet snag at their rims. Todd's collection of exotic cacti have been moved into the basement. My mother grabbed one and had to be taken to the doctor's, screaming profanities the entire way. The basement has a combination lock on the door because of the tools and the table saw. My porcelain figurines are in the attic, also locked. And in my mother's room Depends are stacked like soft building blocks. The bed has rails. Childproof pill bottles clutter the bureau like a miniature city.

Now, instead of measuring for windows, Todd mows the lawn until it looks like a golf course, or goes for long rides on his motorcycle even in the rain. When at home, he walks around with his wonderfully strong shoulders slumped, hands clumped in his pockets, leaving the room quickly if my mother walks in. My daughter, Jazz, is sixteen, and although she's not Todd's child, they are very much alike. She, too, stays out of my mother's way, spending more time at friends', rolling her eyes, keeping her bedroom door shut. And me, I tiptoe about, trying to say I am sorry to everyone. We are a family speaking in body language. We just don't always listen to what we see.

I thought Todd might actually like my mother better after she got Alzheimer's. When she started swearing, she seemed more human, less well-bred. Throughout all my mother's years, and all her troubles, she has always appeared so well-bred. It was refreshing to see her let loose. Or so I thought, for a while.

As my mother sleeps, I sit in the chair that waits by her bed for visitors: me, and everyone she thinks I am. Her hair is curly brown, mine straight. Her lips are thin and her cheeks high, her eyes green, brighter than mine. She has a nasty chuckle, a drinker's chuckle. My mother doesn't drink anymore, but I am

Pavlov's dog. She laughs, and I see her drunk. What we see, and what we remember, is as malleable as clay; it carries our fingerprints.

She has osteoporosis, so I take calcium pills. She has Alzheimer's, so I remember for us both.

I use what I can: the stories she has told me, the stories I have inferred, the few photos of her childhood, a few letters she has saved, the things she has let slip out, the things I know without asking.

My mother would tell me I'm being dramatic, that I exaggerate everything. My brother and sister would agree. So would my husband. These are people whom I have told *I love you*, and *I hate you*, at one time or another. They can believe whatever they want. I believe everything I say.

Rose is born on the second of March, 1927, in Cleveland Heights, Ohio, and is christened Mary Margaret O'Neill. She's the sixth child, the youngest. Brent, the sibling closest in age, is ten years older; Celia, twelve years older; Ben, fourteen years older; and so on. Mary is a mistake, although such a subject is never broached in her parents' well-kept home. She just appears out of the blue and is quite a shock to all.

Celia treats her as if she's a baby doll for about two years, then abandons Mary for less childish games. Mary's mother, Francine, no longer has the energy to take care of a small child, and a plump, sad woman is hired to look after Mary during the day. They go to a nearby park where there's a small lake and a few ducks, and Mary's expected to entertain herself. She names the ducks Lily, Millicent, and Theodore and brings them bread crumbs wrapped in a white handkerchief.

On her fifth birthday the Lindbergh baby is kidnapped. At the dinner table her parents talk of ransom notes and manhunts. Her brothers and sisters whisper to each other about muddy footprints, homemade ladders, and gruesome tortures until they are told to simmer down and be quiet. Mary blows out the candles on her birthday cake, and it's decided she shouldn't go to the park anymore. Her mother keeps an eye on her at all times, even letting Mary roll a pie dough, rewarding her with a pinch of brown sugar on her tongue for a job well done. A few weeks later her parents agree that there is very little risk anyone would kidnap Mary, and she's led back to the park, free to play. She misses her mother and scrapes her knee when she falls off a swing. Iodine and a Band-Aid are the answer.

In kindergarten there are three girls named Mary Margaret. One girl agrees to be called Margaret. Mary Margaret O'Neill raises her hand. "I want to be called Rose."

Her teacher, a very old nun, claps her hands in glee. "Oh, I like that name. Rose you are!" Her parents and siblings continue to call her Mary, but to her friends, and teachers, she is Rose.

That winter the nuns take up a collection for the poor. Children bring pennies and worn pencils. A yard or two of cloth and old shoes. Grace Mott, whose father owns the bakery, brings day-old bread. But Rose, whose father owns oil wells, brings a dozen cans of salmon, a blue wool coat, and seventeen brand-new packs of crayons. The giddy nun wears the coat in school all day before giving it up for the poor.

Everyone is nice to Rose, even the class bully. Next week she brings a huge bag of penny candy.

By the time Rose is eight, all her siblings have moved out of the house. Rose's home is large and brick and suddenly drafty;

hollows of cold air drift from room to room. She starts wearing two sets of socks and two sweaters. Her father takes to calling her "Orphan Annie." Rose imagines crawling up into his lap, but doesn't.

Her father's oil wells are not the grand, deep, endless oil wells in Texas, but oil wells all the same, all over Ohio and Pennsylvania. He leases the land and mineral rights from farmers, then hires men and drilling rigs. He's a wildcatter, his own boss. It's his money he stands to lose, but his fortune to gain. After a week or two of spudding a well, he decides when they have gone down far enough and lowers the nitroglycerine into the ground. Rose gets to miss school on the days that he tosses the small stick of dynamite down into the hole to ignite the nitro. He says she's his good-luck charm; she was born the day his best well blew. It flowed for four years before it dried up. She stands where her father tells her to, wearing a heavy hard hat meant for a much larger head, and feels the ground explode. It trembles and growls beneath her feet like thunder underground, and then there's a boom she can feel in her heart as the well blows in and the black blood erupts from the earth. Sometimes this last part doesn't happen. Sometimes there's nothing down there but more hard rock, and the men shake their heads and swear in low mumbles. Her father shakes his head, too, but when they drive home, he says, "Next time. Next time we'll find it." Rose loves these trips with her father. He's a different person out in the open with his wells. At home he's quiet and stern, and she's sometimes afraid of him, but out here, he's happy and pats the top of her head.

When Rose is in fifth grade, her father leases some land that he believes will make them rich. It's the most expensive land he has ever leased, and there's hardly enough money left to drill, so he takes out a loan. The first well they dig produces nothing but a whiff of gas, but he's sure they are on the edge of something big. They move the rig a thousand feet and try again. It's a cool day in February, but it hasn't snowed for weeks and the landscape looks bare and dead. "Touch this for me, Mary," her father says, holding out the red stick of dynamite. "Take off your gloves. Give it some luck." She does. The dynamite feels dry and smells of chalk.

As her father goes up to the well, Rose stays back with the men. The ground shakes, the oil shoots up, and the rig bursts into bright and brilliant flame, fire rising in the sky like a red geyser. She is so stunned, so completely unprepared, that she screams and screams, but no one comes to calm her down. From out of the black smoke, her father walks toward them, covered in oil and dark soot. He tells her to get in the car, where she falls asleep crying. As they drive home, he says the gas was ignited by a lantern left too close. "We'll give it one more shot. There's more oil there. Trust me. There's a ton of oil there." What he doesn't tell her is that the rig is gone and he has to buy a new one. He puts their house up for collateral.

On the third try they drill farther down than he's ever drilled. Rose is not asked to touch the dynamite, but before he carries it to the rig, her father kneels down on the ground and prays. Following the explosion, there is nothing. Not a drop. It's 1938. The Depression, which hardly touched her family, is almost over. They lose their home.

Her father gets a job selling cars. People are buying cars again and he's a good salesman. They rent a house in a neighborhood across town where the streets are narrow and the lots small. The wallpaper unfurls from the walls, and now and then plaster drops from the ceilings like heavy tears. Rose's bedroom smells like something is dead under the floor. She's afraid to go to sleep at night. She can still hear the sound of her father's prayers, the boom under her feet, the silence of nothing.

By the time Rose is in sixth grade, her mother's furs are long gone. Rose goes to public school. There are no special treats for her classmates. Rose is angry at her parents, but is too well brought up to let it show.

At least I would be angry. My mother never spoke badly of her parents, even though her father left them.

One night when Rose is twelve, she's awakened by an earache. She lies still for a while, testing the pain, realizing each throb is the pulse of her heart. Moonlight patterns a cross on her blanket, and she traces this shadow back to the window frame. She wants to just lie here, discover what else she can about her room, and herself, but her ear really hurts.

Getting out of bed, she starts toward her parents' bedroom. Angry voices spill out from under the crack of their door. She's unsure for a moment if it is *her* parents who are speaking; they never argue. She stands in the hallway, her bare feet on the cold wood floor, good ear tilted in the direction of her parents' room.

Yes, that *is* her father's voice. "You're just in love with him. You always have been. Don't you see what's going to happen now? He's going to—"

Her mother cuts him off. "In love? Is that what you think? That I can't have an opinion that's not based on an emotion?

Forget it, Henry, I won't argue this one with you. First, you think he's out to ruin your business, and now that you don't have one, you think he's out to ruin your country?"

"You're blind, Francine, if you think this country can survive—"

"Oh, hush, Henry! *Enough!*"

To Rose, the words feel like sharp things breaking. Her mother loves another man. Rose puts her hands over her ears, turns around, and tiptoes back to bed. She dreams she's in an abandoned castle and her ear hurts.

For weeks Rose looks to see if her mother's blouse is buttoned properly when she comes back from the market, searches her underwear drawer for love letters, watches her mother's face to see if she smiles more often, or has been crying. Months later, as they all sit at the dining room table eating an eggplant casserole, her father says, "If Roosevelt calls for a vote on the draft, I will personally send him a telegram, in no uncertain terms, no matter what you think of the man. This is not our war." It's not the words that make her understand everything, but the look her mother gives her father, a look that echos the exact tone of sarcasm that had been in her voice that night they had argued behind the bedroom door.

But even though she now understands that her mother is not in love with another man, only the president of United States, Rose can never hear the president's name, or see his picture in the paper, or hear his voice on the radio, without a hot feeling in her chest. *This* is the man her mother might have loved. A man whom her father hates. What has he done? Why will he be the ruin of them all?

In eighth grade Rose volunteers on the *Roxboro Rocket*, the school newspaper. She interviews her classmates, writing their exact words in her notebook. "What do you think about President Roosevelt?" she asks. "Do you think we should go to war?" "What do your parents think?" Rose reads the *New York Times*. She learns the names of countries she never knew existed, like Moravia and Bohemia, and pronounces them under her breath as she walks to school, tasting the sounds of the world.

A year later, when Pearl Harbor is bombed, Rose understands exactly what it means. Nothing has to be explained to her, even her father's abrupt turnaround. Ben, her oldest brother, joins up the next day. Brent, who has already been drafted and is living in Arkansas at a training camp, writes home that he's packing up to move out. Rose interviews her father for the school paper. He says he would join up himself if he weren't too old. She asks him how old he is, and he tells her that's none of her business. She asks him what he thinks about President Roosevelt, and he says, "I am very proud of our president." Pushing her luck, she asks him who he voted for in the last election. He says, "That's enough now. Go to bed."

Her mother, standing under the arch between the kitchen and dining room, holding a dish towel, winks at Rose. It is the only time her mother has ever winked at her. Forever after, a wink reminds Rose of bombs and the beginning of war.

Although her father now loves the president, people stop buying cars because they can't get gas or parts. He finds a job selling insurance, and a second job selling Bibles. He's bold enough to offer them both at the same time. He actually makes good money. He leaves the house humming "The Star-Spangled Banner."

. . .

Rose's mother has donated most of her pots and pans for the war effort, but there are still a few left. Kneeling down on the kitchen floor, Rose opens the cupboard and hands a saucepan to her mother, who places it in a cardboard box. There's only one more saucepan and a well-worn cast-iron skillet, and they will need these, but in the very back of the cupboard, shoved far against the wall, is an old, blackened rectangular baking tin. Rose pulls it out and hands it up to her mother.

"No," her mother says. "Not that one."

"You never use it," Rose says. "It's old."

"Not that one," her mother says again. Her mother takes it from her, holding it against her chest. "It was my mother's."

Rose's grandmother died a long time ago, when her mother was very young. Her grandfather had died a month before her grandmother, both deaths from influenza.

"It was on the counter by the sink the day she died," her mother says. "She baked me a birthday cake. I thought that if my mother had baked a cake, she must be better, but I was wrong. She was dead in her bed, and I just didn't know it."

Rose's mother stands clutching the pan to her chest. Rose stays quiet, studying her mother's face, intrigued by this woman who hardly ever shows how she feels, except behind closed doors. Also, Rose loves stories about great losses and great love.

In a calm, indifferent tone, Rose's mother tells her the story of the pan. "I was wearing my Sunday clothes, but they smelled musty. I'd dug them out of the bottom of the laundry basket. My father had just died. My mother was sick, but she refused to go to the hospital. She said they would never let her come home if she went. So I got dressed and went downstairs. The wood-stove was out. I didn't know how to light it.

"The pan was covered with a thin towel, and I peeked at it.

It was a cake, my birthday cake. So everything must be fine, I thought, and I sat and waited for everything to be fine.

"My aunt Rebecca came. She went upstairs and came back down a little later. My mother was dead, she said. I had to come home with her. She asked me if I had a doll I wanted to bring. She was trying to be kind. I said no, I wouldn't go, but she took my hand and pulled me off the stool. I twisted out of her grip and grabbed the pan with the towel still on it. I took it with me to my aunt's. I never went back in my house. My aunt wouldn't let me eat the cake. Germs, she said. My mother's germs."

Now Rose's mother turns the pan over in her hand, feeling its weight. "A few bullets?" she says, in a strange dead voice that sends shivers up Rose's spine. "A half a helmet? I suppose I should, but I can't. I'm sorry."

Her mother looks down at her, and still holding the pan in one hand, brushes her fingers against Rose's cheek. Rose is as surprised by this as the story of the pan. Her mother's fingertips are rough. She thought they would be soft. They were, once. "I'll give you the pan, when you get married. You'll take good care of it, won't you, dear?"

"Yes," Rose says. She will, too. It's just the kind of thing Rose knows she will be good at, and she is very touched her mother has assigned her this task.

A few years after my father died, when I was fourteen, I made brownies in this pan that my grandmother gave my mother, and took them, in the pan, to the school bake sale. I never brought it back. When my mother found out that the pan was lost, she went nuts.

"I should have known you'd lose it! I told you how important it was! It was my mother's. My *dead* mother's. Don't you care about anything?" She slammed a cupboard door and kicked a wall, leaving a dent.

I didn't remember her telling me about the pan. If she did, it was long ago, when I was very little. How could she expect me to remember something for so long?

I bought another baking tin for her birthday, the same size and shape, but new, to become old, handed down from mother to daughter until it was old again. She said, "It's not the same thing."

I didn't mean it to be the same thing. I meant it to hold the story of me saying that I was sorry for losing part of her past. When we packed up her stuff to move her here to Todd's house, it was nowhere to be found.

I told Todd the story of the first pan, when I couldn't find the new one. He said, "You baked brownies in a pan that was over eighty-five years old?"

"Yes, I did," I said. He nodded, but his eyes were amused. We continued packing my mother's things in silence. I was mad at him for days, until I needed him to take Jazz to the mall for me.

Chapter Two

My mother rolls over and her arm flops through the opening between the bed's rails. I take her hand. Once, at the zoo with Jazz, we watched two chimpanzees reaching through their separate cages to hold hands. All day I wondered how long those chimps held hands. How long was long enough?

Her eyes flutter and open. "Tiffany?" my mother says. Tiffany was one of the women we had come live with my mother, those years she began to lose her mind, those years I thought of, then, as more than I could bear.

"No, Mother," I say. "It's me. Jenny. Your daughter."

She nods. "Oh, yes." But I know this nod, this vague reply. She doesn't know who I am, but she has good instincts and has been confused long enough to be wary. "Where's Tiffany?"

There's fright in her voice. She's on the edge of losing the reality she thinks she has.

What's the point? I wonder, giving up. "She'll be back in a minute. Would you like some ginger ale? Are you hungry?" I prop her up with an extra pillow.

She nods again.

I knew she would be thirsty and have brought one up with me. I open the can, fill the plastic cup halfway, and stick in a straw, pretending I'm a soda jerk at an old-fashioned drugstore. It's a game I'm getting good at, being anyone but me. Sometimes it's easier this way. Sometimes I quite enjoy it.

"Here you go, ma'am. Just as you like it."

"Thank you, miss," she says with hesitation, as if a few words might betray her.

I'm right. She's forgotten me again. But being right doesn't make me feel so special. It used to. I used to be so good at being right.

"Are you hungry?" I repeat.

"No. Just thirsty."

These times when she's alert but not raging are when I want to ask her questions, prod her, get her mind working again, but if I ask the wrong questions, she'll get confused and upset. The problem is, I never know what the wrong questions are.

"Can I go home today?" she says.

What can I say to that, that won't upset her? I think about the advice people have given me. Don't contradict a person with Alzheimer's unless you absolutely have to; let them believe what they want. I could tell her she'll be going home tomorrow, and tomorrow she won't remember. I tried that before—we spent the day packing up her belongings, then I put them all back again at night while she slept.

But Alzheimer's patients are easily distracted. I reach under the bedside table for the photo albums. They're old and thick, the covers in browns and reds, and I imagine the pictures tumbling out of them like fall leaves; pressed memories, whole vacations in a picture or two. I wonder if these pictures shrink our memory, until the entire trip to the amusement park is that wave from the carousel. What happened to the hours when no one took pictures?

I grab a red album because it doesn't look as familiar to me. I open it, and there are Simon and my mother at some party. I know my mistake immediately, but as I go to close the album, my mother says, "Let me see."

I could distract her again, but part of me says, *Okay, let her see.* I lean over the rails and place it in her lap. The light in the room comes from an overhead globe, designed to cut the glare so there's nothing to hamper the vision of what she sees but her own mind. "Who is this man?" she asks.

"That's Simon," I say. I don't want to explain that this is a man she dated after my father died. I'm not ready for my father to die. I'm going slowly through her life so I don't get there too fast. I distract us both. "Do you want me to brush your hair?"

"Yes."

I close the album. "Let me get you turned around." This takes some time. I have to put down the rails, fold back the blankets, move her legs to the side and over the bed. I get the brush and climb up. Brace her against my legs so she leans slightly backward, not forward. Brushing her hair, I clock off five minutes, just as I did when my daughter was two: a plastic book in her high chair after lunch could keep her happy for five minutes while I did the dishes. Ten minutes with a pot and a wooden spoon. Five minutes to change her diapers and clean her bottom. These minutes added up so slowly, but they eventually got me there; to her nap time, a time I always found emptier than I expected.

My mother's hair is not the thin of old age, and I think while I brush the almost grayless brown curls that maybe this is what she sees when she looks in the mirror, just the hair of her youth.

Jazz walks in the room. "I need twenty dollars," she says.

I concentrate on brushing my mother's hair, try to relax my arm. This is nothing uncommon, this request for twenty dollars, but I always want to get upset. I want my daughter to think she's asking for too much. When did five dollars become ten, ten become twenty? When did I stop being sure what she spends her money on? "What for?" I say. And then, under my breath, as if my mother can't hear me, "Say hello."

"Hi, Nana," she says, with just a quick look and a nod. "I'm going to a movie."

"Movies cost twenty dollars?" I don't know why I say this. I already know she'll find some claim to my twenty.

"Aurora, Turtle, and I are going to Mongolian Barbeque for dinner."

"I'm making dinner."

She rolls her eyes like I'm crazy. "It's Saturday."

I know what she means. I never make dinner on Saturday. Saturday is my day off. Sometimes Fridays, too. I welcome any excuse not to cook. I have cooked dinners since I was twelve. "But I *am* making dinner tonight, and I expect you here."

"What are you making?"

Once again, I know what she means, and it's satisfying that I know her this well. She's testing me. There's no food in the fridge for dinner. She's calling my bluff.

"Fettuccine with clam sauce and garlic bread." Garlic bread's a stretch since there is no French bread, but a little garlic butter on white bread, then toasted, will do. But this is only a game, this answer.

"Well, I made plans. Aurora's mom's already on the way here, and Turtle's dad's picking us up after the movie because I knew you wouldn't drive, so I took care of all that. So don't blame me 'cause you decided to cook dinner on a Saturday for the first time in a hundred years."

"Don't talk to the help like that!" my mother spits out. "How dare you! You apologize to Tiffany right now, Jennifer, then go to your room!"

Jazz and I are stunned into silence. How could my mother make this mistake? This girl standing here, this downright beauty, this near woman who astounds me every day with the fact that she came from me; how can my mother think Jazz is me?

Jazz rolls her eyes. "I need twenty dollars. I'm being picked up in two minutes. I'll pay you back if I have to with my birthday money." On the turn of a dime, her face changes. She smiles. She bats her long mascara-covered eyelashes. She pouts her purple-colored lips. "Please, Mommy?"

I nod, and she turns to leave with a skip, turns back with a smile. "Thanks." She knows this much, to thank me. She's no dope. She's just rude and spoiled, and I love her too much. I am still brushing my mother's hair. My arm aches.

"She shouldn't talk to you like that," my mother says. "She can be very rude. I just don't understand her at all."

For the first time in days she can fully express herself, and I want to run screaming from the room. My mother never understood me. I want to grab her shoulders and shake her. I want to say, come back to me and I will tell you why. I imagine her brain like a friendly prison guard. *Don't go there*, it says. *You'll get hurt.*

I fix her hair, get her into the chair, turn on the TV, and tell her I'll be back.

That woman and the rude child are gone. Rose thought the rude child was her daughter, but now she's not so sure.

That *was* her life, that story the woman told, and it was a little too close for comfort. The woman couldn't have known about her listening to her parents talking in their bedroom that night, her fear that her mother was having an affair. Rose doesn't like it, that these things are being said about her, even to her.

And the stuff about the ducks was plain dumb. She never named ducks. But before she can work up any real steam, any real anger, she becomes unsure what the woman said, and what she didn't; what Rose listened to, and what she really heard.

There's a fluttering in her chest. Was she just a child, moments ago, and now she's old?

How old?

Rose looks at her hands, and her breath catches in her throat. *No.* She looks around the room. Is she in a hospital? No. It feels like a home. Whose home?

She closes her eyes, thinking she'll go back to that time in the apartment, but instead she's listening to her parent's talking loudly from behind the bedroom door. Her ear hurts, but Rose stays where she is. What are they saying? Why is her father mad?

Rose is a child again. All over again. And again.

. . .

I'm washing dishes when the phone rings. At the same time, Todd walks into the kitchen through the back door, done finally with raking the leaves, a project that has taken him much longer than it should considering the backyard's not all that big. He's wearing a black T-shirt with the sleeves cut off, even though it's chilly outside. He's warm-blooded, my husband, but more so, he's proud of his muscles and the tatoo that circles his left upper arm. He also has one pierced ear with a small diamond. I like the tough look, but right now pieces of torn leaves are stuck in his hair and there's a smear of dirt across his cheek, as if he's in camouflage from my mother. Hell, it might work.

The phone has rung three times. I get it. It's the nursing home. Kethley House, the good one.

"We have a room for your mother. Are you still interested?"

"Yes," I say. "We are." What else can I say, with Todd standing here? I've made him a promise, too, that if the very best home becomes available, we'll put her there. *Put her there.* It sounds like I'm moving a couch.

"Well, we would want her to move in on Tuesday. Will that be possible?"

Three days away. It's too sudden. Todd raises his eyebrows, turns his calloused palms up, asking who it is. I mouth *nursing home* to him. His eyes widen and he nods. I have to be careful what I say.

"Yes, I think so."

"Well, we would need a commitment from you. There's a long waiting list."

"I understand. Can I get back to you?"

"I suppose. But I would need to know by Monday morning. No later."

"Fine," I say. "Thank you. Thank you very much. I'll call you then."

When I hang up, Todd looks at me. "Well?"

"Kethley House has a room available. Tuesday." My chest hurts with these words. Words do hurt. That nursery rhyme is a big fat lie.

"And you didn't say yes? What's up with that?" His shoulders hunch up, stay there, waiting.

"I'm not ready," I say.

"No one ever is."

When I don't say anything else, he closes his eyes and sighs, slowly shakes his head. He's still standing by the back door. He won't come in further until he takes off his mud-spattered boots, and he hasn't yet. "She needs to go into a home," he says, gently, trying hard not to start a fight. "I'm not telling you anything you don't know, Babe. If you need me to be the bad guy, then, okay, I'm the bad guy."

"No, I am," I say. "I'm just trying to make up for it."

"For how long?" he asks.

"I don't know. Another month?"

He shuts his eyes again, closing me out. I notice the age spots above his temples that mark him as older than he looks. Todd has one of those soft, boyish faces which belies the biker image he's going for—like a rottweiler wagging his stubby tail, you can tell he's friendly. I think my mother's the only one in the world who doesn't like him, and only because she forgot she did.

"You said that last month, Jen. Hell, can't you see she's consuming you? We don't have friends over. You never laugh. You act like you're guilty for everything, for being married to me, for being happy. She's making life miserable for all of us."

"It sounds like *I* am." I go over to the window by the kitchen table. The backyard looks beautiful, the green grass uncovered and fresh looking, the flowers rimming the yard like a frame for all that perfect green. I imagine Todd removing the last leaf by hand, standing back and looking at a job well done. He likes manual labor. He planted the garden before I moved in. I don't know anything about flowers. He said those white flowers are called *mums*. I remember him telling me that because that's when I told him how I was never allowed to call my mother *Mom*. It was *Mommy* until we were old enough to call her Mother, at about the age of six. She hated the word *Mom*. Thought it a lazy, common word. *Mom* is what Jazz calls me.

"I'm sorry," I say. "Look, I chased away every man she could have ever married. She's alone because of me. I have to do this."

"Hey, I've heard the story. I don't buy it." He stomps his feet to get off some of the dirt, but it looks as if he's marching in place. Leaning over, he starts to unlace his boots. After he changes into his moccasins, he'll step outside and shake off the backdoor mat, and then sometime tonight he'll clean off his work boots in the basement with a stiff brush. He says he can't afford not to take care of his things. He's said that more than a few times in the last two months, since I haven't been working.

"Okay, let's get practical about this," he says. "Don't you have to go back to work sometime? We could use the money."

I pause, not saying what I'm thinking—that for the past three years I've been making twice as much as he does, which means, technically, I could take off three years and we'd be even. "They'll understand," I say. "They'll give me more time. We'll be okay."

"Will we? It's not just money. You know what? I don't mind the overtime. It gets me out of the house. Is that what you want? You want to be on your own again, feeling tough and independent? Am I in your way here?" He's bent over, untying the second boot, looking up at me through a mop of soft brown hair. He looks like a big kid who needs some hot tomato soup. Mad, though. He's definitely getting pissed.

"No. You're not in the way. That isn't what I said."

Todd hardly gets angry like this, but it is happening more often now. He really lost it a few weeks ago when my mother pulled the curtains down in her room, tearing the hardware right out of the wall. She wadded one up and stuffed it in the toilet. He actually swore at her. He's a sweet man, so when he turns mean, he frightens me. I am afraid I have mistaken him.

In the silence between us, Todd stands up, sticking his hands in his pockets, making fists under the fabric, as if he has carried large rocks into the house. The muscles in his upper arm pulse.

"One more month? Please?" I say. "It took her longer than I thought to adjust to moving here. She trusts me now. She may not know who I am, but she trusts me. One more month?" I pause, look at him. "I'd do the same for you. Is that so bad?"

He grins, those oh-so-even teeth a reminder of how I love him at the oddest moments. "You're good. Very good," he says. "But will they wait a month?"

"I'll call them back. I'll ask. I'll beg."

"I just want what's best for us, as a family. Is that so bad?"

"No, that's not bad at all. It's just that she *is* my family."

He doesn't say anything, but I can tell he's giving in. He really doesn't like to argue. He's so good. How can I be so lucky?

I walk over and hug him. It's all the words I have.

While Todd's in the shower, I call my sister Betsy to tell her that the nursing home has a room available. I've talked to her more in the last year than in the last thirty-five years, if talking is what you call it. We trade necessary information. She and her husband will pay two-fifths of the nursing home. My brother and his wife will pay another two-fifths. The rest will come from my mother's Social Security, and a bit from Todd and me. Todd's embarrassed by this, so I only talk to my sister about these things when he's in the shower, or not home. Which gives me plenty of time to talk with her, but I don't.

I time this call perfectly. They're not home and I get the answering machine. I leave a message about the nursing home, and then I tell her I've decided to keep Mother here a bit longer anyway. In a very sweet voice I say, "Call me back, if you want to talk about it." Her turn.

We don't sit down for dinner until eight, and it's takeout Chinese. A mistake. Both the timing and the choice of food. My mother gets edgier as the day wears on. I think there's a constant struggle to make sense of what she sees—the details of the present must hammer away at her fragile belief that the time is somewhere around 1960, a time period she finds the most comfort in. I should have fed her earlier. Hindsight now. And Chinese food is not easy to eat; the rice splutters to the floor with each forkful. Bean sprouts trickle out of her mouth. Soup just spills, like soup.

It's not so much that her hands shake, which they do, but that her right arm is weak; the spoon and fork are never held quite level. The mess doesn't actually bother me so terribly—I have cleaned up worse—but it bothers her.

"To hell with this!" she hisses.

Her sweet, kind-lady disposition was fraying by five, when she insisted on a shower even though she already had one. Thus the late dinner.

"If they're going to feed us . . . crap, then I'll just starve. Who cares? Not me." She tosses the spoon with the wonton and more broth than I thought possible across the table. She has wicked aim. It lands directly on Todd's plate.

Todd holds perfectly still, but I see the tension in his jaw. Very slowly he slides his plate to the side.

"I would like to go home now," my mother says.

"Hey, lady, that's fine with me," Todd says. "I'll drive. Let's go." He pushes his chair back, picks up his plate, carries it into the kitchen.

I wonder where all the rules have gone. Such as, when you sat down for dinner, it was a time to be polite and grateful. And the rules I thought I understood about Alzheimer's? Last week I asked her a simple question about her brother, Uncle Brent. I wanted to know if he got hurt in the war. She couldn't get two words right in a row. She talked about someone called Jimmy. Who was Jimmy? And did Jimmy get hot-pierced with the thingamabob in the left pat-her-thigh, or Brent? Why is it that whenever she wants to tell me how bad I am, she has every word she needs? Who made these goddamn rules?

Todd comes back from the kitchen. "I'm going on-line. Thanks for dinner." He always says thanks for dinner, even when it's takeout and he's gone to get it. He's a wonderful guy. My mother, who believes Todd is going to drive her home, is walking toward the front door.

I feel like I'm going to cry, so I shake my head hard like you do when you're driving and nodding off. I don't know why it works, but it does. The tears I felt coming hold off, waiting for the next time.

"Mother," I say as she rattles the brass front door handle. It's locked.

"Will you stop calling me that!" She turns at me. Her eyes are squinted tight with hatred. "How dare you!" she says.

With those words, I lose thirty years of growing up, and suddenly I am fifteen, dressed in torn bell-bottoms and a flowered peasant blouse, wearing white lipstick; I can feel it on my lips like a pale thought. On the floor, tattered and stomped on, are the remains of a carton of Viceroys, each and every cigarette broken in two. "How dare you!" she shouts at me. I have destroyed every cigarette in the house and poured two bottles of scotch down the sink. The house reeks of booze and nicotine and the heady smell of my own power. But really, I am powerless. Every nerve in my body twitches. I can hardly swallow. My heart is right in my throat; I can feel it choking me, I can feel it wanting to be thanked. I believe the things I say, and do, can change her. Holding my breath, I wait for her to say, "Oh, God, you're right. I'll never smoke again. I'll never drink another drop." But I was not, nor ever have been, a reason for her to live.

"Mrs. Morgan," I say now in my calmest tone. My father was a director, and even though he died when I was young, I learned a few things from him, and inherited a few more—my straight hair, my long fingers, rosacea. "Would you like me to take you upstairs? Would you like to play gin rummy? Take a shower?" I say the last just to amuse myself. I need a little amusing. I need to make fun of her, even though she doesn't know it.

"Gin rummy," she says, holding her chin up. "Gin rummy," she repeats. I unlock the gate at the bottom of the stairs. I have asked Todd not to step over it when my mother's watching so she doesn't get any ideas, but I have asked so much he must feel it's only right to ignore something. As I walk my mother up the stairs, I realize I would rather give her the third shower of the day than play a single game of gin rummy.

Passing the computer room, I see Todd furiously typing away to someone I don't know, telling them something he needs to say, to someone else besides me.

He was on-line last night, too, and the night before.

Chapter Three

When I wake up, Todd's already gone. He bought the motor-cycle after his divorce, and since then goes off riding on Sunday mornings, sometimes with a friend, but more often than not, alone. When we started dating, he'd take me along, but I'd keep telling him to slow down, or complain about the wind. He started saying I didn't have to go if I didn't want to, and finally I took the hint.

His first wife left him, stunning him with the news she was having an affair. He told me he would never allow himself to be blindsided like that again. There was an edge to his voice that said he understood quite well that I had left people behind; that he would leave before he was left again. I remember that every Sunday morning when I wake alone. Might he, right now, be riding with someone who doesn't complain about the wind, who doesn't have a crazy mother? Someone he was talking to on-line last night? I'm too tired to think about it, and it's still just morning.

He burned the mattress after his wife left him. He dragged it out to the backyard and set it on fire. The fire department came running, sirens blaring. He got a good stiff fine and had to see a psychologist. As sweet as he is to me, he admits he used to have a bad temper. He won't explain exactly what that means. "I never hit a woman," he says, but that's all. He says he works hard to stay calm, that he's a changed man, and I believe him. I think he told me that story so that I would never take him for granted. But the Todd I know is so good, that I do.

I left him a note on the counter to pick up some chicken breasts at the grocery on his way back, and I know he will. Bug-splattered from the ride, he'll go into the store and get the chicken. Even if he's having an affair. I shake my head. Go away stupid thoughts, I think, and it works for a while.

I take my mother to St. Ann's for Mass, even though I wasn't raised Catholic and my mother has sworn off religion for the rest of her life, not knowing that the end of her life would be a foggy, veiled version of the beginning of her life, and she now gets to relive her mistakes, like believing in the grace of God.

My mother's dressed in a white blouse and a green plaid wool skirt, stockings, and black thick-soled shoes with good traction. I hold on to her arm. I don't know who I am today. We haven't discussed it yet.

We sit in a back pew in case something happens. She might start talking out loud. She might remember that she hates God.

This would not be a good place for her to suddenly remember that.

If my mother is Catholic again because she has forgotten she isn't, what about confession? What does she confess? Old sins? What becomes of the new sins she can't remember? Does confessing that she took the Lord's name in vain when she found out she was pregnant, being forgiven for it a second time, null and void the fact she spat at my husband last week, calling him a "dirty bum"? Where does ignorance fit into His game plan?

My mother makes a soft guttural sound and begins to stand up. I press a hand on her thigh, and she sits back down in the pew. The priest begins to speak and I look at my mother to see if she is going to do anything else, but she just closes her eyes.

Something about the church bothers Rose. It's her church, St. Ann's; she knows that—as she walked up the steps past the towering pillars and under the high stone arch she felt so proud to belong here, still . . . She looks around again. The stained-glass windows are the same as the last time she was here, but the tabernacle is new, rather plain looking if you ask her, and where are all the candles? And the people; none of them are familiar. Where are the Spencers, who always sit in the same row with her family? And where *are* her parents?

Oh, she's in the wrong pew! Way in the back instead of in the fifth from the front, where they always sit. She begins to stand, but a woman presses her hand on Rose's thigh and she figures there's some special reason to sit here today, but she's forgotten what it is. Still, what an odd thing for a perfect stranger to do! Looking down at her lap, Rose is startled by her clothes. They're so dowdy. Jeepers, she's wearing a wool skirt, like her mother's! What exactly *is* she doing here today? It's not Jimmy Miller's funeral, is it? No, that was last month. She remembers that.

The priest begins to speak, and Rose closes her eyes against the strangeness. *Dear Lord in Heaven*, she begins to pray, and then doesn't know what to ask him for. *Help me*, she tries. Will that work?

The sound of the priest's voice soothes her, and she keeps her eyes closed. Nothing could really be wrong, could it? She's in church, after all. If anything is wrong—if *she* has done something wrong—she simply has to ask Him for forgiveness.

Even with the protection of God, Rose's life is a cascade of ration stamps, air-raid drills, headlines in bold letters, and death. The Bibles her father sells are piled along the walls like extra bricks to keep their family safe. On her way to and from school each day, she passes the Millers' house, remembering Jimmy Miller's face: narrow with bad skin and small eyes. His funeral last month was her very first funeral. She couldn't keep her eyes off the flag-covered coffin. She felt her skin crawl at the thought of being inside that small, cramped space. There were latches on the sides? Why?

Still, at the funeral she felt more alive than ever before. Everything was so bright, so clear. Just brushing a hand against her cheek she felt shivers ripple right through her whole body. Her tears for Jimmy Miller were warm and comforting, and so salty. Had she ever tasted her tears before? Rose was surprised by the thought that feeling alive had nothing to do with happiness.

There are good times, too. She and her friends go to movies

every Friday and Saturday night. Musicals with film reels about
the war that make her heart pound. There's so little gasoline to
go anywhere that boys siphon gas tanks in the dark, and sometimes everyone has to get out of the car and push it up a hill.
Rose and her best friend Penelope swear on her father's stacks
of Bibles that they will sign up as WAACs as soon as they graduate. They write to Rose's brothers, and soldiers they have never
met, on the thin, blue airmail paper. The letters they get back
have whole pieces cut out, and she and Penelope fill in the mystery words with the images of film-reel war. Sometimes they forget the war altogether and paint their toenails red on Sunday
nights, listening to *Fibber McGee and Molly* and giggling like
little kids. "It ain't funny, McGee!" they shout while elbowing
each other in the ribs. Penelope says, "Gosh darn it," when she
gets mad, and Rose says, "Hell's bells!" On Mondays they go
back to school, where there are announcements on the loud-
speaker. A boy's name, a moment of silence.

Her father is gone for long periods of time, and her mother
cleans the house day and night. Dust under a chair sends her
into a fit. She cleans the corners and the toilet and the stove with
toothbrushes that she soaks in cups filled with Clorox bleach.
The air is so sharp in Rose's throat that she drinks tea three and
four times a day. Penelope asks her if there's something wrong
with her mother, and Rose gets so mad she doesn't speak to
Penelope for days.

Sometimes her mother calls her by her sister Celia's name,
not correcting herself. Rose's brothers are at the war, and her
sisters have all moved out of town. She imagines their lives as
brave, and interesting, and a bit messy.

· · ·

One morning in late April, Rose walks to school and looks up at the sky. The trees have buds on the tips of each branch, and they remind her of the tightly rolled horoscopes that sit on the counter at the corner drugstore. She jumps, trying to touch the curled leaves, even though she knows she can't jump high enough. A leap of faith, she tells herself, pleased with the thought. Her smile fades as she realizes that school will end soon; she needs to find something to do this summer or she will go mad. She could get a job at the drugstore, or the dry cleaners, but she wants something more, something daring.

That day the assistant principal calls Rose into his office. He introduces her to a new student, an odd-looking girl with deep-set eyes and a white cane. Beatrice is blind and will need some-one to escort her through the halls to her classes. Rose has been selected. She's proud at being asked, as if she's been drafted for something brave. At first she's nervous being near this strange, blind girl. Rose describes everything to Beatrice: the gray color of the walls, the windows above the classroom doors, the water fountain. Beatrice feels the metallic silver case of the water foun-tain with her fingertips, presses the button, touches the water, then finally takes a sip. Suddenly Rose sees the water fountain as a strange and beautiful thing. She knows she will have to touch the water herself, when no one's looking.

Beatrice is not afraid to talk about herself, a fact that sur-prises Rose. She tells Rose about Parma, the town she moved from, and about her family. None of her brothers or sisters are blind, a fact that somehow relieves Rose. As they walk from class to class, Beatrice tells Rose all about a summer camp for the blind, where they have arts and crafts, and swim, and follow ropes around to get from building to building. It is only an hour from Cleveland, in Geneva, Ohio. She says the camp counselors are the greatest.

On the way home from school, Rose notices that the buds on the trees have opened. Above Rose's head are thousands of glossy, light green leaves. She says "Amen," as if this new growth is a prayer that has bloomed right out here in the open sky.

At home she gives her mother a hug and tells her about her plan to be gone for the summer, volunteering at a camp for the blind. "You're a sweet girl, Celia," her mother says. "I'll miss you. Will you come back next year?"

"Yes, Mother," Rose says.

"Well, that's nice." She brushes her hands on her starched white apron and looks around for something to do. Rose's chest flutters like a bird in a cage that will soon be opened. She's worried about her mother, but she doesn't know what to do. She goes upstairs and pulls her suitcase out from under the bed, where she has stored it like a girl placing a slice of wedding cake wrapped in a napkin under a pillow hoping to see the face of the man she will marry; Rose has slept above her suitcase with the dream of leaving home.

That summer Rose learns to guide the blind, memorizes the braille alphabet, and spends her days with people who can't see her. They put on plays and do pottery, they row boats and go on hikes. She spends one day with a blindfold over her eyes, inching forward, her hands out like the antenna of ants. She learns she can laugh and make jokes with people who at first seemed so sad and pitiful. She writes letters home like the airmail letters she received from soldiers, leaving out whole pieces of her life; when she tries to write the words that might explain how she feels, they seem less than what she meant, and she crosses them out so no one can see even the curve of a false word. She's writes the facts, lists the activities, as if her day were a simple series of scheduled events instead of a headlong tumble through mistakes and small successes.

When she goes back home at the end of the summer, she thinks she is a different person. Her mother is still the same. Her father is not around.

Near the end of twelfth grade, President Roosevelt dies. Rose is terribly upset; it's more than just losing a beloved president—she has lost a man who has, in her fantasies, replaced her father. Rose is not one for silly fantasies; this is the only one she has. Her father's away so much, he could be just about anyone. Rose's mother cries for days after Roosevelt's death, but she still cleans. Sometimes she twitches when her husband is mentioned. Rose is the editor of *The Black and Gold*, the star swimmer on the swim team, and the first female president of the student council. She thinks her father would be very proud of her.

She goes to church and prays, but sometimes it doesn't make her feel better. Sometimes she wonders if God cares much about her at all. What an awful thought. It is she who has to care about God. What is the matter with her?

Before Mass is even over, my mother is crying. Thin streams of tears streak her cheeks. I don't know what the priest might have said that brought this on. I take her arm and lead her out of church. When I ask her what's wrong, she doesn't answer.

Jazz is still sleeping when we get home. Todd's still gone. Upstairs, I help my mother get out of her Sunday clothes and into sweatpants and a sweatshirt. She hates sweatshirts and sweatpants. The only way I can convince her to wear them is to buy the kind that look fancy; white with gold lamé designs and rhinestones. I need her to wear something easy to get in and out of, no buttons or zippers or tie strings.

I ask her if she would like to sit downstairs in the living room with me and have some coffee. She nods. She hasn't said a word since we entered the church.

I carry out two cups of coffee, placing one on the table by her chair, a table I inherited when I sold her house. There wasn't much furniture left since she sold it off piece by piece to support her "traveling bug," as she called it. The years before her Alzheimer's developed, she rented out her house and roamed the country, staying in rooming houses or with old friends, and living with both Betsy or Peter for a month now and then. When in Cleveland, she stayed with me for a few days, just enough time to sell some furniture.

All that was left besides a few odds and ends was this table, a bookcase with glass doors, and my grandfather's rolltop desk, which Betsy and Peter said I could keep. Well, sure, I thought. It weighs a ton.

"I want . . ." my mother says. She doesn't know the words for what she wants; I don't know what I want.

"Sugar in your coffee? I already put in two teaspoons." I should let her watch me put it in so she'll believe me, but I never do. She takes the first sip with puckered doubt. I told Todd that my mother trusts me now. It was a lie.

"Did you like church?" I ask. *Did you ever love me?* I want to say.

"No," she says, and I take in a breath and hold it, then remember what I really asked her.

"Why?"

"Because!" she says, as if my tone had been accusatory. I

drink my coffee. She drinks hers. We glance at each other across the few feet that separate us. *Wary*. That's the word that comes to me. As she loses her words, I have begun to collect my own. A bunker of words. The more words I learn now the more I will have when, and if, I begin to lose my own.

All my grand and noble plans to reconstruct my mother are built on the hope that someone will do the same for me. Not someone. Jazz. And when it comes time for her to tell the story of me, I want her to remember I took my mother in.

"What did you do after high school?" I ask.

"I worked as a . . ." Her eyes go hazy, and I am about to supply the word *secretary*, because, of course, I know, but then her eyes light up and she smiles like a kid getting the right answer. "Typist! I worked . . . where those men worked."

"A law firm?" I ask.

She nods briskly. "Yes, yes."

And this I never understood; why go from wanting so much, being the first female president of the student council, to being a secretary? But it's a question I haven't probed too deeply, because it can turn around and bite me. I worked for eight years in a Free Clinic, and now I work at a hospital. The ideals of free health care went out the window when I had to support my daughter.

"Why?" I ask now. "Why a typist?"

"For the . . ." She rubs her fingers together. I see the word *money*. "I needed the . . ." and she does the motion with her fingers again.

I say, "Money?"

She nods theatrically, like I'm stupid. "Yes, the . . . the money. It doesn't grow on . . ." With the back of her hand she waves to the window. *Trees*, I say to myself, then repeat it in my head, forcing an image of a tree, connecting those synapses one more time but not really believing I could ever forget the word *tree*.

"Why didn't you go to college?"

"He wouldn't pay."

"Who?" I ask.

"My father."

"Why?"

"It was a waste of a girl's time." She's gaining her words back. Sometimes she's like a car, you just have to get her jump-started.

"Why a waste?"

She looks at me quizzically. "Who are you?"

She's trying to distract *me*. This works two ways. "Did you forgive him?"

"Did I forgive who?"

"Your father. Did you forgive him for not sending you to college?"

She snorts. "I did just fine. I was a typist. Did I tell you I was a typist at that place? I was very good. I typed eighty things a minute. I made good . . ." She rubs her fingers together without a hitch in her sentence. "I got lifted up twice in the first year. The others were jealous of me." She pauses, and I wait. "Of course I forgave my father." But then she sags, as if every muscle has lost its strength. "I should have gone to . . ." She makes the shape of a box.

I supply the word. "College."

She nods. "I wanted to be a . . ."

I wait, not knowing what she wanted to be.

She puckers her lips together, mad. Closes her eyes. About ten seconds later she shouts, "Journalist!" The effort seems to exhaust her and she starts to cry. I wince and think, *shit*. Still,

I'm glad to have found this out, this thing she wanted to be. Her crying gets louder, and I hand her a tissue. Time for distraction.

"Did you ever have a cat?"

She pauses. I imagine neurons trying to find the word *cat*, the textile sense of fur, the sound of a purr, the warmth in her lap. It takes a while, but then she nods. "Lovely." She raises a hand as if she is going to stroke something. "Lovely."

That's what she named it. At thirteen I had to go outside at night and holler, "Here, Lovely. Here, Lovely, Lovely." My mother was always the one to name our cats. Peter, Betsy, and I had no choice in the matter. When I was twenty, I got two cats and named them Pine Cone and Buttons, because when I was twelve I promised myself that someday I'd get a cat and name it either Pine Cone or Buttons, and of course, true to myself, I had to take it one step further. Get two cats. I never loved them as much as I should have because I named them out of spite.

I may have named Jazz out of spite, too, but I love her.

But Lovely's not the cat I was thinking about. "What about that other cat, wasn't it called Tulip?" I can't help testing her, testing this Alzheimer's. It wasn't called Tulip.

My mother looks at me. She's suddenly young, smiling. A giggle on her face. "No, silly. Daisy. It was Daisy. My first cat was Daisy. White, with a yellow spot. Right here." She points to her forehead. "A white cat with a yellow spot." She taps her forehead again.

"What happened to Daisy?" I ask.

"Oh, she's dead," my mother says with a flick of her hand.

I look at her closely. This *is* my mother. This is exactly what she *would* say to me, just to show me that I hadn't gotten to her, to show she was tougher than me by far. All our troubles stem from the fact that neither one of us could give in first.

"How long ago did she die?" I ask.

That gets her. She blinks and looks around the room. A worried look crosses her face. Then she squints at me. "Who the hell are you?" she says.

Both my parents have asked me that. Neither of them meant it in a philosophical sort of way.

"You know, Mrs. Morgan," I say, "I heard you were quite the femme fatale when you worked in that law firm."

She straightens up in her chair as much as she can. The curve of her spine holds her in the slight shape of a question mark. That will be my spine someday. I sit up straighter, too. We look like two women with sticks up our butts.

"I dated my fair share of . . ." She doesn't even try to make the shape of men with her hands. "Nothing wrong with that."

"You broke their hearts," I say, nicely, as if that's what's expected; to be beautiful and break men's hearts.

"I suppose," she says. "They got over it."

After graduating high school, Rose volunteers at the camp for the blind again, but it's only a summer job. She needs a real job, since her father won't pay for college. There seems to be very little money for the amount of time he works. The thought that he might have another life somewhere crosses Rose's mind like a plane across the sky. She would have to peer too closely to be sure of the shape of her father's deceit. She can't and doesn't want to. The thought that her father might be keeping another woman is a vapor trail, it disassembles; she can't touch it.

Rose gets a job as a secretary in a law firm in downtown Cleveland. She and her mother pass by each other going into and out of the kitchen. They say "Good morning," and "Good night," and "How are you?" Neither wants an honest answer.

One day Rose finds a white kitten with a yellow spot on its forehead meowing pitifully in a parking lot outside her office building. A kitten in downtown Cleveland won't last an hour, so Rose picks it up and brings it home. Her mother gets hysterical.

"You must take that thing out of here at once!"

"But it's a kitten. It's been abandoned."

"Out! Out! Out!" Her mother stamps her feet like a child, pointing to the front door as if Rose doesn't know where it might be. "It will have fleas! Get it out of here right now!" Then, frightening to Rose, her mother bursts into tears and pleads. "Please. Please get rid of it." Her eyes are hollow and huge. Stunned, Rose nods.

Rose walks out of the house holding the kitten, and takes a bus to her friend Ginny Hartman's apartment, where she lives with two roommates.

"I have to stay with you until I find a place of my own," Rose says, skipping any greetings, losing, for once, her inbred politeness.

"Huh?"

"I found this kitten and my mother won't let me bring her in the house."

Ginny takes one look at the kitten and says, "Oh. All right. Come on in." The next day Rose buys a cot from the Salvation Army and sets it up in the living room. Leaving the kitten at the apartment, she goes home to pack up.

"You're moving out?" her mother asks. She hasn't asked where Rose was last night. She hasn't used Rose's name. Her mother is fifty-eight, and something more than senile. Rose has seen her talking to the furniture, the plants, the dishes. She drives to the market and the hairdresser's, but she doesn't go anywhere else. Some days she seems perfectly normal. Three out of four days her mother is just fine, Rose tells herself as she packs.

"It's time," Rose says. There are two suitcases at her feet. She holds a stuffed tiger under an arm, trying to decide if she can carry all this and an umbrella. It's not raining, but it might, someday.

"Well, good luck," her mother says. Rose leans over and kisses her mother on the cheek and walks out the door.

She holds her head up as she carries the two suitcases, the stuffed animal, and the umbrella to the bus stop. She could have waited until later, asked a friend with a car for a ride, but she didn't. She's nineteen and can certainly take care of herself.

Rose doesn't have to sleep on the cot for more than a week before one of the roommates announces she's pregnant and going to live with an aunt. Rose is appalled at the girl's stupidity but wishes her luck—then gets her bedroom. She turns the mattress over and buys new sheets.

Ginny, and the other girl, Dot, are popular. Rose is popular, too, but knows she's considered a tease since she doesn't put out. Too bad. She couldn't care less what other people think. She reads the *Wall Street Journal* and the *New York Times*—just to get both sides of the story. But slowly—she doesn't even know how it happens—she's spending more money on clothes, spending time looking for matching shoes and a belt. She gets her curly hair professionally straightened and bobbed. She begins to drink. A martini with a green olive is a pretty thing.

Girls rotate through the apartment like door prizes being

handed out at the fair. Ginny Hartman moves out, and six other girls come and go. Now there's only a girl named Laura, and Rose. Laura is blond and slim and dates a series of bashful boys who duck their heads in the morning when they leave. Some come back a few times—Rose recognizes the bobbing tops of their heads, the shy waves. She wonders where Laura finds these boring young men. Even after three or four drinks, Rose has the good sense to stop a boy's ambition to defrock her. She's not interested in boys—or getting pregnant. It's not to say she doesn't like to have fun, but she has some standards. She holds a memory in place that gives her the strength to say no.

It was during the second summer at the camp for the blind. There was a girl named Susan who was not pretty but would never know that. She was trying to explain to Rose how blind people see.

"When I touch your face, I learn things about you. How kind you are, by the easy way you allow my touch, and by the fact you don't tense up. I can feel, on a face, anger, thoughtfulness, disdain, goodness, and evil. Here, give me your hands." Susan had taken Rose's narrow, thin hands in her own soft pudgy ones, and lifted them to her face. "Close your eyes. Now, feel my face." Rose did what all the other blind people at camp had done to her. Felt from the top of the head down; the soft kinks in her hair, the flat skin of her forehead, the deep outer sockets of her eyes, the curve of her cheeks; moving her thumbs toward the center of Susan's face to feel the shape of her nose, lightly brushing her lips, ending with the boney ridge of her jaw. It was strange, and interesting, but what Rose felt was the shape of the face she already knew. With her eyes closed, Rose saw only Susan: not pretty, but sweet. Blind. A curious girl who could easily share her own thoughts. But Rose already knew this. She tried to feel something more, working longer at Susan's face than the blind ever had done on her. Susan had laughed. "Okay, I guess that's enough. What did you learn?"

"Nothing, I guess," Rose said, because she *had* learned, here, that lies showed in voice. "But thanks."

Susan smiled. A big, wide smile showing all her crooked teeth. "I thought so. But that's okay. We get some privileges, being blind, so we can pity you, too."

But the thing Rose remembers best is the next thing Susan said. "Someday, when I fall in love, I will touch someone's face and feel their soul."

Rose is waiting for that moment, when she can feel someone's soul in her fingertips. Then she will get married, and make love for the first time.

Chapter Four

"So, how many marriage proposals did you get?" I ask my mother. I say it simply, as if it's a light thing, with no weight; a porcelain cup of air. I want to know if Simon asked her to marry him, or Joe, or any of the other men I scared away. How serious was my crime?

She glares at me. "I know who you are! Don't pull this shit on me. Don't . . . Don't you . . . dare!" With this, she throws her cup of coffee on the floor. It breaks, as cups do. At least there's no carpet for the coffee to stain. The dark liquid pools on the floor like an oil slick.

"Mother!" I say, with the voice of a woman reprimanding her mother for throwing her cup, and of a child calling out in the dark. "Look what you've done." I head to the kitchen for paper towels and a garbage bag.

From behind, I hear her mimic me in a singsong voice. "Look what you've done! Look what you've done." Then, under her breath, "Your mother. As if!"

When I come back into the living room, she's climbing over the gate to the stairs. Once over, she straightens up, raises her chin, and walks regally up the steps. When she's halfway to the top, Jazz comes down in that skipping, easy way that I can no longer do. I have to watch my feet.

"Hi, Nana!" she says to my mother, loudly and a bit too cocky for my taste.

My mother just nods once, and continues up.

My daughter looks at the mess on the floor and laughs. "She sure is nuts."

Should I tell her that my mother is only what we will become? I bend down to pick up the pieces.

"I need a ride to Caeli's," Jazz says. "We have to work on our history project. Jesus, Mom, you should have made her clean it up."

I'm going to try a new way of dealing with my daughter's caustic remarks. Don't say anything at all, let her words hang in the air; that way she'll hear just how nasty she sounds. I read about this idea in a magazine while waiting for my mother in the doctor's office last week. So now I just look at her. She rolls her eyes. She's *imagining* what I would say, and getting huffy about it.

"I can't keep asking Caeli's mom for rides, just 'cause you don't want to take Nana along. I'd really like to get out of here before more things break."

I try not to say anything, but my jaw hurts. I'll probably get TMJ from this.

"I can't take you right now," I finally say.

"Oh," Jazz says, crossing her arms under her ample bosom, a bosom that is beginning to make me nervous. "So, now you're going to ask me to wait until Todd gets home, and then you'll take me?"

I was.

"Then you'll ask *him* to take me, and he will. He does anything for you. Doesn't that embarrass you?"

"Jazz! That's enough!"

"Mom, all I'm asking for is a ride that takes five minutes. When was the last time you drove me anywhere?"

Wrong question. "Just two days ago," I say. "Who do you think took you to the swim meet?"

"That was Wednesday! Four days ago! Oh, forget it. I'll walk. I'll hitchhike. I'll goddamn fly before I ask you again!" Jazz grabs her backpack and throws it over her shoulders. I can hear the thud when it hits her spine, a sound that makes me immediately guilty. Still, she shouldn't yell at me.

"Jazz! What is your problem? I just asked if you could wait a—"

"I'm done waiting. What should I wait for? You to tell me you can't do it anyway? You to ask Todd? For Nana to die? What do you want me to wait for?"

I can tell she knows she's gone too far by the way she stops talking, and her face looks stony. I don't say anything. The trick works. She blushes. I know she's embarrassed. She's my daughter.

"I'm sorry I said that," she says. "But I have to go to Caeli's now. We have a lot of work. It's worth two hundred points. I have to go, or I'll fail history."

"I'm ready," my mother says, coming down the stairs. We

both look at her. She's wearing her little brown hat with the torn veil, the sweatshirt top with the big gold leaf, and the green plaid skirt. I look over at Jazz, warning her not to laugh, trying not to myself.

"Move this," Nana says, waving at the gate across the steps.

"Oh, Jesus," I say. "Fine." Unlatching the gate, I ask her if she would like to ride along while I drop off Jazz.

My mother stops moving in mid-step. She does this a lot now when I ask her questions. It's too much for her to walk and think at the same time—not enough brain cells left to do both. I've told Jazz that that's what pot will do to her.

"You can drop me off at the place," my mother says. "I need some . . ." She pauses, points to her legs.

"Stockings?" I say. "You need stockings?"

"Yes. Just drop me off at the place."

"The store?"

"Yes, the store."

"Sure, Mother, I'll just drop you off at Kmart. How's that? You can walk home or get a cab. Will that be all right?"

I can't believe I said that. Now everyone's silent, letting *my* words hang in the air. Looking down, ashamed, I see that my mother is barefoot.

"All right, Mrs. Morgan, we'll go to the store, but first let's get your shoes and coat on." There, that sounds like a caring daughter, doesn't it?

On the way to Caeli's, no one talks in the car. I drive through three yellow lights. When the car comes to a stop, Jazz hops out, shouts thanks for the ride, and runs up the driveway.

"Who is that girl?" my mother asks.

. . .

Rose watches the pretty, dark-haired girl wave to her. Funny, she thought that girl was called Tiffany, but now she's not so sure. She must be a new secretary or something. She'll have to find out tomorrow. It's been a long day at work. Maybe that's why she's so tired and out of sorts. She loves her work, but really, it takes the strength out of a girl. Thank goodness she has arranged to get driven home today. If she just closes her eyes for a minute, she'll feel better.

But at work the next day Mr. Wellman crooks a finger in Rose's direction, beckoning her over. Jack Wellman is the head of the firm where's she's worked now for four years. Instinctively, she looks down to check on her outfit. Is her skirt too short? No, she's just fine, thank you.

"Miss O'Neill," he says, leading her into his office. He doesn't ask her to sit down, but does close the door. She can feel her palms dampen.

He clears his throat. "Mr. Burt Thompson will be joining the firm tomorrow, and I'd like to offer him our very best secretary. You're it, my dear. Mr. Klein has agreed to let you go, with a little arm twisting I must say, so please show Margaret Gallagher what needs to be done to take over for you there. You'll need to clean up Mr. Halverson's old office today. Make sure it looks spiffed up. Mr. Thompson's bringing us a great deal of clients, Miss O'Neill, a great deal of prestige. We'll want to keep him happy. It'll be a lot of work, I'm sure, keeping up with him, but if anyone can do it, you can. By the way, you'll be getting a raise. Not enough to buy a new car, I'm afraid, but maybe a new hat." He chuckles.

She laughs along with him. "I don't even have an old car yet," she says, but he just smiles tightly and glances back at the papers on his desk.

"Well, thank you," Rose says, and steps out of the office. She's quite flattered she's been chosen. She just wishes the other secretaries had heard what he said.

Mr. Thompson arrives the next day, followed by office boys carrying a load of boxes. He's about forty-five and smells of expensive cologne. Rose thinks he's nice enough, but it bothers her that he calls her *Honey*. "Honey, get me a cup of coffee," "Honey, bring me the Klippard file." "Honey, come here a moment." Rose is twenty-two and dating a sweet guy named Cliff, and even he's not allowed to call her *Honey*.

After one week of this, Rose is ready to explain, as nicely as she can, that her name is not *Honey*. He's on the phone all day, but at three o'clock, Mr. Thompson calls her into his office.

"Close the door behind you, would you, please?"

She does. The light through the wooden blinds is dim from the gray of a advancing snowstorm. On the floor are a dozen boxes filled with files and plaques and Certificates of Merit. She'll have to find someone to hang up all those plaques.

"Would you take a letter for me?" If he had said *Honey* this time, she would have begun the careful speech she has planned. It starts out: *Mr. Thompson, I regard you with the highest respect, and I hope we can work together for a long time, but I'd like you to understand that calling me* Honey *is out of place*. . . . She imagines she would only have to get that far before he would raise a hand and say of course, she's right, and ask her what she would like to be called, at which point she will say, *Rose would be fine*. But now he simply says, "I'll need this letter typed and sent out today." Rose says that will be no problem at all.

The problem is where to sit. There are boxes on the two leather chairs that face his desk. There's a clear spot on his desk, and he pats it. Well, it won't be the first time she's sat on the edge of a desk to take dictation.

It's a long, windy letter, full of two-dollar words. She's taught herself shorthand and is quite proud of that little feat since she never went to secretarial school. When he says, "That's all, thank you," Rose braces a hand on the desk so she can slip off with out stumbling. Just as she's about to move, Mr. Thompson covers her hand with his. "Freckles and green eyes. Are you Irish, honey?"

Rose tenses. She's furious—at him, and the fact that her little speech is now quite inadequate. She pulls her hand away, but before she can open her mouth to say something—she's not sure what—he touches her cheek. Still sitting on the damn desk, she slaps him, a good solid whack, then thrusts herself off the desk, takes a step and stumbles over the nearest box, falling flat on the floor. She looks up to see steely blue eyes staring down at her and no hand to help her up, which she certainly would have refused anyway. She stands up, not retrieving the pad of paper or the pen, and walks out of the office. Who should she go to, to report this? Not a single name comes to mind. There are five other lawyers in the firm, all who would profess outrage, but not one of them would do a damn thing about it. Mr. Thompson has brought with him clients worth hundreds of thousands of dollars. Rose is a good secretary, but there are hundreds of thousands of secretaries.

She gets her purse and leaves without a word. She calls in sick for three days. In her mail, on Monday morning, is a note terminating her employment, with a check for sixty-two dollars; a two-week severance pay.

. . .

Every Sunday, Rose goes home to visit her mother for dinner. She brings a bottle of wine, and they drink from her mother's spotless wineglasses. The two of them sit at the highly polished mahogany table with the overstarched white linen napkins and the too-shiny silver serving spoons laid out like bright dreams.

Each time, when she leaves, Rose writes her name and phone number on a slip of paper and places it on the table by the phone. Her mother never calls her, and the next Sunday, the piece of paper is nowhere to be found.

One Sunday, when her mother opens the front door, Rose's father is there, standing in the hallway. She hasn't seen him for almost a year.

"How's my little girl?" he says. He has a mustache; a thin line across his upper lip. Both the mustache and his hair are darker than she remembers, both slick with some kind of hair grease. It looks ridiculous—he's at least sixty-five. Who is he trying to fool?

"I'm not a little girl," she says, thinking of Mr. Thompson. This is her father, she reminds herself. He just doesn't seem like her father at all.

"Of course you're not, sweetie. But you're my little girl. And not married yet? Are you having fun, at least? Dating the boys?" He lights his pipe, his cheeks sinking in as he puffs hard to get it started. The pull of his cheeks and the smell of his pipe are so familiar that Rose wants to cry, to touch him, to say, *Oh, Daddy, come back to us. Stop whatever you're doing and come back to us.* But then he winks at her. "You're a pretty girl, Mary. I bet you're having a real good time, huh?"

"What are you doing back here?" she asks. She doesn't care that she sounds a bit angry. Her mother stands by the front door, which is still open. Rose knows her mother is desperate to

get the lit pipe out of the house, maybe even the man holding it.
It's a new thought—that maybe her mother is happier without
him. Living in her own life.

"Had to meet with the big guy, then I'm back out again,
probably tomorrow."

Rose has a bizarre thought—that the big guy is God, since
her father sells Bibles. She laughs, a harsh giggle. She would like
to go home now.

"What's so funny?" he asks, eyeing her over his pipe. His
eyebrows are too thick for the rest of his image—they are an old
man's eyebrows. She pictures a cartoon weasel, smoking a pipe.
She almost laughs again. It's just nerves. She could really use a
drink right now, she thinks, feeling the weight of the bottle of
wine in her hand. It feels solid and comforting.

"Nothing's funny," she replies. "Are you still selling Bibles?"

"Nah, that stopped a few years ago. Just insurance."

"Dinner is ready," her mother says, closing the front door
with a snap of her wrist. "Why don't we eat." It's not a question.
Suddenly Rose's mother is in charge. She tells them where to sit,
passes the platter, moves them through dinner at a fast clip. She
removes the plates without asking if anyone wants seconds.

"Dessert?" her mother says, carrying in a pie, already cut
into pieces, plopping it down on their plates before they have
time to say yes or no. Her mother is trying to get them through
tonight quickly, right into tomorrow when her father will leave.
Maybe this woman, who Rose starts thinking of as Francine,
has not been abandoned by her children and her husband.
Maybe she has finally gotten what she wanted all along. Rose
could understand that. Rose has not been in love yet, and isn't
quite sure it exists at all. She has dreamed of love all her life—
but it is certainly something grander that what she sees now.

. . .

Rose writes to her brothers and sisters, sends her nieces and nephews birthday and Christmas presents. In turn, they invite her to come visit; *why don't you come visit us someday*, they write, not *next week*, or *for Easter*, or *for the third week in July*. Rose knows exactly how they were raised: to offer proper invitations, not to accept improper ones. She also understands that the distance between them is greater than miles.

Her brothers and sisters, and their wives and husbands, and their children, hardly ever come home for visits. Her sister Celia did once, three years ago. She and her husband and three children had to move into a hotel before the end of the first day. They never came back. In all the bright and cheery letters Rose writes and receives, no one mentions their mother's dustless home, that the silver-framed photos of their family gleam behind glass so clear that the faces are masked by the glare of sunlight through the clean, vinegar-smelling front window.

After walking out of the law firm, Rose has given herself three weeks to relax before looking for a new job. Her twenty-third birthday is next month—it's time for a whole new life to begin. She will never work for lawyers again. She thinks about working for the newspaper and sends them a résumé, but she never hears back. In the classifieds there's a notice for a receptionist at the local theatre. The theatre. Well, why not? That sounds fun. She desperately wants to have fun. She wants to go out dancing, to movies and plays. Why not work where it would be fun?

Rose looks around the apartment that she shares with Laura and decides to move out, get a place of her own. She never doubts for a second she'll get the job as a receptionist. By the end of the week she has moved into a new apartment, a one-bedroom, and will start work at the theatre in two days. Standing in the middle of her new living room, she shouts, "Yippee!" It's the stupidest thing in the world to shout, so she shouts it again and bursts into a fit of giggles to beat the band. She forgets to go to her mother's for Sunday dinner. She even forgets to call her mother and tell her she has a new address and phone number. She doesn't really forget, she just doesn't do it.

The next week she feels so guilty she brings flowers along with the wine. "How kind," her mother says. They say grace. They eat their meal. When Rose leaves, she doesn't write down her new number on a slip of paper to be thrown out.

The theatre is alive like nothing Rose has ever seen before. During the day, actors pace the floors, stretch their voices, gossip in back hallways, rehearse on empty stages that gradually fill with props, furniture, and hand-painted sets. Techs argue as they carry flats down narrow halls. Saws buzz and hammers wrench nails from wood to be used again and again. Costumes are cut and sewn, recut and dyed. Wigs are dusted and men walk around with makeup on. Flats fall over in dress rehearsals and spotlights miss their marks, but sometimes everything goes perfectly and the feeling of a small miracle makes everyone happy and excited. Actors, techs, designers, directors, and the women who work in the box office go out for drinks in the evening, not getting home until two in the morning. The few men who call her Honey call *everyone* Honey.

A little after a year at the theatre, Rose is fixed up on a blind date with a pharmacist, a man with a grin like the Cheshire cat;

his mouth seems too large for his face, and when he smiles it's almost frightening. She says yes to the second date because there is something fascinating about him, she just can't figure out what. He lives an hour away, and at first they see each other only on Saturdays nights; months and months of Saturday nights go by, and each time he drops her off at her apartment building, kisses her goodbye at the front steps, waits in his car until she turns on a light, then drives off. He hasn't tried anything sexual; at the end of five months they have only kissed—and awkwardly. His mouth is just too big; his lips are like soft mountains, and she's not ever quite sure where she is. But he's a terrific dancer.

One Saturday night, he tells her that he loves her. "You're Catholic, right?" he says, immediately after proclaiming his love. He know this, so she just nods. "I don't believe in sex before marriage," he says, then, "Will you marry me?"

Rose is intrigued by the fact that he's still a virgin. They must be the last two adult virgins on earth, so maybe they are meant to be together. She hasn't felt his soul in her fingertips, but that's just a fantasy of her youth, and she is no longer young. She's twenty-four. She tells him she'll think about it, then a week later she says yes, because she's curious what saying yes might do to her. Will she love him more if she says yes, and will he want to make love to her, if they're officially engaged? Neither of these things happen, and they go on as usual, except now they see each other on Fridays and Saturdays. She begins to notice that he doesn't have much to say, and wonders why she didn't notice it before.

Ten months after her engagement, Rose realizes there's nothing fascinating about him at all except for his large mouth. She breaks off the engagement as kindly as she can, and finds she doesn't have the energy to cry about it for very long. A month later she begins to date again, with a vengeance. She's sick to death of being a virgin. She almost goes all the way with an actor, a funny man who can make her laugh so hard she cries, but she pulls out of his arms at the last moment, saying she's sorry. God, she's so stupid, she tells herself that night as she sleeps alone. Why not do this, this thing her body so obviously wants? Why does she get so tense? A few weeks later she sees her funny boyfriend kissing an actress behind a stage wall. Heck, she will give up on men. She's done with them. She's just fine on her own, thank you. She gets another cat and names him Pinocchio.

On February 7, 1953, the same day that Ginger Rogers marries Jacques Bergerac, Rose walks down the theatre's back stairs, and a man she's never seen before comes bounding up, carrying a stack of scripts under one arm. He has a mass of black hair, and his skin is the pale white that actors tend to have, shaded by dark stubble as if he's forgotten to shave this morning. He has deep-etched wrinkles splaying from the corners of his eyes and his ears are large. His eyes are black, like his hair. Rose notices every detail in the few seconds they stand there on the stairs staring at each other.

"And who might you be?" he asks Rose.

"Rose O'Neill," she says.

"Well, I'm Michael Morgan. Very pleased to meet you, Rose." He steps up one step and offers her his hand. There is a slight electrical twitch as they touch—from the dry air, she tells herself firmly. His hand is warm. His knuckles large.

"It's nice to meet you, too." She wants to ask him what he's doing here, on the stairs in her theatre, but the cat has caught her tongue. He's smiling at her, looking her right in the eyes. She slips her hand out of this much-too-long handshake and blushes. Damn it, she hates blushing.

"Well, Rose, I'll be seeing you," he says with a smile.

Rose feels she has been promised something. She goes back to the box office and acts as if it is just an ordinary day. At lunch a girl from costumes mentions there's a new director at the theatre, a man named Michael Morgan who's been hired to direct just one play. "*Romeo and Juliet.*"

That night Rose has a vivid dream. She's an old woman who remembers loving Michael more than anyone she has ever loved, and being loved that way in return.

Chapter Five

My mother's fallen asleep in the car. We haven't gotten her stockings, but she'll never remember she wanted them. And she looks so peaceful I don't want to wake her up. Just as I used to do when Jazz was a baby and asleep in the car, I turn on the classical station and drive out of Fairmount until the houses become sparse and the trees take over. It's raining gently. The trees are a deep, wet black, and the gold and orange leaves plait the ground like a damp Oriental rug. Crows perch on the high, bare branches as if they own the world.

I pull into the gravel parking lot of a public park and turn off the car. I feel very alone here in this car, the rain blurring the world. I miss my daughter; the baby asleep in the car seat. I miss my mother, the one I used to know and tried so hard to love. I miss knowing my aunts and uncles and cousins. I miss my husband. I wonder why his name has come to me last, and why I should miss him at all, since he has not left me, yet.

She's still asleep when I pull into my drive. I close the car door carefully behind me so it doesn't bang and wake her up. She should be safe enough in the car for a few minutes. Todd's motorcycle is parked in the garage. I'd like some time alone with him, just a few minutes would be nice.

He's in the kitchen, showered and changed, so he must have been home for a while. He's wearing those well-worn jeans that look so good on him, and a soft, old gray sweatshirt that's older than our relationship. I don't say anything, just walk over and lay my head against his shoulder. Then we both speak at once, in whispers; we are so used to being overheard. "Hello," he says. "She fell asleep in the car," I say. There's a moment while we're both afraid to speak again, to interrupt something that feels fragile and rare. He tilts up my chin and we kiss. His hands are calloused and rough against my skin, and our kiss gets pretty hot. It's been a long time since we kissed like this.

Todd nods his head toward the stairs. "If she's asleep, can we . . . ?" I know what he means. Why can't he ask me to make love, and why can't I say I love you? We are like kids, whispering, sneaking about. Afraid to speak about sex or love.

I want to go upstairs with my husband but my mother could wake and wander out of the car, go off looking for her home, which, in her case, could be anywhere from the East Coast to the West Coast, depending on her time frame. If I go upstairs with Todd, I'll be worrying the whole time and he'll know it. But I have a better idea. A way to make him happy—which will make me happy—and keep my eye on my mother.

I smile as slyly as I can and walk over to the kitchen door to look outside. The car's in full view through the window. The bottom half of the door is wood. I can see my mother's curly head of hair pressed against the glass of the car's window. She's still sleeping. "Come here," I say to Todd. He looks puzzled. "Trust me," I say.

I move him around so his back's against the door and he's facing me. I glance out the window one more time. She's not moving at all. I have a few minutes, at least. Enough time. I lower myself to my knees. I hear Todd protest, a sound between a *no* and a moan. I say, "Shhh," and unzip his fly, then reach inside his pants to pull out his cock, which begins to straighten out immediately. I put my mouth around it and hear him moan again. His hands are on my shoulders, and they press down. I know him; he is torn between thinking I shouldn't do this— please just him—and wanting this so badly that his hands hold me in place against his better instincts. I can't help grinning with his cock in my mouth. I hope he can feel that, my grin. It takes less than two minutes. There's a lot of moaning coming from above me. If someone were in the backyard, they could see me through the hall window. It makes me very excited.

When I'm done, I stand up. He opens his eyes, a stunned look on his face. Behind him, through the window, my mother still sleeps.

"That's not quite what I meant," he says.

"Complaining?" I ask.

He shakes his head no. "But what about you?"

"I got what I want," I tell him. And I did. As hot as I am, I am completely satisfied. I feel so accomplished. I've made my husband happy and not taken the chance that my mother might wander off. Superwoman. I feel like cooking something complicated and serving it on fine china. Painting the bathroom. Cleaning the whole basement while singing opera.

"Will you keep your eye on her while I go brush my teeth?" I ask, blushing. He nods. We're both smiling idiotically, but upstairs, as I look in the mirror, I start thinking. I didn't say I love him, and yet I'm satisfied. Is he? As I come back downstairs, I see the red light blinking on the machine. It's my sister. "Jennifer," she says, "it's me, Betsy. I guess you're not home. Just remember, money's not a problem. If the home's good, maybe you should get her in there before things get worse. Let me know what you decide to do. Bye." I hear in her voice the same relief that was in mine, that she got my machine, not me. I also hear the question in her statement: *Why* are you not home, her voice says. And I hear a smugness in her mention of money. And I wonder how many sisters have to say who they are. I've read all this into a fifteen-second recording of a voice a thousand miles away.

Why the hell do I want her to like me so much? I erase the message.

Rose wakes up and wonders what she's doing in a car. Panicked, she looks around. *Where am I? Whose car is this? Is it locked?* She's not the type to wake up in a strange car—or is she? Reaching for the handle to open the door, Rose cries out at the sight of her wrinkled hand. Just moments ago she was twenty-six. She was happy. In love. Not old!

She opens the car door, so relieved it opens that her chest hurts. She steps out, but her legs don't work as she thought they would. Old legs! She stumbles and falls to her knees on the grass just outside the car. With the shock of hitting the ground, she remembers getting into this car with a nice lady and her daughter. The word *daughter* sticks in her head like a piece of taffy—thick, something she has to pull at to get the taste and shape. My knees hurt, she thinks. Then she can't think right. Just the word, *stockings*. Then, *daughter*. She begins to cry, and calls out, "Michael!" But he's dead. She knows that. Then she doesn't, and she yells his name louder.

A lady comes running out of the house. "Mother! Are you all right?" Rose knows this is her daughter. Just look at her face! Of course it's her daughter. But then she wonders, *is it?* She could be wrong. Maybe the woman said *Mary*, not mother. She has already forgotten what was said. If this woman is not her daughter, and Rose calls her Jennifer, they will think she's crazy and lock her up. She's terrified of being locked up. She'll have to say something but hide the fact she's so confused. Rose tries to get up on her own, but the woman who she thinks is her daughter takes her hand and helps her up.

"Thank you," Rose says.

"Are you hurt?" the woman asks. Is this Tiffany? The name Tiffany is strong in her head, like a rock marking the place for something. She knows, at least, that whoever Tiffany is, she likes her. She is not so sure she likes her daughter. Sometimes she does. Not always.

"No," Rose says. She looks at the house. She lives here. She doesn't know why, but she does. She remembers thinking she didn't live here, getting angry and screaming at someone, and she's embarrassed that she made a fool out of herself. *Hell*, she thinks. *Screw them.* This is what she says when she gets upset, and she's oddly satisfied that she knows that about herself. *Screw them all*, she thinks again. She walks toward the house. *I'm not going to throw any fits*, she thinks. *I will simply go into this house and up to my room*. The image of what that room might look like wavers and won't take shape.

The woman walks beside her with a hand on Rose's arm. They go in the house, through a kitchen with dark cabinets. The room needs some color. Something red or orange. She can't imagine living here. Does she? "Stupid house!" she says. So what if she said it out loud.

The living room doesn't even have rugs. Who would live in a house with bare floors? There's a gate across the steps, and that upsets her. She stops. This gate has something to do with her. It's to keep her locked up. She tenses and thinks she will turn and run, but two things occur to her: One, she probably can't run very fast with these stupid old legs, and two, it's a pretty sorry excuse for a gate. She laughs, knowing her laugh is a bit of a cackle—she was told that once. By whom? Then before the woman can unhook the gate, Rose steps over it, holding on to the banister, using every muscle she owns not to trip. Then she walks upstairs. She doesn't know where she's going, she can't picture it, but her body seems to know what to do, and she's going to trust it.

Rose walks into a room that has a bed with rails, and adult diapers in the corner, and words written on things, labels meant for some stupid old woman. *Me*, she thinks. I'm some stupid old woman. "Hell's bells," she says.

The woman, whoever she is, has followed her into the room. "Let me look at your knees," she says.

"Leave my goddamn knees alone," Rose says, and then is immediately afraid. Is this someone she can offend?

"I just want to make sure you're not hurt."

"Rat's ass," Rose says. Then, "I'm fine. I'm . . ." The word she wants is not there. It's nowhere, not even on the tip of her tongue. It's a word not invented yet.

"Tired?" the woman says.

"Yes!" Rose says. *I'm goddamn tired*. She doesn't think she said this last part aloud. She sits in the chair by the bed. "Leave me alone," she says, not caring anymore if she's being rude.

"Are you sure?" The woman looks both worried and relieved.

"Oh, go on." Rose waves her away.

"I'll be back up soon," the woman says, with a nod. "We'll play cards."

"Oh, fine," Rose says, just to get rid of her. She wants to be alone and think. She's very afraid to think, but she's desperate to do so. "Close my door," she says.

The woman nods and does as Rose asks. She could be my daughter, Rose thinks. I suppose she is.

Rose closes her eyes. Inside is a woman of twenty-six. With her eyes closed, Rose can see very well.

Chapter Six

Every time Rose turns a corner at the theatre, she sees Michael standing there, looking at her. She has this crazy idea that he's doing it on purpose, waiting around corners for her.

One day he comes to the box office. "Hey there, Rose, will you do me a favor?"

"And what favor would you like, Mr. Morgan?" Rose asks. The older woman who works with Rose in the box office busies herself studying a brochure.

"We're out of the greenroom and on the stage. We need an audience. Will you come watch? They're getting tired of my face."

"Sure," she says. As if they could really be tired of his face, she thinks.

She watches a run-through of the first act. He doesn't interrupt the actors as other directors do at this stage in rehearsals. Michael lets them stumble through it, then when it's over, he goes up on the stage and draws the actors around him like a cocoon. Reading notes from a yellow legal pad, he talks so softly she can't hear what he says. The actors nod. Some ask a question. This takes time, but she stays in her seat, transfixed by the whole silent scene. She is taken by this man so many look to. When he's done, he hops off the stage and struts up the aisle. He knows she's watching him. He's a director, but she can see the actor in him.

"Still want to watch?" he asks. She nods. He sits down right next to her. He smells warm and musky from the hot lights.

"Good," he says. "I told them that if you didn't cry this act, they were all fired." He says this quite seriously, but then laughs. "Just kidding. It's a love story. What I really told them is that if you don't fall in love with me, they'll have to do it over and over again until you do."

"It will be an awful long night, then," she says.

"Not if you're sitting next to me the whole time." He stands and hollers at the stage, "Once more, with feeling!" He sits back down and whispers to her, "Always wanted to say that. Sounds pretty damn stupid, if you ask me."

The actors move into place. She watches, afraid to blink. Something has happened. They have just become a couple. She can feel it. It's like a dream. God forbid she wake up.

That night, after the rehearsal, Michael asks her out to the nearby bar. They sit in a dark corner and drink gin and tonics. She asks him where he lives.

"Everywhere," he says, cupping his head in one of his large

hands and leaning on the table, gazing at her. "I'm a roving director. I've moved from play to play for four years now and have completely forgotten where I started from. I hope I didn't leave the stove on."

"Seriously," she says, looking at him, noticing again the wizened skin under his eyes. She wonders how old he is. "Don't you have a home base?"

"Not anymore. But I have a lot of friends. And I know a few hotels rather more intimately than I might have ever cared to. Where are you from?"

"Here," she says. "Born and bred in Cleveland, Ohio." She knows now, as she says this, that she is ready to leave her hometown tomorrow, that she wants to travel, like he does. She's so tired of the same old streets, the same buildings, knowing exactly where she's going. To get lost in a new city . . . It sounds romantic. She feels romantic. Her faces flushes as if Michael could read her thoughts.

He offers her a Viceroy and she wonders if he knows it's the brand she smokes, how much of this could be real. He's debonair and goofy, something she suddenly finds is an extremely attractive combination. There's such intelligence in his face, and kindness, and mystery. She wants to touch his cheek, run a finger down his nose, feel the curve of his chin. She is beginning to have expectations. She wants to make sure.

"You've lived here your whole life?" he asks, sounding astonished.

"Yes."

"Well, we'll have to do something about that." Nat King Cole comes on the jukebox, singing "Unforgettable," and Rose feels a huge grin come over her face and has to cover her mouth with a hand. All around her is smoke and murmurs. Right in front of her is a man she knows she is crazy about. She's living right smack-dab in the middle of a love song.

That night they make love in the narrow bed in his small, dark apartment. She tells him she's a virgin as he unbuttons her blouse, and his hands stop mid-motion.

"We can wait, if you want," he says. She shakes her head. She is more than ready for this. Mind and body agree.

She closes her eyes to feel what he does to her, then, after a while, she opens her eyes, to see. At first he's very gentle, moving slowly down her body, and she's gentle, too, but then things speed up and she's not quite sure what's happening, just that she feels pressure, pain, then pleasure. He kisses her all over as he's inside her, even as they toss and turn. There's one moment when she actually thinks *this is nothing at all like dancing*, which is how she imagined it, and then she comes. She knows what an orgasm feels like, she has touched herself—she's not a prude, really, just stubborn—but this, with Michael inside her, kissing her now, is completely different. This is really fun.

The combination of love, and lust, and being a virgin at twenty-six, takes her right over the edge of desire into addiction. She can't get enough of him. For three weeks they make love two times a day—morning and night, or morning and lunch, or lunch and lunch. And she gets better at it all the time. There is so much more than touching a man's face. She wonders if the blind girl Susan ever found that out.

They're married by the justice of the peace eight days after opening night of *Romeo and Juliet*. It's only when they fill out the marriage certificate that Rose discovers Michael is eleven years older than she. Rose's mother won't come to the wedding because he isn't Catholic. Rose's father hasn't shown up by the time they leave town to move to Chicago for three months so Michael can direct *King Lear*. Rose says she will call her mother, to give her an address when they get there. She doesn't.

Rose loves Chicago. Three months later they move to Tulsa, Oklahoma.

Two months later they move to San Francisco.

Moving is more work than she ever imagined, but she likes it; the organizational skills, the frugality of what they take, even the lifting and carrying of boxes. She's good at this. Wherever they move, she buys maps and locates the interesting sights to see, checking them off her list after she visits them. Michael's too busy directing to come with her, and she pretends it's her job: she's an investigator, a journalist. She takes notes, storing them in different colored notebooks for each city, and saves the title page of the newspaper the day they arrive, and the day they leave.

Rose tries to make the apartments they rent seem like a home. She hangs curtains she sewed in Chicago, lays down a small braided rug she bought in Tulsa, puts books on the shelves. She scrubs and cleans these places she will soon leave, but she's careful to leave some dust under beds and couches to prove her own sanity. She's disturbed terribly, in the eighth month of her pregnancy, at the urge to haul the bed across the room, scrub the floor underneath it until it shines. She dreams of washing the walls and woodwork and windows of the small apartment, but she won't allow her hands this relief. She is not her mother; she is nothing like her mother.

She's ashamed of being pregnant so early in their marriage; she feels as if she has bought an expensive appliance without asking. When she told Michael, she actually apologized, but he hadn't even blinked before hugging her. She wants time alone with him, something rare enough as it is; after rushing home to eat dinner, he runs off again for the late-night rehearsal. Sometimes they go out to see a play at a competing theatre, but even during those times he's lost to her. Rose loves plays; she's just beginning to love them a little less.

She has never, not once in her whole life, held a baby. It could be too late to start, she thinks. She won't be able to do this.

One rainy day she writes her sister, Celia.

Dear Celia,

Hello! How are you? I wrote to you when we moved here, but since I never received a letter back, I assume you must have been too busy with four children to write. I'm exhausted just being pregnant. Michael's doing quite well, and they've asked him to stay and direct another play, Who's Afraid of Virginia Woolf, *even though his trade is really Shakespeare. The man who was going to direct it canceled with no excuse (can you imagine!), so Michael said yes. He's now going into dress rehearsals of* King Lear, *and starting the blocking of* Virginia Woolf. *It's getting harder for me to keep up with him, being the beached whale that I am. I'm due in two weeks. If there's any possibility of your coming for a visit and giving me some pointers, I would greatly appreciate it and would love to see you. I do understand it might well be impossible, but I want to make the invitation all the same. The sooner the better, since I never had a younger sibling, and I don't have a clue how to change a diaper or mix formula.*

I haven't been able to talk to Father since moving

here, actually for more than a year now. Do you know if he's all right? Have you spoken to him at all? Do you know where I can reach him? If you do talk to him, please give him my address and phone number. I call Mother on Sunday afternoons. She seems to be doing fine, in her own way.

I am well and happy. I miss work. Not the work, per se, but the friends I had there, even the deadlines and accomplishments. These days I feel accomplished by merely dragging my bloated self out of bed. Oh, I long to sleep on my stomach! Tell me things get better.

Please write back. I can't talk to any of the rest of our crew as easily as I do you. I always feel I should start my letters by reminding them I'm their sister. Mother says they're all fine.

Hope to hear from you soon.

Love,
Rose

Rose gets a letter back from her sister a week later.

Dear Mary,

I see you're still calling yourself Rose, but I just can't seem to do the same. I am sorry, but I won't be able to come visit you. I just can't leave my children behind, and to let you in on a secret I haven't shared with Mother yet, I'm pregnant again and due in five months. I'd like to say I'm getting good at this, but unfortunately, that's not the case and my ankles are

*already swollen. I'm tired beyond belief and must tell
you that it never gets easier. Walter is now thirteen and
trying to ape the older boys by combing his hair back
and wearing those tight jeans. I suppose I'm spoiling
him rotten by allowing him to go out of the house looking as he does, but it's all in innocence and I know he's a
good boy. Bonnie, Melanie, and Dorothy are still too
young to care about the latest fashions, so I get to dress
them as I please, but that won't last forever. I'm hoping
for another boy this time, just to even things out. There
are little girls' clothing scattered all over the house like
weeds. If you have a girl, let me know and I'll send you
some clothes.*

*I haven't heard from Father, either. Enough said. I
don't care anymore. If he doesn't want to be a part of
our lives, then so be it. I won't beg for his love. As for
Mother, she must be getting money from Father, but she
doesn't talk to me about these things, and I don't ask. I
have my own family to look out for, and it keeps getting
bigger. I don't have the energy for her problems, or anyone else's.*

*Good luck with your delivery. I will pray for you.
Children are a wonderful blessing. I hope to meet your
husband someday. He sounds like a very talented man.
Congratulations!*

*Love,
Celia*

Rose goes into labor while she hangs underwear to dry on a
clothesline rigged up in the bathroom. She feels a moment of
great power when she calls the theatre and has them interrupt

the rehearsal. Michael leaves work and drives her to the hospital. They put her to sleep. When she wakes up, she has a baby girl. They name her Jennifer.

Two months later, after the second play opens, Michael accepts a job in San Antonio, Texas, but they don't have to move for another three weeks. He paces in the small apartment like a caged tiger, holding the baby as if it were a script, looking at it, prodding it, sizing it up to see what it might become.

"She's so serious!" he says. "Like a little banker. But look at these hands! Oh, she's going to be a tough one, just like you. Feel that grip! She won't let go of my finger! What a face! Look at those gray eyes. They're almost violet. The next Elizabeth Taylor! Not that I think she should be an actress! Well, maybe. Just think of it, Rose, this little tiny child could grow up to be anything, anything she wants. A doctor, a magician, a playwright! It's fantastic. She's fantastic! Don't you think?"

"Would you like to go to the grocery store for me?" Rose asks. "Could you?"

"Sure, sure!" Michael says, handing her the baby so he can find a sheet of paper and make a list. He licks the tip of the pencil, a habit that is just beginning to annoy her.

"Milk, certainly," Rose says. "And three pork chops for tonight. A few potatoes. Oh, how about a can of peaches? We can pour that over ice cream tonight. And a newspaper, please."

"Okay," he says. "Got it. Anything else?"

The way he looks so hopeful, his eyes wide with a need to get her something else, she adds peanut butter and celery to the list, even though she stopped craving peanut butter and celery after her fifth month of pregnancy. "And don't rush. It's time for her nap anyway."

"All right. I'll be quiet." He kisses her on the forehead,

which she should love, but doesn't. It feels dismissive. It reminds her of her father.

Michael kisses the baby on the forehead, too, then her fingers. *I'd like my fingers kissed*, Rose thinks. Michael leaves, asking twice more if there's anything else he can do. She wishes there were.

She looks down at the child in her arms. Jennifer. She doesn't like Michael calling her Jenny. Jenny's a silly name. Rose doesn't want a silly daughter. Rose always calls her Jennifer. It's a beautiful name.

They can't have cats because of their moving about so much. She had to leave Daisy and Pinocchio behind with a friend. Rose misses that part of her life, the small soft creatures that would crawl into her lap, sleep awhile, then go off somewhere. A baby is nothing like a cat.

She pushes the baby carriage down the sidewalk to a nearby park. One lone cloud is left in the blue sky like a lost sheep. It's hard to get used to the idea that it's February and warm, but San Antonio is a beautiful place. Lying on her back, three-month-old Jennifer waves her fingers, wearing a pink hat, wrapped in a pink blanket, her tiny feet covered with knitted pink slippers, all sent by Rose's sister Celia. Rose thinks her daughter looks like a bundle of cotton candy. Even her own thoughts seem to be about soft, shapeless things. Some days she walks a mile to the library just to read the local newspaper and then stares at the pages as if they are written in Greek. What is this about the U.S. getting involved in Indochina? She just can't keep up. The budget's so tight she's given up all sorts of things, like perfume and new shoes. She makes meat loaf that lasts for three days.

All her siblings sent presents. Bibs and picture frames, bibs and pink sweaters. Her mother sent a check for fifty dollars. Her father sent a check for two hundred dollars and a nice note that said absolutely nothing, with no return address. She wrote a thank-you note she keeps in her bureau.

At the park, children climb metal jungle gyms and slide down slides. Rose sits on a bench, pushing the carriage back and forth with one hand. A woman walks over, dressed in sharp plaid capris and the newest sandals, and Rose wants her clothes. "May I?" the woman says, her arms reaching out toward Jennifer.

"Certainly," she says.

The woman picks up Jennifer and makes cooing sounds. Rose has never gotten into the habit of making those noises to her baby, nor anyone else's.

"They grow so fast," the woman says. "My name's Libby. That's my Stephen over there. I can hardly pick him up any-more, not that he'd want me to. He's no momma's boy, that's for sure."

The child across the playground is maybe five. *They do grow up*, Rose thinks. She bets he can play by himself for hours.

She wants to ask this woman a thousand questions, and none of them about babies. *What's happening with Indochina? Did you go to college? Did you want go to college? What do you think about working mothers? If you could have any job in the world, what would it be? Who did you vote for?* But she wants this woman to stay and talk to her. "Your son can really climb," she says, as brightly as she can. "When did he start to walk?"

They talk children for a half hour until Stephen runs over

and tugs his mother's arm. "I gotta go," he says, hopping from foot to foot. Libby laughs and says they will have to leave. She has held Jennifer the whole time and now hands her back.

With a friendly wave, Libby and her son walk off.

Rose feels abandoned, like that cloud that still sits in the sky, waiting for a breeze. It will dissipate, before it gets anywhere. The sheer pity she feels for herself makes her laugh out loud, a harsh laugh. Jennifer jerks and begins to cry.

On the way home she passes a small market that has fruit and vegetables displayed outside on crates. Going inside, she buys oranges, a pineapple, and peanut butter and celery.

Seven months later, in Milwaukee, she has a son. They name him Peter.

Four months later, in Tallahassee, she has still not gotten her period back.

Rose knows she should see a doctor, but they're moving to Boston in a week. Two weeks later, boxes unpacked, cribs set up, a dozen trips to the local drugstore for diapers and formula, she sits down on the shabby couch in their rented duplex and bursts into tears. She wants peanut butter and celery so badly she could scream. She tries to convince herself that if she just doesn't eat them, everything will be fine, as if eating peanut butter and celery were what got her pregnant.

A month later, while drying dishes, she throws a clean sauce pot against the wall. "Damn it to hell!" she shouts at the wall, at the dented pot, at the dingy kitchen. *Hell's bells* won't do anymore, she can see that.

Michael runs into the kitchen, holding Peter. He's a wonderful father. He makes up silly stories for the children that make Rose grit her teeth. She reads them *The Wreck of the Hesperus* and *O Captain! My Captain*! She reads them biographies of

Roosevelt. She does this privately, when Michael's gone. She could read them *War and Peace* in two days, he's gone so much.

"What happened?" He looks around the kitchen bewildered, as if there should be some foe he can fight off. He understands so little, she thinks: it is her own body that is her foe. Once set free, she has found her sex drive to be a dominant need in her life. She thinks about Michael inside her at the stupidest times. She sees, while picking out apples, his eyes looking into hers as they push and twist their bodies, tastes the sweat on his forehead, smells the heat off his chest. It can blind her; she will pick out bruised fruit and never notice until she gets home. And it never shames her because this urge comes with such love she feels surely she must be blessed. But right now she feels cursed. She kicks the nearest kitchen cabinet, yelling, "Damn Him! What the hell is He doing to me?" Maybe God is punishing her because she doesn't go to Mass anymore, and Michael is a lapsed Protestant. Who has time to *find* the goddamn church? She plops to the floor between the cupboards and the fridge, and can't cry. The tears of just moments ago have burned off. Her face and eyes are hot and dry. She has nothing left in her, except another baby.

Michael lowers himself to the floor. "What is it?" he asks softly. In his arms, Peter has started crying, and now Jennifer can be heard wailing from her crib.

"I'm so sorry," she says. "I just don't remember trying out for the role of the pretty brunette housewife with three kids."

"I'm sorry," he says. Then, "Three?"

"Oh, hell," she says. "I'm pregnant."

"Oh. That's great." He takes just a second to put the right face on, to get the tone right. He's pretty close, and now she does cry. Michael shifts his position on the floor, and hoisting

Peter onto one hip, he pulls out a white handkerchief from his pocket, handing it to her. "But, are you sure?"

She can't blame him for asking. *She* can't believe it. She nods.

"Well, that's wonderful. Three kids, all so close in age. They'll be great friends. What a crew we'll have!"

She just closes her eyes. Leans against him.

"Are you okay? What did the doctor say?"

"I haven't seen a doctor yet."

"Why not? Don't you need to?"

"For what? I could do this in my sleep—if I could sleep." She laughs, and cries. He kisses her wet lips.

"We'll do fine. What's a few more diapers? I'll just have to direct more plays."

That's not what Rose wants to hear. She can't imagine what she wants to hear. That *she* go back to work and he stay home with the kids?

Peter has stopped crying in Michael's arms. He does this: cries, then stops, distracted by any little thing. He touches her face and plays with her tears like finger paints.

"I can't stand more diapers," Rose says, a hitch in her voice, hysteria just around the corner.

"Then we'll move somewhere warm and leave them all outside naked."

"Okay," she says. "All right."

He draws her head to his chest with Peter trapped between them in a warm, wet hug. In the next room, Jennifer screams her lungs out.

Rose opens a window and kneels down to rest her arms across the windowsill. Immediately she realizes her mistake; the small house they are renting in Jackson, Florida, is cooler inside than the day outside.

With her eyes closed, Rose imagines she's back in Cleveland, a spring day with a breeze; she's ten and waiting for the ice-cream truck.

A gush of sticky, hot water runs down her legs.

This baby is three weeks too early. *I will just stay here on the floor for three weeks, then get up. I'm sticking to the plan.* But the first wave of a strong cramp makes her moan. Jennifer and Peter are both taking a nap. Holding the windowsill, she rises, careful not to slip on the slick surface of her broken water. She's dizzy with the thought of swimming in cool water. Help me, Lord, she thinks, then spits out the window. Something tastes bad in her mouth.

Michael has just left for work and won't arrive at the theatre for another ten minutes. They have been in this town for less than one week. She walks out the front door and looks around at the row of identical stucco houses along the narrow street. She turns right for no particular reason, walks over to the next house and rings the doorbell. *Avon calling*, Rose thinks. She'd laugh, but she's having a hard time breathing right now.

A woman opens the inner door and takes one look at Rose. "Oh, my God, honey, come inside." She pushes the screen door open, but Rose is standing too close to the door. She has to think to step back.

The woman is around forty, with wrinkles around her mouth of a longtime smoker. Rose wants a cigarette and almost asks this lady for one, but then remembers why she's here. She steps inside. It's hotter than her own house.

"Hi, I'm Rose, your new neighbor. I have two children

asleep next door, and my water just broke. I need to get to the hospital. Do you know where the hospital is?"

"Oh, honey. Let me call you an ambulance."

"Okay. Call me whatever you like, but could I sit down?" She smiles. Damn it if she's going to have this baby now. What she really wants to do is sit down and tell good jokes. This lady could be her friend. She looks friendly.

"Sit down. I'm Betsy Tarken. Sit down anywhere. I'm gonna call you an ambulance and your husband, and then I'm gonna go over to your house and watch your babies while you go off and have this one. My son's sixteen and don't play with me no more. If he comes home for dinner, I'm lucky. I won't mind being with your babies at all. Trust me, okay?" Rose slips into a lounger and thinks she will never be able to get up again. Betsy dials the phone and tells someone the address and to hurry up.

When Betsy asks Rose the number to call her husband, Rose says she doesn't know. "It's on the phone table, by the couch."

"I'll go get it. What's his name?"

She has to think a second. *Romeo* she wants to say. There's a stabbing pain in her lower back. "Michael. Michael Morgan."

"I'll call him. You just rest there." When Betsy comes back, she says Michael wasn't at work yet, but they'd tell him to go right to the hospital. "What's your babies' names?" Betsy asks.

"Jennifer and Peter."

"What a lucky lady you are," Betsy says.

"Thank you." She has been taught to say thank you to compliments. "I'll name this one Betsy, if she's a girl."

"Oh, don't be silly," Betsy says. But she's smiling like all get out, and Rose decides she will have a girl, come hell or high water.

She does. And she names the baby Betsy, even though it's a silly name. She said she would.

Michael finds a job directing his next play in another warm place, another town in Florida. The lawn is only a few feet deep and the street so busy there is no way in God's green acres Rose can let her children run around out there, naked or not.

Making love is never the same again. She's not a good Catholic anymore, but still can't face the idea of using a diaphragm. She marks the days on the calendar that might be safe; a few days on each side of her period—which she gets now every month, relishing even the cramps and inconvenience—and even then, on these safe days, she's scared; she makes him pull out before he comes. Sometimes he doesn't. Sometimes she allows him this because he's such a good father, but those nights are sleepless and she holds a grudge against him until she gets her next period. But she still gets horny; she still thinks of the things they do, the way she puts her mouth on all of him, tastes all of him, the way he tells her to move this way or that, to bend over—the things they say in bed. When she thinks of making love, her arms ache, her back gets tight, and she will snap at Jennifer for any little thing, or ignore Peter as he calls for her from his crib, or forget to heat the formula for Betsy, and then, knowing what she's done, she cries as she makes it up to them, she cries as she pushes Jennifer on the swing, she cries as she gives Peter a cookie, she cries as she holds Betsy against her breasts, and sometimes she cries as she makes love. But she always cries silently, and they don't know. They think she is just wonderful.

One night, after all the children are asleep, Michael asks her to sit on the couch with him. He tells her that he's been offered a job running a small theatre.

"What do you mean?" she asks.

"It's a year-round theatre, in the Finger Lakes. I'd be the executive director. I'd pick the plays, cast them."

"We'd live there year-round?"

"Yep. What do you think?"

She doesn't know. Moving around isn't easy, but it still feels like an adventure—and she still pretends it's her job. What will she do? She rolls her eyes and holds back a laugh. Raise kids, apparently.

"I guess it's okay." She shrugs. "Sure." They kiss, but it feels more like a handshake.

Chapter Seven

I come downstairs after getting my mother settled back into her room, and now the memory of Todd and me at the back door makes me feel guilty and ashamed. How can memory change what really happened? It was good, what we did, and now I want to crawl under a rock and hide from myself.

"She okay?" Todd asks. He was in the basement when she fell, cleaning out the dryer vent. He can't tear down walls, so he does the small things. He's running out of small things to fix.

"I guess," I say. "I can't believe I left her in the car like that."

"You kept your eye on her. It was an accident."

He's not using this "accident" as another reason I should put her in the nursing home because I have a few hours of grace after doing that thing by the back door. I look down at my feet.

"I'm going to Ron's to watch the game. That okay with you?

I got the chicken. It's in the fridge." He rolls his head around on his neck. I hear things pop.

"Sure, go," I say. "Thanks for getting the chicken."

We look at each other for a moment. He doesn't watch Sunday games here much anymore. I miss the sound of football, sitting next to him, asking what's happening. But sitting in the TV room, listening to the roar of the crowds, blocks out the sound of my mother. She could be doing anything. Once, I thought she was sleeping and I sat down to watch a game with Todd. She tossed all her medicine and cups down the laundry shoot, then anything she could find that would fit, and then things that couldn't fit. Most Alzheimer's patients wander, but not my mother. When she gets really lost in her head, she stuffs things into small spaces, like the curtain into the toilet. Maybe she thinks she's packing.

"Have a good time," I say.

He kisses me goodbye on the lips, with just a hint of tongue. He wants me to know he still loves me, still finds me sexy, thank me for the thing by the door, hint I'll get mine later, and say he's sorry for leaving. I smell the scent of dryer lint on him, and touch his Sunday stubbled face. I've seen pictures of him with mutton chops. I'm glad he got over that phase. "Be good," I say. I'm pretty sure he really is going to Ron's. He's wearing sweatpants. You don't wearsweat pants off to have an affair, do you?

"Love you," he says.

Todd's gotten enough chicken for a week of chicken dinners, and I freeze most of it, leaving just enough for tomorrow's dinner. The lasagna in the freezer will have to do for tonight.

It was my plan to take some more photos up to my mother's room this afternoon, to get on with building her life brick by crumbling brick, resurrecting the dead if I have to. I'm wary now of any such ambitions, and worried I might hurt her even more. I go into the living room and sit down with one of the albums I haven't taken up yet.

Here's a photo of my brother Peter and me, when we were three and four years old. We're playing with pots on the floor, banging them with wooden spoons. My brother's hair has just been cut within an inch of its life and sticks up like short, neatly trimmed brown grass. He looks frenzied. Attention deficit disorder they would call it now. An active little boy, they said then. The wooden spoons are raised high; he's ready to hit those pots with all his might.

The next picture is of my father holding my baby sister, my brother and I looking over his shoulder. I remember her at that age as only a tug on my sleeve. And here's my mother, in a white-and-blue-striped dress, sitting on a patchwork quilt on the lawn, the three of us children arranged around her, so perfectly placed that I can almost feel my father's hands directing my arms and legs into smooth and lovely shapes, hear his deep voice say, "Now, hold still . . ." And I do miss him, this man I swore I would never forget.

And here, out of sequence, is their wedding picture, taken at the courthouse: my mother in a blue A-line skirt and matching jacket, a corsage with a yellow rose pinned too high, near her shoulder; my father in his gray pin-striped suit, a huge grin on his face. The photo is black-and-white. I add the color.

My mother used to tell the story about meeting my father. Girl finds the man of her dreams after waiting for so long. Stayed a virgin until her honeymoon, then had three perfect children. But I believe my mother wanted a man, not children. As she told me once when she was drunk and furious with me for something, "If we'd had the pill back then . . . I would have used it, Pope or no Pope." This quick succession of children was the beginning of her fight with God. The death of my father was the straw that broke God's back.

I remember what I can, without her help. This is my story now, not just hers.

When I am four, my father gets a job running a small repertory theatre built along the shore of one of the thinnest of the Finger Lakes in upstate New York. During the winter they do a few dinner theatre plays, but it's the summer, when the "name" actors come, that draws the tourists. I meet Joel Grey and Dom DeLuise. I am too young to be impressed; later in life I will throw these names around as if they were my best friends.

We rent a farmhouse on a country road, with acres of mowed grass surrounded by deep woods. My mother finds she does enjoy this, too, this staying still for a while. The refrigerator is the same damn refrigerator that she put that bottle of ketchup in a whole year ago, and she opens the door just to peer at the sheer wonder of it all. She gets a cat and names it Eleanore.

When I am six, she shows me how to pick up a baby kitten and hold it to my chest so it can hear my heartbeat. The kitten purrs like a tiny motor and I am in love with it. I ask my mother if I can hear her heart, and she lets me climb in her lap and put my ear to her chest.

My mother plants a vegetable garden with neat rows and generous spaces between, not a weed in sight. The vegetables are healthy, well fed, thick. She picks some spinach and puts it straight into her mouth. I do the same, as if I know exactly what I am doing. The taste is strong, and dirt sticks to my teeth, but it is good for my dry mouth. Tiny drops of hidden water escape; spinach holds on to the rainfall like a miser.

Someone driving by will see my mother bent over, a bright yellow hat shading her face. She carries a small bucket of water she drops insects into. They make a tiny splash and hold tight to the surface of the water. Marigolds border the garden; short soldiers. Their smell keeps the scaly bugs out. My brother, Peter, sits in a rusty red wagon. "Pull me. Pull me," he bleats, lost in the repetition of his own voice, five years old and lonely for friends.

She decides the peas are ready and fills the basket with them, one pod at a time. Her hands are covered with thin red scratches and her nails are black with dirt. At the kitchen sink she washes her hands until they turn pink from the hot water. She says peas are a special pleasure, tiny wrapped gifts. She is happy to pop them open while sitting at the table. Our cat plays with the ones that fall to the floor.

My father walks in and they kiss. They always kiss. Quickly though; my father does everything quickly. At a young age I learned to walk fast.

"I have to be back at the theatre by six," he says.

"All right. Do you want tea?"

"Yes, please. And something sweet." He winks at her.

It is a code, I think. I need a decoder ring.

"Hello, honey," he says to me. "What did you do today?"

I don't know why he even asks. He's had our only car all day. This house is miles from anywhere.

"A bull jumped the fence and chased Peter," I say.

"Really?" he asks my mother.

"No," she says.

But it was *my* day he was asking about. Maybe it *did*.

She hands him a cup of tea. "Dinner will be soon," she says. He will leave again right after dinner, and won't be back until past midnight. After the final curtain, after the stage is swept with the green sand, he will go to a bar with the actors and discuss the show. This short time now, with the tea, is theirs. He tells my mother that there's trouble with Act Two.

"Ken can't build the anger slowly enough. He needs to justify it before he starts to yell at Miriam. He can't seem to get it."

"He will," she says.

I am sitting on the steps. Another kiss will mean dinner's ready. My brother plays with two trucks in the gravel driveway. He smashes them together, yells, and smashes them again. I wait for the bull to jump the fence.

Grandmother Francine comes for a visit. She is my mother's mother and very strange. She lives all alone in a house in Cleveland. I never met my grandfather. He's dead.

My mother warns us to be good. "Treat Grandmother Francine nicely." We smile, a bit nervous. We never know what will happen. Something will. Last time Grandmother busted her hip. She jumped from a chair. No one knew why. Sometimes she washes dishes that are clean, but my mother will yell at her if she does that. My mother doesn't always treat Grandmother Francine nice, but we are supposed to.

This time Grandmother shows us her mole, under her left armpit. It's big, with hair growing out of it like a little head. Peter and I have friends over. She shows everyone. We stare, then laugh; embarrassed by the size of the bra we see as she lifts up her pink angora sweater. Acres of white elastic, bursting with spotted flesh.

My mother walks in. "Put down your sweater, Mother." She doesn't yell. Or laugh. Or cry. She wants to, though, to yell and shake Grandmother Francine like a bad child. I can tell. "Go outside," she says to us, mad, as if we had encouraged her to perform. Maybe we had. It would be so easy.

"How could you do that?" she scolds Grandmother Francine.

"It's so big, don't you think? Should I see a doctor?"

"Yes, do."

My mother has patience. Her mother will leave soon. She won't be back for a year. She may never come back. She's old and has strange spots on her skin.

Sometimes my mother makes us go to bed early. "Go to bed," she says. "You need your rest." My father joins in. "Today was longer than most days. Didn't you feel it? I think there was a whole extra hour there, somewhere. You kids must be exhausted." He laughs. "Life is just amazing, isn't it?" Sometimes, like these times, he kisses her right in front of us, longer than a hello or goodbye kiss. Then he kisses us. "Good night," he says. "Off to bed."

I knew it was because they wanted to be alone without us around. I didn't know what they did alone, but now I do. Still, I can't imagine them like Todd and me. They were probably very sweet lovers, very quiet and gentle. That's all I'm going to imagine. Some things I don't need to know.

. . .

My father decides to buy a farmhouse, a different one than the one we're renting. The old farm he finds has lots of land, with a long lane, so the house is way back off the road. He says he got it for a song, and I ask, "What song?" He picks me up and kisses me on my hair. The house needs a lot of work. My father is very happy.

The grass around the house is not grass but head-high hay. Peter, Betsy, and I play hide-and-seek, making a maze of paths through the rough hay. Our world is made of thin, green stripes that crinkle loudly if we move too fast. We don't.

We hardly notice the work being done. One day we have a toilet, the next, a bathtub with clawed feet like an animal. With deep red paint he draws naked women on the bathroom walls, with breasts as large as whole planets. A few days later he paints over them, covering the walls with the red paint so that going into the bathroom feels like walking onto a dark heart. I imagine the women hidden under the walls, and sometimes I just pee outside. Downstairs, my mother can't decide on which floral wallpaper she likes best, so he papers each separate wall with a different pattern. He covers the lampshades with the leftover paper. The house is busy, and my mother laughs out loud at every bad joke my father makes. Sometimes she sings "White Coral Bells" as she follows my father around, sidestepping paint cans and sawhorses.

When he's not working on the house, my father takes us into the woods for a walk. We are surrounded by thin poplars, ancient oaks, and red maples. He finds a large branch lying on the ground and, taking out a knife, carves it, cutting off twigs until it has two arms, a body, and a face. He waltzes with it in the old woods where the ground is clear. My mother dances next to him. My brother thinks this is all pretty stupid, but I am charmed.

The next summer my father builds a stage, a wide platform at the edge of the hiding-hay, near the mountain ash. The banging of his hammer scares off the crows from the treetops, and small animals huddle in their holes.

He holds rehearsals here for the plays that take place outside. The first is *A Midsummer Night's Dream*. My mother brings out an old patchwork quilt for us to sit on, to watch the kings and fools and fairies. My father plays Theseus, as well as directs, his voice filling the air, his hands waving about his head as he tells everyone what to do, where to move. My mother never takes her eyes off him. She sits cross-legged, leaning back and balancing her weight on her hands. Her waist is slim, her face tan, her shoulder bare. My father winks at her between the scenes. During the scenes he forgets that she's there. He is Theseus.

I love to watch the rehearsals. I love the way the actors get out of their cars, laughing and gossiping until my father calls them together, the way they become someone else instantly as they step onto the stage. But more, I love when they move the play back to the theatre, where the heavy blue drapes mask out the daylight, where the world smells of sawdust and makeup and hot lights, and I am allowed to sit in the wings behind the heavy curtain and watch the play unfold, the audience entranced and quiet, or erupting with a laugh. My mother gets a baby-sitter and sits in the eighth row center for every performance. My brother Peter comes only for opening night; he thinks plays are barely tolerable. But I think plays are the only important thing in the world, and that my father is the greatest actor alive.

I am eight. Someday I will be a great actress. My father will teach me.

One day in September we get a phone call from Aunt Celia. Grandmother Francine died in her sleep. We have to go to Cleveland, to the funeral. It's a six-hour drive, and my mother is very quiet. My father keeps his hand on her thigh as he drives. We are dressed in our best clothes because we are going right to the funeral. My father tries to keep us happy by telling us the story of *Twelfth Night*, quoting all the lines he can remember, and I don't know how I will ever be able to remember stuff like that. Peter likes the fight scenes, and when my father says, "Put up your sword," Peter pokes me hard with his finger and I hit him. He hits me back. My father pulls the car over to the side of the road.

"Cut it out," he says. "This is not the time to fight." He glances over at our mother, who has her head in her hands. We are both ashamed, and nod. Betsy is perfect and hasn't moved for hours. We drive on, and I think about how hard I'll punch Peter back when it *is* the time to fight.

The funeral's in a big church, and my grandfather is there. He's small and wrinkly with enormous eyebrows. I'm confused because my mother said he was dead. There are so many people, aunts and uncles and cousins that I've never met, everyone hugging each other. I can't remember anyone's names and I know I will never be an actress because I can't remember well enough. No one hugs my grandfather, and that makes me think he must contagious or something. I just got my shot for measles, but I still don't want to hug him.

"I thought Grampa was dead," I tell my father. My mother's

surrounded by too many people to talk to her. No one's talking to my dad much.

"Well, that's a long story," he says, so I get ready for him to tell it, but he doesn't.

After the funeral we go to Grandmother Francine's house. I've been here two times before that I remember: the time we came and visited the museum with the dinosaurs, and when it was Nana's birthday, but with my memory, I could be wrong. Maybe I have been here hundreds of times. It smells like lemons and emptiness. My mother shows me her old bedroom, and I sit on the bed. It has a pink spread with fluffy raised lines, and I run my fingers along them. They're soft, and I want a bedspread like this, but not this one. I'm afraid of Grandmother Francine's things. My mother sits next to me on the bed. Betsy's asleep in the car, and Peter is with my dad downstairs talking to an uncle about my grandmother's car.

"I'm very sad my mother's dead, Jennifer. It's okay to be sad. Do you remember when she made you that cake for your fifth birthday? She loved you very much."

I don't remember the cake at all, not one little bit, and it was only three years and ten months ago. I feel stupid and start crying. My mother puts her arms around me, and she cries, too. "It's okay, honey. It's okay," she says. We cry until my father and Peter find us. My father touches my mother's cheek, then picks me up in his arms. It makes me cry harder, and I don't even know why, because I feel good being held.

"I think everyone's here," he says. "I can't remember anyone's names. Jesus, there's a lot of them."

I am so happy now that my father can't remember their names, I start to hiccup.

"Let's go home," my mother says.

"Really?"

"Yes."

"You don't want to spend some time with them?"

"No."

"Okay. Let's go."

We walk out, my dad still carrying me, my mother holding Peter's hand. We drive back to our farm. I forget to beat Peter up.

We see very little of my father. He works late hours and is seldom home. But during the summer that I am ten, he begins to come home in the middle of the day, to take a nap between the rehearsals and the performance. At these times we have to whisper and walk on tiptoes, or stay outside. I spend whole days in the woods—even though we finally have a TV—pretending I am lost in Africa, and starving. I have cookies in my pockets for the times I call intermission.

For almost a whole year my father takes naps that get longer and longer.

One spring evening I am watching *Lassie*. My sister sits next to me. My brother's at a friend's. I am eleven and too old to be watching *Lassie*, but my father won't let us watch much TV, so I watch whatever we are allowed, no matter what it is. In the kitchen my mother cooks soup, cutting vegetables, tossing strange bones into a large pot. She is almost content, but something nags at her. Something is different, but she doesn't know what, or she doesn't want to know what. Every time these thoughts creep into her head, a door inside slams, and she cooks.

My father walks down the stairs. We see him at once. His

face is contorted. "Who are you?" he yells, so loud. "Who the hell are you?" It's an entrance in a play, I think. He's just acting. My mother runs in, stops, and stares at my father. He looks at her. We are so quiet, all of us, that when Lassie barks my sister starts to cry. My father shouts, "Where the hell am I?" He smashes the wall with a fist. "Who are you!" He is terrified. He is not acting.

"Go outside," she tells me. "Take Betsy. Go to the Brands'. Stay there till I call."

I hear my father start to cry, and I realize I have never been so scared. I have to tell my legs to move. It's a half mile to our neighbors. I never think of turning back.

My mother is brave and strong. She explains to us what cancer is. What it might mean. How people will react. She continues to help with our schoolwork, clean, cook, take us shopping. We go to the hospital every day after school. Sometimes, for months, my father comes home, even goes to work. Sometimes he is in the hospital for days or weeks. Neighbors visit with pies and brownies dusted with powdered sugar. Some of them say stupid things. "Be brave." "Be good to your mother." This goes on forever.

He looks much older now. He has spots on his skin.

One night, when he puts me to bed reading *Huckleberry Finn*, he keeps stopping to take a deep breath. Betsy is asleep in the other bed.

"Dad," I say.

He waves a hand. "Just a second." Then he tries reading again, but his voice is all scratchy.

"Don't," I say, because I don't want to hear his voice like that. My voice sounds scratchy now, too. He closes the book. My eyes hurt, and I close them.

"I promise I'll get better," he says.

I open my eyes and stare at him. "You promised me you'd take me to the amusement park, but you didn't." It's already late August, and he promised to take me for my fifth-grade graduation, which was a long time ago, but then he got sick. Sicker.

"Is that very important to you?" he asks.

"Yes," I say.

"Then we'll go tomorrow."

"Just you and me?"

"If that's what you want." He brushes the hair out of my face with his hand, and I tense. I love him, but sometimes I am afraid of his body.

Just before lunch my father and I drive off. It's only a small amusement park, but I love the Tilt-A-Whirl and the flying swings. I can't believe he is really taking me without Peter and Betsy, and that scares me a little. I wonder what it means.

He tells me on the merry-go-round. He makes us sit together on the goose, which has a seat for old people and doesn't even go up and down. So far, I have gone on every ride by myself—he says they will make him nauseated. It's not so fun alone, so I don't mind sitting with him on the goose, except he ruins it.

"You're right, Jenny," he says, putting an arm around my shoulder and leaning down to talk to me, right in my ear, so I can't possibly not hear him. "Sometimes people can't keep promises. It doesn't mean they don't want to. Do you understand?"

I nod. This was supposed to be a fun day.

"I will do my very best to get better."

"Eat, then," I say. I had a hot dog, onion rings, and popcorn, and he wouldn't eat anything. He's getting thin and his bones show. If he wants to get better, he has to eat. I know that.

He doesn't have an answer for this, or any promises. We go around a whole time, just looking at our laps.

"I'm trying," he says to his legs, like he's talking to his body.

I don't look at him. "Make the doctors make you better," I say, my jaw tight. "Make them."

"They're trying their best, Jenny," he says, and then the ride stops.

"She doesn't love me as much as you do," I say, and get off the goose. People are moving around on the merry-go-round, and a girl bumps into me. "Boy oh boy, are you dumb," I say to her, but she doesn't hear me.

I walk quickly, but when I turn around, my father is way behind me, walking very slowly. I stop and wait for him. He takes my hand, and we walk back to the car. Only when we are both inside the car does he talk again. "That's not true," he says. I lay down across the seat and put my head in his lap, and he turns on the car. He drives home with one hand on my head, and I try really hard not to cry. I am asleep by the time we get home.

That night he eats a lot of dinner. Waving a forkfull of pot roast at me, he chuckles. "Think you have cotton candy in your hair, kid," he says, and I do. That night he throws up loudly, and my mother cries.

"He's taking me to Putt-Putt tomorrow," Peter says. "You better not have gotten him too sick."

But my father goes back in the hospital before he can play Putt-Putt with Peter. I never find out what he promised Betsy.

. . .

He comes back home a week later, for almost three weeks, but he never gets out of bed. Then he goes back to the hospital for a long time.

My mother says we can't visit him. He doesn't want us to see him as he is now. There are only weeks left. She sits us down and tells us we must be strong and help each other. This is the talk she has been putting off, but it is her job to do it. Duty is holding her together: a rope tied with knots of *must dos*, and she knows when the knots are gone, everything completed, she will have no more rope.

I want to see him anyway. I force the issue, and she relents. "He may not recognize you," she says. I don't believe her. This is not real, any of it, so I am going to the hospital to say, "Stop it. This is enough. You're scaring me, so stop it and come home."

I go in first. She follows like a shadow and sits down in a chair by the door. She's angry at me, at herself; she knows she shouldn't have brought me.

He is bald. His black hair is all gone. He is deaf, almost blind. He is very old and shrunken, tucked under the white blanket like a child.

Reaching for my hand, he calls me by my mother's name, his voice a whisper, not a stage whisper but small and fragile; his voice barely makes it across the few feet separating us. I hold his hand, but I can't talk, all my protests forgotten. I cannot take my eyes off the brown spots on his bald head. Who is this? This is not my father. I want to leave. I turn to my mother, who nods her head toward the door, but this man will not let go of my hand. She comes over and helps me. She takes his hand, and I walk out quickly. I wait in the hall. I wonder why she stays in there so long.

. . .

My mother calls her friend Betsy Tarken in Florida, whom my sister is named after. "He's going to die," she says. I hate my mother for saying this. If he dies, it will be her fault. Betsy says she will fly in tomorrow. My mother says, "Oh, no." Then, "Well, if you insist." Then, "Thank you. Oh, God, Betsy, I can't live without him." She says this while I am right there, in the living room. I'm really scared now. I saw *Romeo and Juliet* a dozen times. I know how it ends.

He dies while I am in school, two days before Thanksgiving, two days after my twelfth birthday. The day before my birthday, the day Mrs. Tarken arrived, I heard my mother tell her, "God, I hope he doesn't die on her birthday." As I blew out my birthday candles, I hoped he wouldn't die. At least she got her wish.

Mrs. Tarken comes to get me. I see her walking hesitantly toward me while I'm eating lunch in the crowded and loud cafeteria, and right away I know what has happened. The room grows silent, or at least I think it has. Before my mother's friend has even reached our table, I turn to the girl next to me. "My dad's dead. I gotta go. See you tomorrow." I say this last part without really thinking. I don't do much thinking for the next few days.

The funeral is at the theatre; this place is all the religion my father had. Fellow actors speak about him, elegantly, in deep, full voices, standing on the edge of the stage, and this is when I know he didn't really die—wasn't even sick. It was all an act, a grand and tragic play. This is the last act, when we cry. Then the cast of characters will come out for the curtain call. I wonder vaguely if I'm to go up on the stage. Don't I have a role in this play?

When he doesn't appear, even after I give him days and days, I decide he has gone to Canada. I've heard about people going there, escaping something, but I can't figure out what he's escaping. Maybe he went to act in the Shakespeare Festival that I heard him talk about. He loves Shakespeare.

My father invades my dreams. I see him walking down the street, away from me, his thick black hair bobbing in and out of a crowd. He turns the corner as I run after him. I wake wondering if I will see him today. I am twelve. Reality and fantasy have thin boundaries. As I walk to school, my eyes search in the distance for a black-haired man with a quick stride.

Then I get angry at my father for leaving me. I know deep down inside that he's dead, but get mad at myself for even thinking that. I believed he wasn't sick, but my mother wasn't as good as me at pretending, and in the end she gave up and he died. How will I be a great actress now? I want to yell at him, but he's not here. My mother is, though, she is right here and so easy to hurt.

In the spring my mother sells the farm because we need the money, and we move to Cleveland Heights, Ohio, where my grandmother lived. My mother has an old friend there who gets her a job as a secretary at a public relations firm. We rent one side of a duplex on Oak, a street with lots of kids roller-skating and shouting all the time. I keep thinking that I am at our farm and kids are playing in my yard, and I get mad at them and want them to go away. Then I realize I am in this stupid house, where we can't turn up the TV because there are people right on the other side of the wall.

My mother drives us by the house she grew up in, when her

dad was rich and owned oil wells. It's large and brick, and the street is wide, not narrow like ours. "Is your dad really dead yet?" I ask my mom. Mine is. I sure would never have said he was dead if he wasn't, like she did.

"To me he is," she says. She doesn't sound sad at all. I wanted to make her sad.

"Why?" I say.

"Oh, forget it, Jennifer. I'm mad at him, that's all. He's not really dead, but we don't talk. That's all."

I remember getting mad at my dad for not taking me to the amusement park, and then, how he did. If he hadn't taken me, he would have gotten better.

My mother gets a cat and names it Lovely. She pretends she names it Lovely because it's so pretty, but I hear her talking to Mrs. Tarken on the phone. She says, "Yeah, I named it Lovely because life is just so goddamn *lovely*, isn't it." At night I have to go outside and call for it. I am twelve and am embarrassed to death.

I paint my closest walls with black paint and carry in a mirror. I take a candle from the living room and put it on a cookie tin in front of the mirror. I call to the dead. No one answers, but I have just begun. I will grow up to be a witch, and then everyone had better watch out.

A year after my father dies, five months after we move into this duplex, my mother begins to drink. Drunk, she calls my father on the phone. "Michael. Come home. Come home, Michael." I take the phone from her, but there's no one on the other end. Or, if there is, he's not speaking to me. I start to wonder if he just couldn't stand to be near me anymore. Maybe he knew I couldn't memorize lines. I yell at my mother, who sits crumpled up on the floor, wedged in a corner. She just keeps crying.

My sister is ten and retreats into quiet. She hardly speaks. My brother spends hours in the basement nailing boards together, wiring batteries to potatoes, making lights go on and off.

My mother is perfectly straight when she goes to work. It is only when she comes home that she drinks.

I cook the dinners. This is my job now. Pork chops, mashed potatoes and gravy. Beef stroganoff, rice, and peas. Chicken Kiev. I can really cook. My mother taught me. I cook dinner. I set the table. I put the food on the plates, hot and smelling so good. I do not call anyone in for dinner. They can go to hell.

Chapter Eight

Now, sitting on my couch, I close the picture album and think of calling my brother, but I'll never find him. He's on his way to some mountain with a number. The fifth highest, or the sixth. He's working his way up to the big one, the one everyone dies on. I am supposed to cheer him on.

I should call my sister, but I don't. One challenge at a time, and I am working on my mother while she still has the time.

When Todd and I began dating four years ago, I showed him these photo albums. *This is me*, I'd say, as if by looking at pictures I would never have to explain anything to him. I showed these pictures to other boyfriends, hoping the same thing. Showing them to Todd, I thought, *I can't do this again*, this opening myself up and hoping to be loved for who I was. There are too many men who have seen my baby-plump body in a striped bathing suit, my friendly wave as I sat on my new tricycle, my crooked-toothed smile as I sat on our old gray couch. I wanted every one of those men to love me, but I never loved them. Then there was Todd, and somehow I love him.

Or, I have *said* I love him. Said it even to myself. What you say becomes true.

Jazz calls to say she won't be home for dinner, she has to keep working on her school project. My mother won't come downstairs, so I take her a plate of lasagna and sit with her. She keeps her eyes on her food but her chin held high, which makes eating even more difficult. I ask her if she would like anything else, and she snorts.

I turn on her TV and tell her I'll be back up soon.

I set the table and wait for Todd to come home. When he does, he notices the table is set for two.

"Just us?" he says.

"Just us," I say, happy and guilty at the same time. How come I can never feel just one damn emotion at a time?

"This is nice," Todd says. He gives me a kiss on the cheek. Now he smells like beer and cigarettes, and I go around the other side of the table and sit down, try to shake off those smells so I can eat. He sits down and waits for me to pick up my fork, take the first bite. How could his ex-wife have ever divorced him? What woman would not have done anything to keep this man? I want to tell him that he's the prize in my Cracker Jack box of life, but it would sound so stupid right now. Maybe I can work it into the conversation later. Or whisper it in his ear tonight in bed.

Still, I want to offer him something. "I'll drive her over to the nursing home tomorrow. Maybe she'll have forgotten she already saw it, and said she wouldn't go there for a million dollars. It was last month. Who knows what short-term means to someone her age?"

"Jen . . ." He looks at me sadly. I hate it.

"Sorry. But I should take her again. The more she sees it, the more she might think she already lives there. And I'll work on my . . . project." What a lame term for what I am trying to do. But then again, what am I trying to do? Unfortunately, Todd picks up on this.

"What project? What are you trying to do? I don't get it."

"I have to resolve something with my mother." As soon as I say it, I hate what I have said. *Resolve* is too politically correct for what I mean. What I want involves blood and guts. I want her to know what I did and why. I want her to remember what she did.

"What the hell needs to be resolved?" Todd asks. "You've told me all the stuff that happened to you, and yeah, it sucks, but I don't get it. She tries to kill you both, and now you want to resolve something? It's too late, Babe. Let it go."

I haven't gotten there yet. To that night in the car. That's why I'm remembering so slowly. She has never said she was sorry for what she said, so I could never say I was sorry, too.

"I can't let it go," I say.

"Then take it out of the house," he says. "Go on *Jerry Springer,* or something."

I actually stop chewing just to stare at him. What the hell happened?

"Sorry," he says. There's real kindness in his voice. He means it.

"You are the prize in my Cracker Jack," I say, then I cover my face with my hands, embarrassed.

At least he laughs. "You're nuts," he says.

"And caramel corn," I say. "I'm crunchy but sweet."

"I think you need to work on the sweet part," he says, then winces. I know it was just a joke, so I don't get mad.

"Put a little whipped cream on me, then," I say, tilting my head, batting my eyes.

He looks down at his half-eaten lasagna, his untouched green beans, then back up at me. "I'd like to pay you back for this afternoon," he says with a sly smile. "But your mother . . ."

"She's not speaking to me right now. And she's watching a *Columbo* rerun. Jazz won't be home for at least an hour. I'd like you to pay me back, very much."

"Really?" He says this like a kid hoping to hear Santa's real, and I get all choked up. I was getting in the mood for sex, but now I want to make love to him. I want to kiss his eyelids. I want to be held. Standing up, I walk around the table and take his hand. He follows me upstairs, both of us gracefully stepping over the gate as if gates have always been a part of our lives, as if we are good at this.

Rose wakes, sitting in a strange chair. Nearby is a hospital bed. She's in a hospital? She turns her head and looks out the window. A brown-haired girl gets out of a car, waving good-bye to the driver. It must be Jennifer. It's hard to tell from so far away.

She stays in her chair, too tired to move. After a little while, the door to the hospital room swings slowly open, and Jennifer peeks in.

"Well, it's about time," Rose says.

"Hi, Nana," Jennifer says, not coming into the room, just standing there in the doorway like an old stone.

"It's not contagious. Come in."

Jennifer comes in. She looks so young, and her clothes are too casual for a hospital, and what's that on her lips? Purple lipstick? It looks awful. Well, she's not going to start a fight now, although she should. It took Jennifer much too long to get here. "Sit on the . . . thing." She points to the bed. "Go ahead. The nurses won't mind. Sit down."

Jennifer goes over to the bed and sits down cautiously. What does she have to be nervous about? She works in a hospital, for God's sake.

"I almost died, you know. I could be dead, and it takes you a week to show up? Your brother and sister were here. Peter just left. Did you see him?"

"No." Jennifer shrugs, looking around as if Peter might still be here. Rose wants to tell her to sit up straight.

"They're going to let me out tomorrow. You'll pick me up? The doctor will tell you what time. Where's your daughter?"

"Ahhh . . ." Jennifer says, obviously stalling for time. Rose doesn't wait for her to answer.

"Play cards with me. I'm bored out of my gourd here."

Jennifer shrugs again. "Okay, but I was just looking for my mom."

Rose doesn't understand this. Did she hear her right? She must mean she had trouble finding her room. Well, she's here now, anyway. "Pull that table between us. You deal."

They play a game of Rummy and Rose wins. As Jennifer deals the next hand, Rose says, "I wish you'd stay at the house for a while. You're a good cook. Remember when you made us that duck? You must have been fourteen. So goddamn pissy all the time, then you'd make a duck with orange sauce. Asparagus, right? Didn't you make asparagus with that meal? Whatever came over you?"

Jennifer stares dumbly at her. What's the matter with her? Is she stoned?

"Well?"

Jennifer shrugs.

"Oh, stop that shrugging and play cards. God, Jennifer, do you always have to be so difficult?"

Jennifer folds her cards down. "So, I was a pretty bad kid, huh?"

"Well, angry, that's for sure. It's not like your father's death was my fault, but you acted like it was. I never understood why you ran away."

"I ran away?"

"Twice. But who's counting?" She puts her cards down. "I'll tell you a story," she says. "You want to hear it?"

"Sure, I guess," Jennifer says.

Rose tries to figure out how to say this. The harder she thinks about it, the more the words vanish. Frustration makes her head start to shake. Damn it.

"I went to the . . . bell place to swim away and I didn't. Down by the . . ." She moves her hand back and forth and that helps. She can feel the water. "Lake." "There was this lady . . . I went there to swim away, but I didn't. Then he died, just like I knew he would. It wasn't fair!"

"Nana, it's okay. Don't worry about it."

"I'm trying to tell you a . . . story. Just be quiet."

. . .

Rose wants to tell the story about the time at the Bell Tower. She's furious that she can't make Jennifer understand. The memory is right there, she's just not sure she's getting the words out.

When your father got sick, I couldn't bear it. My mother was dead. I couldn't even tell you what state my oldest sister lived in. Ben was in Vietnam, and Celia had seven children and lived hundreds of miles away. The people from the theatre didn't want to believe your father was dying, and neither did he, so I just went along with the program. Then he went into the hospital that last time, the time you insisted on coming, remember? He told me to tell everyone not to visit, just wait till he got better and came home. Jesus, he was going to die, and I had three young kids, and what I really needed was to tell him how scared I was, but he wouldn't let me, so we made plans about what we would do when he came home.

I went down to the lake around sunset. I stood out on the point, where the old Bell Tower stood, and I cursed God out loud, to the lake and the sky. But then I asked myself if I even believed in God anymore, and I didn't. Not one damn bit. God was a ruse. A phony. I had been an idiot to believe in Him in the first place. That terrified me. I felt more alone than ever. So, I thought, I'll just swim out into the middle of the lake and tread water till I drown. But I was a good swimmer and the lake wasn't all that big. I could probably tread water for an hour or more and still swim back to shore. I began crying, the kind of crying where tears just stream down your face. There I was as the sun set, staring out at a lake that I couldn't even drown myself in, knowing full well I'd go home and the phone would ring and someone would tell me Michael was dead. I should have gone back to the hospital, but they said he had a few more days and I should get my rest. What a stupid thing to say.

*After about fifteen minutes of standing there silently crying,
the sun set, and I thought, well, I'll just get in my car and drive
to a bigger goddamn lake. I knew I had you kids, but I was
empty. It was like I was made out of papier-mâché. I had no
bones or muscles or blood left. I couldn't even walk to my car
because there was nothing in me that knew how to walk. And
then this lady comes up behind me. I didn't even know she was
there until she cleared her throat. "Oh, I'm sorry to bother
you," she said, "but I just had to talk to you." When I turned
around, the sky behind her was dark. With the sunset behind
me, she couldn't see my face, that I'd been crying.*

*"I have to tell you, I was walking by, up there," she said,
pointing up the hill, "and I saw you standing down here, with
your hair glowing in the sunset. You just stood here for so long,
so peacefully, the waves lapping at your feet and the seagulls flying overhead. The sun set right behind you. I've never seen anything so beautiful in my life. So serene. I felt as if I shared a
moment with you, as if there was some bond. You seemed so
content to just stand here, to take the time to watch the sunset.
I just want to thank you."*

*I didn't know what to say, so I said, "Thank you." She
said, "Well, good evening. I'm glad I spoke to you." She left
and I walked over to the car. I got in. I drove home. I never
thought about killing myself again, although I know you don't
believe that.*

"I didn't try to kill myself!" Rose shouts. The sound of her
voice feels rough and loud in the small room. Sitting on the hospital bed, her daughter looks stunned. God, it makes Rose tired.
This sharing of her life. Still, she's glad she has finally told Jennifer all this. It's about time.

"I'm tired," she says. I want to go to . . ." She can't find the word for the thing Jennifer sits on, so she just points.

"To bed?" Jennifer asks.

Rose nods.

"Can you brush your teeth by yourself?"

"Certainly."

"Okay, while you brush your teeth, I'll get a nurse."

"Thank you, Jennifer. I'm glad you came. I was waiting for you to come back."

"You're welcome," she says.

Chapter Nine

Jazz comes out of my mother's room just as I'm headed down-stairs. When did she get home? My face heats up as I glance at the bedroom door. It's closed. Todd's still getting dressed.

"Nana wants you to get her ready for bed," Jazz says. "And, by the way, she thinks I'm you, and you're a nurse, okay?"

"Okay."

"And, Mom, she's acting a little weird. I mean weirder than usual. She was talking really good, she was telling me how you cooked a duck, but she thought I was you, then she got real quiet and she looked like a zombie or something, then she shouted, 'I never tried to kill myself!' What's that all about?"

My heart starts racing. "She said that?"

"Yeah. So what's it mean?"

"Nothing. I'll go get her ready." I walk by Jazz, go in my

mother's room, and shut the door behind me. She's standing in the middle of the room, just a few feet away, holding her toothbrush.

"Hello," she says. She says it like you say hi to someone that you walk by on the street.

"It's me, damn it," I say. "Your daughter, Jennifer. Remember me? You have to remember me. Come on. Oldest kid? Black sheep? Took you into my house so you didn't have to go to a nursing home? Remember?"

She drops the toothbrush.

"Oh, God." I rub my face, embarrassed. I shouldn't be shouting at her. It's just that Jazz upset me. I lean over and pick up the toothbrush, shake it.

"What did you tell my daughter?" I ask.

She cocks her head. Squints one eye. Sizing me up.

"What did you say?" I try to say it calmly, but I don't.

"The bell place," she says.

"The bell place? What's that?"

"It's none of your business, is what. That's between me and my daughter."

"I am your daughter!"

"I would like to go to box."

"*Bed*," I say. "*Bed*, not box."

"Yes." She looks at me. Grins. "Box."

Jesus, I swear she's doing this on purpose, just to get me mad. I wouldn't put it past her. "So go to box," I say, and then I have this sudden picture in my head that makes me dizzy. My mother in a box.

It would be easier for everyone if she were dead.

It's not the first time I have thought this. I know it's normal to think like this. At least, I hope it's normal. I wonder if Peter and Betsy have had thoughts like this.

I get her ready for bed, reminding her to put on the Depends, which she does with no complaint. If I keep bedtime to a specific routine, she follows along nicely, which means it has to be me to do this every night, and means Todd and I don't go out.

I get her into pajamas, watch her take her pills, tuck her in, pull up the rails, turn down the lamp with the dimmer switch that Todd installed, go back to her bed. Every night I say the same things to her before I leave the room, a little litany of reminders: I'm her daughter, she's in my house and I hope she's comfortable, that we love her and care for her, and that she shouldn't try to get out of bed until I come back in the morning. But tonight I pull up a chair. I will try talking very calmly, hypnotize her with slow peaceful words. See if I can find my mother if I lull just the Alzheimer's to sleep.

I go backward in my story of her, before my father's death. I have missed so much about back then, but that's only an excuse—before my father's death is the time I would go to, if I had this disease. But I don't believe in Alzheimer's. If I don't believe in it, it won't be true.

"A long time ago, when everything was good." I stop there, remembering what Jazz said, try to shake it off. "You had a garden, remember, with iris, and mums, and black-eyed Susans, and vegetables? Peas, and tomatoes, and lettuce, and zucchini." I make a long list with all the things I can remember in the garden, using a steady, rhythmic pace, making even me sleepy. "And actors would come to our house for parties, and they'd rehearse plays in our yard." I list their names, my voice getting softer, slower, the pauses longer. After a while I get the actors confused with the characters they played and know I'm tired and lost when I mention Hamlet. My eyes are getting heavy and I feel my head bob up and down once. I look at my mother, and her eyes are heavy lidded. I don't want her asleep quite yet so I skip a few things. I know where I'm headed, even if I don't want to go there. "And you cooked soup, and you taught me to cook, and then Daddy died.

"The funeral was in the theatre, and so many people came, like that lady you liked who always walked the terrier by our house, and the doctor—it was so nice of him to come. But no one came from your family, just Aunt Celia, and afterward—"

"They came," my mother says.

"Who came?" I say it gently, trying not to scare her away.

"Everyone. My brothers and sisters. All of them."

"No, just Aunt Celia. I remember how mad you were."

"You're wrong. They came. They stayed at the Hilton."

I can't believe her Alzheimer's is making up facts like the Hilton. "Really?"

"Yes."

"But I thought you were mad that they—"

"*You* were mad."

"No, I was sad Daddy—"

"You don't get sad. You took the easier way. You got angry. Just made it hell for everyone else."

No, she's wrong. I was sad. I just got mad when everyone else stopped being sad, when they thought it wasn't the time for being sad anymore.

"I didn't want another father."

"Well, you didn't get one," she says. "Happy?"

"No." I close my eyes. I have no answer. I like the quiet. Suddenly my head jerks. I open my eyes. My mother is sound asleep, breathing slowly though an open mouth. Did I fall asleep? When?

But we were just talking, and she was making sense. Weren't we just talking? And what was that about the Hilton? Now I vaguely remember something about the Hilton. Maybe her brothers and sisters did come to the funeral. Maybe I wasn't even talking to my mother. I'm too tired to know. I close my eyes again. The chair is very comfortable.

My mother was right—or the mother I made up just now was right—I got angry. Anger was something that helped me deal with my father dying, and I didn't know how to give it up. I didn't know how to back down from the hill I had made to defend myself.

A year and a half after we move to Cleveland Heights, my mother buys a house. It's not far from the duplex we rented, and we're still in the same school district, which helps because I'm finally beginning to make friends—not friends my mother likes, but they're my friends, not hers. The house is small, just three bedrooms, so I get the attic. She says we have enough money for the down payment, but we need to be frugal. We get some old furniture out of storage that belonged to Grandmother Francine, and my mother frames posters of distant countries that she buys at Woolworth's. The night we move in, we toast the new house with ginger ale, pretending it's champagne, and play a Roger Miller record, turning up the music as loud as it will go. Peter, Betsy, and I sing along with the goofy lyrics, laughing as we hold hands and dance in a circle.

"It's a new beginning," my mother says, and I stop having

fun. This is when I notice there is nothing of my father here in this house. "To Daddy!" I shout above the music, holding my glass up high. Then I throw it against the fireplace and it shatters. It's meant to be a grand gesture of love. No one smiles. It's me against them. Daddy and me against them.

My mother is forty years old and very pretty. She's lost weight, and skirts are short. Her curly hair falls to just below her shoulders and she pulls it back with a silver clip. The married women at the public relations firm where my mother works make it a project to find her a good man. She tells them to forget it. I hear her on the phone. "No, Gerty, I am not going to be fixed up with some nice man you know. I don't need to be fixed. I'm fine, thank you." Her words slur. "I don't care if you've had it set up for a month, I'm not coming." She's sounding a bit nasty, but I'm all on her side. How dare they? My dad just died. He's still here in the house. I can feel him just behind me, like a shadow with weight.

But a month later she's getting dressed on a Friday night, and we have a baby-sitter, which is stupid, since I'm fourteen. It's all stupid. She's too old to be dating, and I don't need another father. I tell her that her skirt is way too short and she has on too much makeup and Daddy is watching her. Her eyes rim with tears, and I don't feel bad at all. "Just don't go!" I shout.

"I have to," she says. "I'm stuck, this time. It got planned before I knew what it was all about. Don't worry. I'm not getting married." She says it so sadly, so honestly, right to me, that I believe her.

"Just come home early," I say.

"I will," she says.

But she doesn't. I should have known. She was wearing perfume.

The next date, two weeks later, she doesn't even apologize.

But I know how to stop this. I find the photos of Daddy she can't bear to look at that are still in a box in her closet. I stick them to the walls of her bedroom with tape. I pretend to be sleeping when she comes home. She opens her door, and I hear a gasp, a glass breaking on the floor. Then I hear sobs. She must know it was me, but she doesn't come up to my room. In the morning the pictures are gone. She doesn't say anything about them. Her eyes are as red as eyes can get, and I think, *good*. She doesn't go on a date for another two months.

The next time she tries to trick me. She says she's going to the Art Museum for the evening with some friends, but she wears eye shadow and perfume, and I know better. While she's gone, I have a séance with Peter, Betsy, and the baby-sitter, who's seventeen and thinks it's a cool idea. She has no clue. I turn off all the lamps, and in the dim glow of a candle, I call the dead. Then I pretend to have a seizure. My eyes roll back in my head. I talk in a deep voice. "I am the spirit of Michael Morgan," I say. "Where is my wife?" Betsy's too frightened to speak. "She's not here right now," Peter says, so seriously I almost lose it.

"Why not?" I say.

"I don't know," Peter says, his voice beginning to tremble.

"Well, she should be here," I say. I am doing a pretty good imitation of my father. I begin to think I really am summoning him, so I get a little scared, too. The tremble in my voice makes it sound ghostly. "I love Rose. I need her. But she doesn't love me anymore. She wants another man, and I am angry! Bring me my wife!"

By the time my mother gets home, my sister has been crying for an hour, my brother is in a state of shock, and the baby-sitter says she is never coming back.

"Oh, Jesus," my mother says when Betsy tells her that our father's ghost is angry with her. She sits on the steps to the second floor and weeps, holding my sister in her arms. I don't get any hugs, even though by now I believe I really was possessed by my father's ghost. *I will speak for you*, I tell him. I feel him nod and smile. At least he loves me.

One night, a few days later, she comes up to the attic. "We need to talk," she says, walking over to my record player to turn the music off. "What's going on? Why are you doing this to me?"

I don't know what she's talking about. "What?"

"Not letting me go out. With men. What are you so afraid of?"

"I'm not afraid of anything. I just don't need another father. I already have one. How can you forget him already?"

My mother sighs and looks around my room. The words to my favorite songs are written on the walls with Magic Marker, along with drawings of large eyes, the only thing I can draw. I expect her to forget about my question and start in harping about the walls, but she just shakes her head and sits next to me on the bed. "I haven't forgotten him, Jennifer. I never will. But life goes on. My life goes on. I want to be happy again."

"So you're not happy now?"

"What do you mean?"

"Just that, you aren't happy."

"Well, no."

"So we don't make you happy? Peter, Betsy, and me. We're

not enough to make you happy." I don't say it like a question. It's not. It a simple fact.

"Oh, Jesus, Jennifer, of course you kids make me happy, but there's something more than . . ." She looks away. "I'd like the chance to be in love again. I'm still young. I don't want to be alone."

"Well, you and Peter and Betsy are good enough for me! That's all I'm trying to say! We're a family! Us and Daddy, even though he's dead. I don't want someone else sleeping in your bed!" I jump up and walk away, toward the stairs. I don't want to have this conversation. I don't want her to say something that will make me say I'm sorry.

"Jennifer, no one's sleeping in my bed but me, not for a long time. But I deserve a life! I'm the adult here. I am allowed—"

"Over my dead body!" I shout, and run downstairs. "You go out with other men, and I'll kill myself! Just see if I don't!"

It was in the newspaper just yesterday about a teenager hanging himself. I know I won't really do it, but it sounds so good, I repeat myself. "I'll kill myself, and you'll be sorry!" I hear her coming down the stairs, and I run into the bathroom and slam the door. Lock it. I think she's going to pound on the door, tell me not to kill myself, but she doesn't.

It's a little less than three years after my father's death that she meets Simon Burton at a fund-raiser for University Hospitals. I'm almost fifteen, and she hasn't dated for a while. My guard is down.

For their first date she gets dressed in a pale yellow skirt and a white blouse. She ties an orange scarf around her neck, wears new earrings I have never seen.

"He's a pediatrician at University Hospitals," she tells me as she stands in front of the mirror putting on too much blush.

"So that means he likes kids, and I should like him?" I say, not hiding my sarcasm.

"Yes." She sighs. "That's exactly what I meant. You're so smart." Her sarcasm matches mine exactly, and we stare at each other in the mirror.

"What's he look like?" Betsy asks. She's thirteen now, and both overly serious and helplessly naive.

"He has brown hair. A great smile. He's very nice."

"Another nice guy," I say. He may not be a threat after all. The nice guys never make it. Not as long as I'm around.

My mother glares at me. "Please, Jennifer. Give me a break."

"He's here!" Peter shouts from the TV room. Peter's not happy about my mother going out but only because I'm baby-sitting. When Peter asked if he could stay at a friend's, she said no, and we both knew it was because he's really baby-sitting, that she would never leave me alone with my sister. The last time I rolled Betsy up in the braided rug and sat on her. She's a skinny little thing.

"Okay!" my mother shouts back to Peter, then lowers her voice. "Be good now." This is obviously said to me, even though my sister is standing right here, too.

The doorbell rings, and my mother takes a deep breath and rolls her shoulders. This relaxation exercise is a theatre thing. She is using something she learned from my father to date another man.

Simon comes in and says hi to all of us, using our names. She must have told him our names and he remembered them. This doesn't endear him to me as well as he might think it does. I don't believe pediatricians really like kids.

Simon has curly brown hair like my mother, but the curls are tight all over his head like a helmet. He looks Irish, like she does, with a few freckles on his nose. He's wearing a plaid jacket with wide lapels. A real dork.

"We're going to the Top of the Town," my mother says, gloating just a little as she looks at me. "I won't be home too late. Eleven?" She says this last to Simon. He nods and takes her elbow. I can't stand him.

"I expect Betsy to be in bed by then, and the two of you ready to get into bed as soon as I get home."

Yeah, right, I think. She's trying to impress him with her motherly skills. I haven't gone to bed by eleven on a weekend night for well over a year.

"I really appreciate your taking care of your brother and sister so we can go out, Jennifer," Simon says. "Thank you."

I just nod.

"Good night, then." He leads my mother out the door, still holding her arm.

I look at my brother and sister, and go up to the attic to smoke pot. I have just started smoking pot and I like it a lot, although every now and then it makes me slightly paranoid. I am asleep when my mother comes home. She wakes me up.

"Why are your windows open?" she asks.

"It got hot up here," I say.

"I'm not paying to heat the outdoors," she says, closing my windows.

"Did you have a good time?" I need to know.

She turns and smiles, a big, helpless smile. "Yes, I did. Thank you for asking."

Now I *am* paranoid, and it's not the pot. It's my mother's smile.

Before I know it, he's around all the time.

They sit on the couch and discuss Nixon. He says her name constantly. "I think your right about that, Rose." "What do you think about this Kissinger, Rose?" "Well, Rose, we have to fight for democracy sometimes." She still drinks, and I hear them discussing that. "I'm worried you're drinking too much, Rose," he says. "Let me help you." Trying to hear better, I step down one more step and it creaks. They stop talking. I don't know how he plans on helping her. If I can't get her to stop drinking, how can he?

They go out every Friday and Saturday night, and sometimes he comes to our house for dinner on Tuesdays. She'll rush home and make something expensive, like steak and twice-baked potatoes and asparagus; she knows better than to ask me to make these dinners. He joins right in, talking and making jokes, asking for seconds. One day he brings us a microscope to keep, and sets it up in the basement where my brother does his experiments. He shows Peter and Betsy how to see the cellular makeup of plants. I'd have to join in on the big huddle to see what they're doing. I don't. I go back upstairs and turn up my music. I can figure out how to use a microscope on my own, if I want. One Tuesday after dinner, he touches my mother's cheek with a finger, saying, "Look, an eyelash. We can look at your mother's eyelash!" and they all troop downstairs to the basement. I want to puke.

It takes me a while to realize just how serious they're getting—I have become distracted by pot. It's a lovely thing, and makes everything nice. I go downstairs to the basement when no one is around and look at my own eyelashes, fingernails, and pubic hairs under the microscope. I write poetry that I think is really great. Other times I watch Simon and my mother as if they are a B movie with the sound track turned off, until I get some Dexedrine from a friend, and suddenly I am wary. This man is trouble.

Lately, I think they may be talking about me. About my bad grades. My bad moods. How I got caught stealing lipstick from Woolworth's. He's a pediatrician and looks at me funny, like he's taking my temperature with his eyes. How dare she talk about me to *him*?

The first Monday in March my mother tells me that Simon and she are going to go to the Allegheny Mountains for three days, leaving this coming Sunday morning and coming home Tuesday night. A neighbor, a widow named Mrs. Layman, is going to come stay with us. My mother doesn't look me in the eye when she tells me this. Simon has never slept here, and she's never stayed overnight at his house, but I am old enough to know they are not going to the mountains to sleep in separate rooms.

I make a plan of my own.

Two nights before they leave, I pack up a small suitcase and sneak out of the house. It's snowing heavily, and the world is white and soft.

My friend Lisa thinks I am so cool to run away. She appropriates her parents' car while they're sleeping and drives me to a friend of hers, who is older than us both and lives in an apartment by herself. She has cast off her given name, and calls herself Moonglow Sunshine. I am supposed to say the whole thing, she tells me, because that completes the circle of light. After dropping me off, Lisa goes home so she won't get in trouble.

Moonglow Sunshine is into transcendental meditation. The windows are shrouded with cotton paisley sheets, the room illuminated with the flicker of candles stuck in wine bottles, the air thick with the aroma of patchouli incense. It's cold outside, but the radiators are on full blast, hissing at us like fat coiled snakes. We cross our legs and chant "Ohmm," sending good vibrations out to the poor and suffering. We do this for days and find ourselves dizzy with the power of our minds. We eat cinnamon toast because that's all there is. On the forth day I walk to the store to get more bread and maybe a few apples. I'm picked up by the police for being truant. The police officer is a sadist who grins wickedly at me in the backseat of the cruiser. "They might send you to juvenile home for this, little lady," he says. I glare at him, but my lips tremble. Besides being scared shitless, I'm starving. When my mother picks me up from the police station, she offers to take me to McDonald's. I say, "I'm sorry," and she cries as I eat a cheeseburger and fries. For some reason, she stops dating Simon and stays home a lot. She teaches me how to play gin rummy.

Chapter Ten

It's dark outside now, and the house is quiet. My mother's still asleep behind the rails. I wonder how long I have been sitting here, and what Todd and Jazz are doing. I want my life back. I am too old to be a daughter anymore.

I stand up, lean over her bed, and kiss her forehead. I remember that night, when she brought me home after McDonald's. She did the same thing, kissed my forehead as I pretended to sleep. I was so glad to be home, but I never told her that. "Sleep tight," I whisper to my mother, then walk into my daughter's room.

Jazz looks up at me from her bed. "I'm on the phone, Mom," she says, stressing the *Mom*, letting me know I'm not supposed to just walk into her room.

"I know, but I want to talk with you. Can you call them back?"

Jazz closes her eyes as if the sight of me is just too much to bear. "I guess." Then, into the phone, "I gotta go. I'll call you back."

I pick up the unicorn music box off the bureau and wind it up. It plays "My Favorite Things." I remember how badly Jazz had to have this music box three years ago. I would hear it playing whenever she was in her room. Not lately, though. Not for a while.

"So?" Jazz says. "What?"

"I just wanted to tell you I love you."

I watch her face squint up, but she stops herself from rolling her eyes. "Thanks. Love you, too."

She's really not a bad kid. At least she knows what I want to hear and gives it to me now and then. She's just at that age when she's confused and frustrated by her own feelings, and the easiest thing to do is to be tough. Why is being tough easier than being loving? Even now? When Todd tells me he loves me, I can feel my shoulders tighten. "My Favorite Things" slows, then stalls, as if the music box forgot the rest of the song.

"Do you like living here?" I ask.

"I have a choice?" Jazz says, looking at me like I'm nuts.

"Yes, if you had a choice. Would you want to live here?"

"Yeah, I guess. I don't know where else I would live. I mean, maybe if I could live with . . . my dad?" Her eyebrows arch up. I haven't told her who her dad is. She hasn't asked for a while. I kind of hoped she'd stopped asking for good. I ignore the almost question she has asked me.

"But you doing okay? I mean, you're happy, mostly, right?"

"Yeah."

"You sure?"

"Yeah."

"Would you tell me if you weren't? If you had a problem?"

"I guess." She rolls her eyes.

"Well, I want you to," I say. "I want you to be able to tell me if something's wrong."

"Okay."

"Good. Just remember I'll love you no matter what."

"Like if I get pregnant or steal something?" She says this with a smile, and I know she's just trying to shock me.

"Yes. Exactly."

"Okay. Fine." There's very little sarcasm in her voice. I'll take it.

"Don't stay up too late," I say. "Love you."

She half smiles, nods. She's not going to say she loves me twice in one night. There are limits. I understand them.

I walk downstairs, taking each step as if it were a slow, difficult thought. I'm so tired of being the caretaker of someone with Alzheimer's. I'm betting Todd's tired of being the caretaker of the caretaker. The sound of the TV wavers from the family room. I follow the sound to Todd.

He sits on the couch watching one of those shows where a good-looking but down-to-earth couple walk the viewer through building a fireplace from scratch, or installing a Jacuzzi in a newly built bathroom the size of a living room. Todd watches these shows as a way of relaxing, just as I watch the Discovery Channel. No plot, just something to rest your eyes on.

"Hey there," I say.

"Hi, Babe." He slides over to make room for me on the couch.

"If I sit down, I'll never get up," I tell him. "I'm going to go to bed in a minute anyway." I lean against the door frame. He mutes the TV.

"You were up there a long time," he says. "Everything okay?"

"Who knows? I'm just as crazy as she is. I think I just imagined a whole conversation with her. It was like talking to my own subconscious. I don't know if I liked it much. Did Jazz say anything to you about coming home and us being in the bedroom?"

"What's she going to say? And besides, it's normal. We're married."

"Remind me about that," I say.

"Hey, I'm the one who moved over so you could sit down. You'd rather stand against a wall than let me put my arm around you."

"Point taken. At least you're not on the computer, talking with someone."

He doesn't say anything.

"Have you forgotten what we did upstairs?" I ask. "That was more than putting your arm around me."

"Yeah. And the thing by the back door was very good, too, but I think you just did that to thank me for getting the chicken."

"Hey, if that's how I thank you for picking up the chicken, wait till you see what I do when you bring home a turkey."

"I'm not kidding, Babe." The lines around his mouth are tight.

"I know. I just can't think straight. Look, what I did by the back door was because I wanted to make you happy. Is that so bad?"

"I'm confused. You give me this great blow job, make dinner, we go upstairs and have sex, but you won't sit down and talk. You're stumbling backward for something you left behind, and you don't want my help. I'm the only one worrying about the future."

The TV flickers across his face. He hasn't turned to look at the screen once. I know I would have. If I was sitting on the couch right now, I'd be staring at the couple with the saw and hammer.

"Yeah, well, I can't think about the future because the future is that my mother's going to forget how to eat, how to walk, and then she's going to die, probably in a nursing home while I'm not there. I have to watch her so she doesn't stuff shit into toilets, or eat something poisonous, or . . . whatever." I know I'm getting defensive. Getting my back up, my mother would say. "I'm too tired to talk about this right now. I love you. Thanks for getting the chicken."

He only nods, not a good sign.

"Good night," I say.

At least one of us is still talking.

Rose wakes in the middle of the night. There's a dim lamp glowing and rails around her bed. She doesn't cry out. She knows better. It won't do any good. She doesn't waste time with things that won't work. She's practical that way. Michael was never practical, always a dreamer. Wanted her barefoot and pregnant, but then he up and died on her. She got smart quick. Learned to handle a mortgage, invested in stocks bit by bit, saved money for her retirement. All along she knew there would never be another man. Just not in the cards. But Simon . . . oh, she had hoped . . . but he was practical, too. Didn't waste time on things that wouldn't work.

She grasps a cold metal rail with her hand. *This is what holds me in*, she thinks. *Well, so be it.*

For a while, maybe an hour, she is seventy-four and knows it. Knows everything. That everyone thought she couldn't live without Michael, but the truth is, she could. Love could wear thin, and it had started to, before Michael died. No one knew that but her and Michael, and he took that truth with him to the grave. Oh, she loved him, but she loved him more after he died. She loved him then and after, for always. But there were other men.

She will have to tell Jennifer about Simon.

Chapter Eleven

I wake up as the sky begins to brighten. Todd's already out of bed. He'll have made a pot of coffee and laid out the Living section of the *Plain Dealer* on the kitchen table at the spot where I sit, argument or not. He's probably the best damn thing that ever happened to me, and I resent it. I want *me* to be the best damn thing that ever happened to me.

Sitting up in bed, I know I should call Kethley House and tell them we want the room, but before I make that commitment, I'll drive my mother to the nursing home, see if her feelings have changed. I'm sure they have. She has a great range of disgust.

Downstairs, Todd's reading the paper, but the Living section is not at my place. I'm glad he's not as good as I thought. I kiss him on the forehead.

"Thanks," I say.

"For what?" he asks.

"For nothing," I say, and mean it. *Ignore me just a little and I'll be fine*. I'm constantly exhausted by trying to keep up with his good standards. I wonder if this idea to take care of my mother is something I came up with to impress him.

"I'll call Kethley House," I say. "Ask if we can visit again. Tell them we're still interested. I'll see how long they can hold the room."

"Thank you," he says, both words dry and flat.

"Sure," I say, using the same tone.

"Jazz said to tell you she was going to Turtle's after school," he informs me.

"Okay. Thank you." He's wearing his work clothes: jeans spattered in paint, black T-shirt, a red plaid flannel shirt over that, holes torn on both elbows. I used to be up and dressed by now, in a blouse and skirt, stockings and nice shoes. We'd look so odd at the breakfast table, as if I were one of those women who pay him to fix up their homes. One night Jazz was at a sleepover and I kept on my work clothes, overdid the makeup. When he came home smelling of sweat, I wouldn't let him shower. I pretended I was one of those rich woman, employing him, telling him what to do. "Lower," I said. "Softer." It was very, very good, but it was too close to the truth, and we never did it again.

Now, sometimes, I don't even change my clothes for two days.

Finished with the paper, he ties his bandanna around his head now. It's to cover his hair from sawdust and paint, and to look tougher, hide his pretty hair. This man, in his bandanna, always finds work; word of mouth keeps him employed, although he never seems to break even. My salary and health care are what make it possible for the three of us to live as we do.

"I don't know when I'll get home," he says.

"Okay," I say. "Just come home."

He looks up. Our eyes meet. We both know we're falling apart. I'm not the only one here who uses sex as a temporary adhesive.

"I will," he says. He picks up his travel mug full of hot coffee and leaves. He forgets to kiss me goodbye.

He doesn't really forget, he just doesn't.

I tell my mother that we're going to take a ride to the ice-cream shop. I just don't tell her that the ice-cream shop is in a nursing home. She climbs into the car without question. I think of all the times I told Jazz never to to get into a car with a stranger.

"Okay, we're here," I say, pulling into the parking lot. It's a clear, blue day and not too chilly for October. A few old men and women—mostly women—are set outside on benches, cheeks pink, noses dripping. A black woman in a white uniform stands off to the side, smoking a cigarette. I shudder; these old people with deep wrinkles and droopy ears are the good ones, trusted to sit outside with only one aide to watch them casually, as if they are potted plants. I am thankful, once again, for the fact my mother has great skin, that she doesn't show her age. Heredity: When I am old and set out like a potted plant, I will look younger than the rest.

My mother turns and glares at me.

"We're going to get an ice-cream sundae. Remember?" I say.

Her lip curls and she shakes her head. She snorts. I know exactly what she's saying. *Do you think me an idiot?* So I answer her.

"Okay, it's not a regular ice-cream shop. It's Kethley House.

The nursing home I brought you to before. I really think you might like it. Give it another chance, okay? And they *do* have an ice-cream shop. That's the truth. We'll just go in to get ice cream. That's all. That's not so hard, right?"

She rolls her eyes. Either she has been taking lessons from Jazz or this eye-rolling thing is hereditary because they both do it exactly alike, their green irises slowly arching up, then back down like the sun rising and setting—big dramatic gestures followed by a slow shake of their head. Seeing that, from my mother or Jazz, makes me feel small and stupid. And angry.

"Oh, come on," I say. "I'm going to get out of the car and come around and open your door. Just get out and come in with me for *one* ice-cream sundae. That's all I'm asking. Just this one small thing." I get out of the car without waiting for the next show of unspoken words, and with my back turned to her, I pretend she's nodding, agreeing with me. I'm good at pretending. I tell myself that if I get her to go inside, I'll reward myself with a video tonight. Something science fiction, far in the future, on another planet. You never see nursing homes in science-fiction movies.

I open her door, offer a hand. My mother is a statue, hands folded in her lap, legs together, feet planted firmly on the floor, looking straight ahead as if she were deaf. "Come on," I say, a bit loud. The old people on the benches are staring at me with big droopy eyes, and the aide is looking my way. I want to kick the car. "Come on, Mother, just for a few minutes. Please? Ice cream? Pretty, pretty please with ice cream on top?" I try a laugh. It doesn't work. I grab her arm. Sometimes I can propel her about like this. Sometimes that's all she needs. Not this time. It's surprising how strong the muscles are under the soft, flabby-looking skin of her upper arm. A few weeks ago she threw a dictionary at me, and it went a whole lot farther than I thought it would and hit me in the shin. I try to lift her out of her seat, flashing back to a long time ago when I did this same thing to Jazz to get her into the doctor's office. She stiffened her legs and dragged her feet, so it was quite a scene. I have the feeling that if I actually pull my mother out of the car, she will drop like a lead balloon onto the parking lot pavement, with an audience, to boot. The aide will come over and ask if I need help, and I'll burst into tears. I let go of my mother's arm.

"Please?" I ask again, my voice sweet and kind and sounding ten years old.

Her lips are pressed so tight together they disappear. "Fine," I say. "Have it your way." I carefully don't slam the car door.

I don't want to go home yet. Todd will have called, to see how our nursing home visit went. I don't want to go into my house, see that red light on the answering machine. I won't be able to ignore it, it would be rude; that red light blinking like a heartbeat, knowing it's my husband's.

"Do you want ice cream now?" I ask as we drive away.

"Okay," she says. She's smiling now because she won. I drive to Draeger's, a homemade ice-cream and candy shop where I used to take Jazz for her birthday.

After ordering a mint chocolate chip sundae for me, and strawberry for her, I touch her hand to get her attention. She seems dazed. The inside of the shop is brightly lit, and the walls, tables, and floor are the blue and pink of cotton candy. "Do you remember when I ran away from home for four days?" I say. "I'm sorry I scared you."

"You were gone three days," she says.

The sentence is grammatically correct, and she seems to know who I am, but the facts are wrong. "No, I was gone four days. Remember?"

"Oh, bosh!" she says. The waitress has just put the ice cream down in front of us. I smile at her and she nods. Maybe she has a mother.

"Really. You took me to McDonald's after you picked me up. Four days."

She rolls her eyes and eats the hot fudge off the top of the sundae. "I don't like strawberry ice cream," she says. "You know that."

I didn't. I thought she liked strawberry ice cream.

"You and Simon broke up right after. Remember?"

"Simon?" she says. "Oh. I have to tell you about Simon. Good I remembered!"

"What did you remember?"

"Simon!"

"Yes, but what about him?"

"He was the one." She points to her chest. "I want you to know." Then she looks at me and squints.

"I'm Jennifer," I remind her.

She nods, but I can tell she's not so sure.

"So tell me," I say. "Tell me about Simon."

"He was too smart for me," she says. "Damn it. He liked me, though. He almost loved me. He was a children's . . ."

"Pediatrician," I say. She nods.

"You really screwed things up," she says. "And you didn't even know I . . ." She taps her chest three times. I see the words, *loved him*.

My mother tells me the story of Simon, skipping words, using the wrong words, drawing words in the air. I hear all the words she misses. I'm getting good at this.

This is what I hear, although it's not exactly what she says.

. . .

Rose swore that she would never love another man. She made this promise as Michael grew thin in the hospital. She made this promise standing by his freshly dug grave. Even as she goes out on dates with the men her friends have set her up with, she has no intention of falling in love. And then she meets Simon.

He's bright, and makes her feel bright. She feels connected again, both to the world outside her own narrow scope and to the girl she used to be. They follow the elections with an intensity she had forgotten she ever had. They both agree it's a good thing Nixon won over Humphrey, who seems to be a lightweight. And Simon likes sports, something Rose has never paid much attention to. They sit on her couch watching the Olympics in Mexico, and he surprises her by jumping up and hollering at the screen during the fight between George Foreman and the Russian boxer, then shouting with joy when Foreman wins. She likes it that he surprises her. He feels solid, substantial; adult. And he kisses like all get out. They make love at his apartment a month after their first date. He's the second man in her whole life she has made love to. She doesn't cry until after she gets home.

Three months later they have both said they love each other, but there are problems. He says she drinks too much. She says he doesn't know how to loosen up. He says Jennifer treats him rudely. She agrees, but then he tells her that Jennifer treats *her* badly, too, and she shouldn't put up with it, and she won't answer that one. It's not something she cares to admit to. And work is not going well. She has headaches to beat the band. When she arrives late for the third time in a week, her boss asks her if everything's all right. She says, "Everything's fine, thank you," and she's on time every day for the next two weeks, but then she begins to leave early. She says her daughter's taking private skating lessons and needs to be picked up at the rink by four-thirty. It is the first bold-faced lie she has ever told, and it bothers her until the second glass of scotch, when she waves away the worry with a flick of her hand. "Oh, who cares," she tells herself. She calls Simon early in the evening, before her voice gets sloppy. "It's my new routine," she tells him. "Go to bed early, rise early." It's not quite a bold-faced lie, and easy to live with. When she hangs up the phone, she gets a glass and fills it halfway with Johnnie Walker Red, drinks it standing by the sink. Then she fills it halfway again and takes it into the living room. She turns on the TV. She sits straight and holds her head high. She is not the type to slouch.

One morning Rose wakes to find her cigarettes in the sink, smothered in scotch. The smell is nauseating. The need for a cigarette is overpowering. She will kill Jennifer. How dare she! Who the hell is *she* to be so smug, the little druggie? The attic reeks of marijuana. Rose cries over the kitchen sink and cleans up the mess.

That Friday night Jennifer tries to leave the house, even though she's grounded. "You're not going anywhere!" Rose yells. "You're to stay home, clean your room, and stay off the phone!"

"What will you do?" Jennifer says. "Stay home for once and watch me?"

"I have a life! I'm allowed to have a life! You need to listen to me and stay home!"

"Why? Because you're such a good example?"

"Shut up, Jenny!" yells Peter, coming into the kitchen, his fist clenched.

Rose appreciates Peter's concern, but she wishes he'd stay out of this. It only makes it more difficult with two kids shouting.

"Fuck you," Jennifer says to Peter, giving him the finger.

Peter rushes Jennifer and knocks her against the fridge. She scratches his face, and he grabs her arm and twists it behind her back. Peter has been lifting weights, and his arms are muscular. Within a second Jennifer's bent over double, screaming for help. Who the hell is going to help you? Rose thinks.

"Stop it!" Rose shouts.

Simon comes in the side door. At the sight of him everyone freezes. He's never just walked in before. This puts a new slant on everything. He stands there, looking at them. He's furious, his teeth clenched, eyes narrowed.

"Let her go," he says to Peter, with a sigh, as if maybe Peter had done the right thing but must stop now. "Why don't you leave us alone for a minute, Peter. Would you mind?" Peter looks at Simon, shrugs, and walks out of the kitchen. The TV goes on. Jennifer and Simon glare at each other. "Apologize to your mother," he says.

"She thinks she's perfect," Jennifer says. "And you think you're my dad, but you're not. You can't tell me what to do."

"No," he says. "But I can ask you, and you can do it because you should. I know it's hard to lose a father. My dad died a few years ago and I'm still crying about it. But I'm not blaming anyone. Stop blaming your mother."

Rose feels swollen with love for this man. Her heart pounds in her chest, and she hopes these well-said words will do the trick, make everything better. If only that could happen, she would never drink again. She holds her breath. This is not a time to interfere. It's time to let the cards fall where they may.

"I'm not blaming her for my dad dying, Simon," Jennifer says in a dry, even tone that makes Rose's stomach sink. "My dad was what made her happy, not us. I'm just tired of being reminded of that. But now you're here, and she's still drinking. I wonder why?" Jennifer turns away from Simon and looks at Rose. "I'm sorry I yelled at you. I should know better. I should know better than to even bother talking to you. I'll go to my room now."

Jennifer walks out of the kitchen and up the stairs. Rose clamps her teeth closed as tight as she can to keep from crying. There's silence as both she and Simon stand there, not knowing what to say. Finally Simon asks, "Should we stay here, tonight? We could order out."

"No. Let's go. We need to give Betsy a ride, anyway. She's in her room. I'll go get her." She goes upstairs to Betsy's room. Betsy doesn't say a word about the arguing downstairs.

"I love you, Betsy," she says. "Thank you for being a good kid."

"You're welcome," Betsy says.

Rose stares at Betsy, this quiet child who gets all A's on her report cards, who doesn't say much but is kind and polite when she does speak. Too polite, maybe? They are all afraid, just handle it differently. Betsy thinks that if she's very good, no one else will die. Jennifer thinks she can bully death away. Peter's trying to fight it physically; he's not old enough yet to understand that cancer doesn't care if you have muscles. Cancer doesn't give a crap if you're good or bad or if your family needs you.

Sure, she drinks to ignore all this, but maybe she's the only smart one.

As she gets into the car, Rose wonders what Simon does to push away death. That he might love her, to comfort himself, troubles her. It's too much responsibility.

It's Friday night, and on Sunday they're going on a three-day trip to a cabin in Pennsylvania. At the restaurant they talk about the drive, what they'll pack, what they might do there. They grin at the suggestion that they might not leave the cabin at all.

When Simon drops her off, Rose notices the house feels cold and she remembers the time in her life when her brothers and sisters had all moved out. She keeps her coat on as she walks upstairs to the attic. Peter was to be picked up at eight to spend the night at his friend's. Jennifer was to stay home, but that didn't mean she did. No music filters down through the floorboards.

There's a note on Jennifer's pillow, and somehow, Rose was expecting it. Staring at the note, not able to read it yet, she wonders; did she choose to go out, leaving her daughter to her own fate? Possibly.

Don't bother looking for me. I'll be out of the state by the time you read this. Just making life easier for you. Your daughter, Jenny.

A laugh like choking clenches her throat. Her daughter is so theatrical. Michael's genes. Damn it. Don't do this to me.

What should she do?

There's a good chance this is all show, and Jennifer's peacefully sleeping at a friend's house. Still, Rose will have to make some phone calls. It's midnight. God, she wants to just go to sleep and see if Jennifer isn't back tomorrow. She can't, though, can she? How would she ever explain herself? *I was tired?* Still, calling strangers at midnight, admitting that she doesn't know where her daughter is, will be so goddamn embarrassing. Now she's pissed. Now she's really pissed.

"Damn it, Jennifer!" she shouts to the room. "Fuck!" It's the first time she's ever said that word out loud. She will not cry. Her eyes feel hot, but dry. Fine, she thinks. Fine. I have to make these calls.

When she gets to the phone, she realizes she knows only two of Jennifer's friends, who might not be her friends anymore. She hasn't been keeping track. She has been too busy being a god-damn widow and paying the bills. She makes the two calls. Jennifer's not at either place. Rose asks these parents if they have any suggestions, any other phone numbers. They kindly offer her lists of names and numbers. She writes them all down, and hangs up the phone. She can't do this anymore. Not a chance.

Simon will be home now and she can call him. But she won't. He'd have all sorts of good suggestions and opinions he'll want to share. She can't stand anyone's opinions just now. She's too tired. Jennifer will come home tomorrow. Where else could she go? She's only trying to scare Rose; not to get scared is to win this round. She will simply go to bed.

She has one drink and goes upstairs. Outside, it begins to sleet, the pings against the windows sound like someone typing slowly, then faster, a furious release of cold, harsh words. She takes off all her clothes and gets into her flannel pajamas, a Christmas present from Peter. Before she falls asleep, she has this thought: Peter will know what to do. Her fourteen-year-old son will know what to do.

Light seeping through the thin shades wakes Rose, and her first cogent thought is *damn those cheap shades*. When might she have enough money to do things right? She is sick of cutting corners.

Then she feels her head swell, as if while she lies there it fills with a heavy liquid expanding inside her skull. The throbbing will eventually go away, even though it's hard to believe—where does pain go? And then she thinks of Jennifer and wonders if last night was a bad dream. No, it was too ordinary. Rose's dreams are of long halls with no doors, or flying above the trees, or ghosts—Michael to be exact. While she sleeps, Michael walks, talks, and directs plays. He sits down to dinner. He hangs pictures. By sleeping, she is responsible for his life. In the day he is just plain dead.

Rose makes coffee and well-done toast. She can't stand the thought of chewing anything soft so early in the morning. She sits at the kitchen table, staring at nothing, eating slowly. She does not want this day to start. She'll have to search Jennifer's room for phone numbers, possible clues. She's searched her daughter's room before and always found something, a little pipe, a small plastic bag with the remains of what must be pot, an odd pill. At first she began these searches with vigor; she would find something, prove to her daughter that she has a drug problem, and they would both cry and hug and bond. What a stupid word. *Bond*. As if she wanted to be bonded to her daughter. She simply wants to be a good mother.

But after the first confrontation—when Jennifer ranted and raved, swearing it was someone else's pot, even naming a name—Rose simply threw out whatever she found, a statement in itself. *See, I am searching your room.* A lot of good that did.

And now Rose can't stand the thought of pulling out drawers, lifting the mattress. Jennifer had better come home soon because Rose can't bear it. And if Jennifer does come home today, before Simon calls, she won't ever have to tell him that her daughter ran away, and that she didn't call him. Because Simon will not be happy. He will feel betrayed. Damn him. What promises has she made by saying she loves him? What choices does she have to make because she *does* love him?

Jennifer is not home by noon. Rose calls Peter at the house he slept over at last night, and he gives her a few more names to try, says he will get a ride home soon to help her look for Jennifer. He sounds excited by this turn of events. She wonders if it's because he thinks Jennifer may really be gone, or because it makes him look even better. Peter's into making good impressions.

Rose remembers training for the synchronized swim team in high school. She would hold her breath until it hurt, then hold it longer, finally letting her breath out slowly, not allowing herself to gasp. If she gasped, she would add ten more minutes to her practice. But, in the end, she could hold her breath longer than anyone.

Simon doesn't call until five in the evening, a slight blessing—he has been very busy all day. Rose interrupts him as he describes a nasty accident a teenage girl had involving a pencil and her eye. She interrupts him because he will be embarrassed he went on and on when she had something so important to say, and she doesn't want to embarrass him. She's right, he's quite shocked by her news and asks her how she discovered Jennifer had run away. For a moment she thinks to lie; she could say that just this morning she went up to her daughter's room and found the note, but if she tells this lie to him, and he believes her, she will lose respect for him. She tells the truth.

"Last night? And you didn't call me?" There is everything in his voice she expected, and more. Hurt, confusion, anger, and distance, as if already he is eyeing his retreat.

Her heart skips a beat, throwing her off-kilter. She grinds out her cigarette in the ashtray; a blue-glazed, half-moon tin-thing Jennifer made in camp one year at Boys & Girls Club, so long ago. "I'm sorry. I know I should have called you, but I thought it was a prank. Maybe it is."

"And you called everyone you can think of?"

"Yeah. I even searched her room." She told him a month ago how she searched Jennifer's room and found pot. He was so appalled, and offered so many careful, moral, perceptive ideas that she was overwhelmed by her own inadequacies and never told him about the following searches, the things she found and threw away. "I've been driving around to a few spots she hangs out, like Coventry and the mall. I guess I'll go out again now and look some more."

"Would you like me to come help?"

Right away she knows something has changed. The Simon who loved her just last night would have said, *I'm coming over.* This Simon feels unneeded, hurt, and a bit pissed. He warned her she had to do something about Jennifer and she didn't.

"Please," she says.

"I'll be there in ten minutes." He's coming straight from the hospital.

"Thank you," she says.

As they drive around looking for Jennifer, Simon tells her that she should send her daughter to a drug treatment program, or one of those tough-love places where Jennifer will scrub bathroom floors with a toothbrush. His concern is tinged with resentment. All his comments are too pat, too easily said. Her jaw tight, hands gripping the wheel, driving because she knows this part of town—and *her* daughter—Rose says, "You're such a fool."

"You think so?" he asks. His anger comes out dry and held tight. Doesn't he know how to fight?

"Yes. You don't know my daughter at all. Or me. You're pretty damn new to it all, to know so bloody much."

"Yes, I guess I am." That's all he says.

Rose worries. She knows she has gone too far, but this is her life he's judging. "I only meant—"

"Oh, I know what you meant. I really don't want to discuss it anymore, if you don't mind."

She can't drive, not like this. Her sight is blurred; it is as if she is seeing the streets and buildings through a hot, bright fog. She pulls over to the side of the road. Trees hold snow along their branches like deft ballerinas, icicles glisten from the eves of homes, window lit, cozy, warm inside. What she sees isn't real, they are the postcards, she thinks, of places she might have lived if Michael hadn't died. *Wish you were here*. The thought is bitter and she's tired of that taste in her mouth. She's doing the best she can. Damn Simon for judging her.

"Look," she says. "I know I need to do something about Jennifer—but I think your ideas are a bit harsh. She's lost a father. She needs love, not boot camp."

Simon turns away, shaking his head slowly. There's dead silence. The windshield wipers are on, brushing aside the snow with a rhythmic pulse that Rose finds annoying. She almost turns them off, but she's afraid of being closed in with Simon, the outside world gone—because if no one was looking right now, she would climb into his lap and curl up, close her eyes and never open them again. And she can't. Life doesn't work that way. God knows, she's no one's good-luck charm anymore.

"I don't think love's going to do it this time," Simon says.

She has no answer for that, so she doesn't say anything. Once again they just sit in silence. Finally he touches her thigh. Briefly.

"Let's go back to your house, Rose. I think I'll go home now."

She knows it's over. She just doesn't have the energy to fight for his love right now. Maybe if he goes home, he'll miss her. That's how it works for her, anyway. She will miss him terribly in a few hours. She even misses Jennifer right now.

"Okay," she says. "I'm sorry."

"Me, too."

She drives home, still looking out the window for Jennifer, imagining her barefoot in the snow, wandering around, searching for a little warmth. Just for a minute she hopes Jennifer *is* barefoot.

Rose pulls up the driveway and they both get out of the car. Simon turns to walk down to the street, where he parked his car. It's covered with snow.

"Simon," she says. "I didn't mean what I said. I'm tense and tired. I'm sorry."

"We'll talk when you're feeling better," he says. "Please call me when you hear about Jennifer. I'm sure she's fine. She'll be home soon."

"Yeah, I think she will," she says. "I'll call you." Nothing has been said about the trip to the cabin in the mountains. They would have been leaving tomorrow, but that will not happen now. She knows, too, why Jennifer chose to run away.

Simon gets into his car, turns on the wipers, and drives off. Snow blows off the back of his car like a long white wave.

There is at least five inches of snow on the ground. There are no tracks leading to her door.

· · ·

Sunday Rose doesn't call Simon, and he doesn't call her. But she does call the police. They take a description and tell her to stay by the phone.

On Monday she goes to work, thinking that Jennifer might sneak home while she's at the office—it would be just like Jennifer to be home when Rose returns, as if nothing ever happened. It is exactly what Rose believes *will* happen.

But Jennifer does not just appear, and Rose has dinner with Peter, Betsy, and the absence of Jennifer. Peter does his best to cheer her up by talking about a science project that involves building a volcano. Betsy quietly clears the table and does the dishes. Rose could enjoy this, the facade of a family; this would be something she could live with.

She thinks of calling Simon, but she's afraid she will beg him to forgive her for what she said, and she won't do that. She will not beg, so she does not call.

The next morning the police phone her at work. Jennifer has been picked up as truant. Rose goes to the police station, signs some papers, and takes Jennifer to McDonald's because she doesn't want to take her home yet. She doesn't want to begin all over again, being a widow with three children. "I'm so miserable," she tells Jennifer as her daughter eats french fries.

"I'm sorry," Jennifer says. "I'm sorry I ran away. It was stupid."

"Why do you hate me?" she asks, not sure she wants to know.

"I don't." Jennifer looks her right in the eye. Rose wants to believe her.

"I won't drink anymore," she says, "if that's it. I'm done." She doesn't drink all that much anyway, just now and then, when things get really bad, but if that's the problem between her and Jennifer, then she'll stop.

"Thanks. That would help."

"What else would help?"

"I don't know." Jennifer crumples up the wrapper. She ate three hamburgers, and Rose finds some satisfaction in the fact her daughter is so hungry. "I get mad. Sometimes I forget Daddy, like whole days go by, and I hate myself for forgetting him. What's the matter with me?"

"You never cried. Maybe that's it. Maybe you have to do that. How about we go to a counselor? I think we should." She doesn't want to do this; she doesn't want her privacy invaded, but she's pretty sure she won't be confiding in Simon again, and they both might need someone to talk to.

"No. I'm not going to a counselor. I can cry all by myself, if that's what you think I should do. I just can't stand seeing you with men. It makes me crazy. I know that's not fair. I know it. So date Simon. I don't care. I think he's a dork, but do what you want."

"Gee, thanks, Jennifer. Thanks a lot." She looks at her daughter, the long, straight, unwashed hair parted in the middle, the ratty winter coat she got at a thrift shop, her sad, pale face, and Rose feels sorry for her. She herself had so much going for her when she was fifteen. So many interests. "Look. Things have to change. I'll quit drinking, but you have to do something, too. Got it?"

Jennifer nods.

"Okay. Here it is. I'll quit drinking, and you join the swim team and the Spanish Club, and spend weeknights at home doing homework, and no counselor. Deal?"

"Deal. But I get to talk about Daddy sometimes."

"No taping pictures to the walls. I see him just fine in my head, Jennifer. Don't think I've forgotten him. I loved him, too. You know what you don't get, Jennifer? That I know what love is. I want it again."

"All right, fine," Jennifer says. But what her daughter doesn't know, but Rose does, is that it's already too late for her and Simon.

She calls him that night to tell him that Jennifer's back. He says he's glad for both of them. He asks if she's going to send Jennifer to a counselor, or a drug treatment program. This is a test, to see if she wants him in her life.

"No, we've worked something out."

"Good for you," he says.

When she hangs up, she wants a drink so bad that she pours a full glass of plain old ginger ale and gulps it so quickly she nearly gags, then she pours another glass of ginger ale and guzzles it, too. Now there's no room in her for anything else. She goes up to bed and crawls under her covers and screams against the pillow. "Damn you, damn you, damn you!" Jennifer thinks she has forgotten Michael, but she hasn't.

Less than two weeks later, on a Friday night when all her kids are out of the house, Rose takes the bottle of Jim Beam out from behind the mixing bowl and has just one drink. She's all alone on a Friday night. She deserves one drink. Saturday night she has two, because one just doesn't do it.

Drinking gives her an excuse to cry. And she's angry; drinking seems like giving the world a good slap in the face. And, finally, she's an adult and it's perfectly legal.

Chapter Twelve

I added that last part to my mother's story, about why she began to drink again. Her strawberry ice cream has melted in the bowl, but she has managed to scrape out every last bit of hot fudge.

I never knew that my mother loved Simon, or why they stopped seeing each other. I am very sorry for the two of us, who we were back then. No matter the point of view, no matter who you listen to, it wasn't a very good time.

It's 1969, and Rose works as a secretary for a large public relations firm downtown. Sometimes she feels as though she has stepped back in time, to her first job at the law firm where she worked when she was twenty. The styles have changed, but the conceit is the same. This is the world of business. Art is only something to subscribe to. She misses the easy laughter and crude jokes of the theatre people, but she finds that, once again, she's very good at this, being a secretary.

She wonders if she'd sue her employers for sexual harassment if something like that happened again. Yes, she would. Would she marry Michael, knowing he was going to die and leave her with three children and debts she never knew they had? She thinks she would, but she's not sure.

As for her family; Peter is beating himself up with exercise, and Betsy walks around looking at the ground as if it might split in two. Rose has seen Betsy on her hands and knees watching ants crawl into cracks. What the hell is that all about? And her deal with Jennifer? The Spanish Club lasted three weeks, the swim team, four. And just last week Rose smelled pot in her daughter's bedroom, who's seldom home anyway. At least Peter and Betsy sit down with her for a nice dinner. Rose appreciates the kindness her other two children show her, but she doesn't quite know what to do with it. Does it mean she's supposed to be happy?

And the world's so big that it scares her more than interests her now. There's a war her son might be drafted to go fight. Just that thought alone makes her numb. She's a widow with three children and she needs to pay the rent. How can she fight a war? Oh, others do, but they all seem so innocent. People die, no matter what you do. No matter how much you care. Caring is worth a hill of beans. She isn't up to it anymore.

A year and four months after Simon drove off, Rose is forty-three, standing by a lilac tree. She holds a vodka and tonic and talks to Larry Miller, the owner of the public relations firm, and Kathy, his wife—he has a hearing aid and she has eyebrows drawn on like the sharp outline of two hills. It's been hot all day, but now there's a slight breeze. A good-looking man with a gray goatee walks over. He's wearing a well-ironed Hawaiian shirt and crisp beige slacks.

"Joe!" Larry says, holding out a hand. "You came! Kathy, you remember Joe, don't you? The Lutts' son? And this is Rose Morgan. Rose, Joe Lutt. Rose is a secretary in our firm. Rose, I'm trying to talk Joe into joining us. Be nice now."

"Pleased to meet you, Rose." Joe Lutt holds out a hand and she shakes it. "And Mrs. Miller, of course I remember you. You brought over a chicken casserole after my dad died, and we talked in the kitchen for a long time. It's been years, but I remember that talk well. It helped me get through a bad time. Thanks again."

Kathy Miller smiles gently. "Well, we loved your father, Joe. We still miss him. He was a very good man."

Rose watches them talk, thinking she should leave, but she doesn't really want to move from this place that smells of lilacs, where kind people stand and talk about death as if it's something you can get over with some dignity left.

"So, how long have you been with the firm, Rose?" Joe asks. He has a disarming smile.

"Oh, too long, much too long. You're thinking of joining us?"

"Well, Mr. Miller here has made me a very nice offer. I've promised to let them know by the end of next week. They're making it pretty tempting."

"Do you live in Cleveland?" she asks.

"I used to. I work with McMillian and Peters in Kansas City, but . . ." He looks down at his drink, seemingly bashful for a moment, but then smiles that smile again. "I've just gone through a divorce, and I'd like to put that and a few other things behind me."

"I'm sorry," she says. "I didn't mean to pry."

"You didn't," Joe says.

"Joe and my son used to play football on the same team in high school," Larry Miller says, patting him on the back. "I remember that graduation. Nineteen forty-nine. Kathy cried the whole time. Blew her nose so loud during 'Pomp and Circumstance,' I thought she was a trombone."

"You were no dry creek bed, yourself," Kathy Miller says. "So don't pretend you were. Besides, no one wants to hear your old stories. I do hope you'll take up Larry's offer, Joe. Oh, my, I need my drink refilled."

"I know a hint when I hear one. Excuse us, Rose. Joe. Call me as soon as you make up your mind."

"I will."

Rose is left standing by the lilac tree with Joe Lutt, who, she has just figured out, is four years younger than she.

"Do you play croquet?" he asks.

"Not really."

"Then you need to learn. No one's playing right now. We'll have the court to ourselves. Care to try?"

She almost says *no, thanks*. She comes that close to walking away and going home. But then she thinks about going home. "Okay," she says. "You're on."

To teach her how to play croquet, Joe wraps his hands around hers on the mallet and she feels foolish. She's played this game before. Why did she say she hadn't? Within minutes they're making suggestive jokes about the ball going through the hoops. He wins the first game and they shake hands. When she wins the next game, Joe whoops, lifting her into the air and giving her a spin. His hands brush her breasts when he lowers her to the ground. She's not sure how she feels about that—or doesn't like how she feels about that. Either way, she gives him her phone number when he asks.

When she gets home, she knows Joe will call her soon. She'll have to head off the whole Jennifer situation.

She's got to be over it by now, Rose thinks, heading upstairs to where the music from the attic broadcasts Jennifer's presence. Jennifer has her own life now, friends, boyfriends, marijuana. That ought to be enough to keep her occupied. She doesn't need the game of *Get Rose* anymore.

Neither she nor Jennifer have keep their promises, but it hasn't been that bad. They ignore each other very well. It's a shame it has to be that way, but it works.

She opens the door to the third floor and walks up. There's no door at the top. Her daughter is naked in bed with a boy.

"Jennifer!"

The boy turns quick as a cat and pulls a blanket over his exposed privates. Jennifer leans around from behind him. She says, "Sorry, Mother."

"Who are you?" she asks this boy in her daughter's bed. "I want your name."

"Neal," he says. The scared look on his face makes her think he's telling the truth. But it doesn't really matter what his name is.

"Go home, Neal. I don't want you to come here ever again. I don't even want to see you on this block. You understand?"

"Yes, ma'am."

"Get dressed and leave. And you, Jennifer, get dressed and come downstairs. We need to talk." She turns and goes down the stairs. Her legs are shaking. It seems every damn time she is ready to say something, it's not quite enough.

The boy leaves, then Jennifer comes downstairs. Rose waves to the chair across from the couch she's sitting on. She doesn't want her daughter to sit anywhere near her.

"We can't have this," she says. "I can't take it, really I can't. I'd like to be able to leave the house and not worry about what I'm going to find when I get home. Jesus, Jennifer, what's the matter with you?"

"Nothing, I guess. That's why I'm so popular."

She can't breathe. This is *her* daughter?

"I hope you used birth control. I wish I had." She knows she shouldn't have said that, but she's so mad. "Here's the new deal. You live your life, but you damn well better let me live mine. I'm going on a date, and you better not say boo. Got it?"

Jennifer nods. She looks a bit shocked. Good. For once Rose gets the last word. She stands, goes up to her bedroom. Peter and Betsy will be home soon. She will have a good cry, then go make them all a nice dinner.

Sitting on her bed, Rose wonders if there was a moment just now where she was glad about what she saw because it gave her the upper hand. What has happened to her? What happened to the girl who loved politics and ran the school newspaper, who volunteered for the blind and waited for the man whose soul she could feel with the touch of her hand? She has come so far from the little girl who changed her name to Rose. She has become a widow who wants a date so badly she could make a deal like she just did with her daughter. But she has been pushed to it. There's no doubt she has been pushed too far.

. . .

My mother goes out on dates with Joe, coming home at two in the morning. We kids are old enough to take care of ourselves, or not. That's up to us. I take care of myself just fine, and I take care of my boyfriends. But even though I'm sixteen, my mother won't let me drive. She says I smoke pot and do drugs, so I can't drive her car. I can't imagine why she says that, she has no proof. I tell her it stinks. She says I have made my own bed, and now I must lie in it, which is a big fucking joke to her, since I never make my bed. "That's life," she says. She says that a lot.

But we keep fooling each other. One day she comes home with a bracelet in a gift box. The bracelet has different colored stones with flat bottoms. "I thought you might like this," she says.

"Thanks," I say. I do like it. It's something I would really wear.

"Just want you to know I love you," she says.

"Thanks," I say. "Love you, too." It feels awkward to say this, like speaking Spanish—which I did so badly I just gave it up.

"What's for dinner?"

"I forgot to make it," I say. "Pork chops, but they're frozen."

"Pizza, then?"

"Okay."

"Okay," she says. "Pizza it is."

The four of us eat pepperoni pizza and plan a vacation to Maine next summer. We talk as if it might happen. I feel like I'm watching a commercial. It's hard to swallow.

Rose knows exactly what she's getting into; a relationship that won't last. Not only is Joe younger than she is, he's too wild for her. He takes her to dimly lit bars and they stay until the place closes, and sometimes he slips a hand under her skirt, right there in a public place. He's careful not to take it too far; he's never really crass, never really sleazy, but she wonders if he's holding back, playing it safe with the Irish widow. It's like he's slumming in reverse. She imagines his usual girlfriend: blond, teased hair, not too smart. He may be a mover and shaker in the public relations world (his clients include the makers of name-brand products she uses every day), but there's something about his smile; he just looks too pleased with himself.

But when he's looking at her, she's a goner. So, if he's using her to see how far the widowed, hardworking secretary, mother of three, will go, well, she's using him for the same thing; she's curious about how much of a fool she can be. When it's not fun anymore, she'll call it off, if he hasn't already. Already she can see it coming.

Some days, even for weeks, I forget about my dad. I'm almost seventeen; there are a lot of other things to be interested in, and I have found most of them. I'm going to be an actress, and I try out for *The Glass Menagerie*, the play our school is doing this year. The day after the tryouts, I read the cast list posted on a bulletin board. My name is not on it anywhere.

I'm straight today. Believing with all my heart that I would get a role in this play, I haven't smoked or dropped anything, so it's harder now to ignore my feelings. I go out behind the school where the windows are high up and no one can see me, and sit down against the wall, my knees to my chest in a huddle with myself. I can't act for shit and I'm failing most my classes. The cement under my butt is cold. It's December, fifteen degrees out, and these stupid tears are freezing my face.

I walk to the parking lot by the beauty school, and there's a car, idling. The windows are fogged. It's Lannie, who sells pot and stuff to the kids before school. He's nineteen or twenty, with slicked-back hair and dark eyes. I knock on his window and he rolls it down.

"Yeah?"

He recognizes me because I've bought acid and pot from him, but he doesn't know my name. I know his name, everyone does.

"Let me in," I say. "My ass is freezing off out here."

He looks at me for a second, up and down, not hiding what he's looking at. He nods. I go around the car and get in.

"What's up?" he asks.

"Fucking school," I say. "I'm through with it. I'm never going back. I'm done."

"Yeah? And you're here in my car 'cause?"

"'Cause I'm cold and I want to get out of here, and I want to get high. If you're going anywhere, I'd like a ride. I have a ten for a nickel bag."

"Where you going?"

"I don't care."

"And your name is?"

"Jenny."

"You friends with Lisa and Chuckles?"

"Yeah."

He nods, a slight, sexy grin. "Thought so. You like that acid I sold you last week?"

I nod. It was a little speedy, but this is not the time to complain.

"I'm going to my place to lay back. Want to come?"

"Yeah. Thanks."

Lannie puts the car in reverse, laying his arm across the back of the seat. I like the feel of it behind me. He's a tough guy, and now I feel tough.

His place is really cool, a duplex he shares with two other guys. When he kisses me in the living room, with his hand sliding up my blouse, I get tense. "Chill out," he says. "They're asleep." We screw on the couch, then smoke pot.

I don't tell my mother I've dropped out of school. Instead, I wake up at the regular time and go to the school parking lot to meet Lannie. I learn to make nickel and dime bags, always a bit short, but not much.

"Try this," he says. We're at his place, and his roommates are sleeping. They sleep till one or two in the afternoon, crawling out of bed just as we're leaving to go back to the parking lot for the after-school crowd. They didn't like me being here at first, but now they like me. Everyone likes me.

Lannie slides a rimless mirror over and takes a small dark glass vial out of his shirt pocket. Unscrewing the tiny cap, he carefully taps the vial, sifting white power out onto the mirror. It's cocaine. I've never seen it, but I know. I've got drug instincts. I watch him inhale the cocaine through a rolled-up dollar bill, and then I do the same. It burns my nose. In seconds I'm speedy and something else. Talkative. I want to talk.

"Did I tell you what I did to my mom's cigarettes once? You won't believe it. I emptied them in the sink, on top of the dishes, then poured her booze over them. She didn't even mention it. I wonder if she knows I'm cutting school? I don't care. What can she do? Pick me up and carry me? Maybe I should get a job, get my own place, get out of there. I should go fill out an application at Record Revolution. That would be cool, to work there. Do you know anyone there I could ask?"

Lannie nods, rubbing his nose with his palm. I can feel

myself wanting more coke already, but he puts the vial back in his shirt pocket.

"Yeah," he says. "Ask Dan. Tell him I sent you."

"Do you have cards? Let's play cards." I need something to concentrate on. My mind is like bees. He gets up and actually finds cards. They're old and sticky. "Gin rummy?" I ask. It's all I know how to play. We're halfway into the first game when he puts his hand down.

"Let's go upstairs."

I know what he wants. I was thinking about it, too, but thinking about it, not feeling it. I don't want to *have* sex, I want to *talk* about sex. I want him to tell me everything he's done, but I don't want to touch anyone now.

"Hey, I was winning," I say.

"Come on," he says. He points to the steps with his chin, then walks upstairs, not looking back. I follow him. I follow the slight bump of cocaine in his shirt pocket.

The sex is awful, creepy, like my skin's crawling, but intense because I can't shut my eyes. By the time I go home to make dinner, I have a headache and my teeth ache.

"The school called," my mother says as I walk in the door. She's sitting in a chair, waiting for me.

"I don't go there anymore," I say, my chin up.

"Why?" she says. She says this like she really wants to know.

"I'm flunking everything. I feel stupid. They make me feel stupid. They don't know my name, I'm just some dumb kid. I got sick of it. I'm going to get a job and save some money and go to Hollywood."

"Jennifer, you need to go to school."

"Why?"

"Because your father would have wanted you to."

It is exactly the right thing and the wrong thing to say. If I didn't have a headache, if my teeth didn't hurt, if she didn't slur those last words just ever so slightly, I would probably break down and cry, tell her I will go back. But I am just on the other side of the line, where it's exactly the wrong thing to say.

"Well, he's dead, and you have no right to be talking for a dead man when you're sleeping with someone else."

She holds perfectly still, staring at me, not saying a word. I leave the room and go upstairs. It's been a long day, and even I know when I have said too much.

When I wake up late the next morning, my mother's already gone. Standing in the doorway to her bedroom, I look at her neatly made bed, the way the things on her bureau are arranged simply; a brush, a jewelry box, a school picture of each of us. I am so sorry for what I said. For everything. If she were here right now, I would tell her. She would understand why I am the way I am, even if I don't.

I decide to go downtown, to the place where she works. I take the bus, which I hate. I think of Lannie and his car. Of Lannie and his mouth. His coke. I want to go back to his house so bad right now it makes me afraid.

My mother's office is near Ninth and Euclid, and it's almost noon. It's snowing and people walk with their heads bent down, watching their step, avoiding the slush sprayed up by passing cars. Crossing the street, I look toward the door of the building, where she works on the seventh floor. I see Joe coming out the revolving door, his arm around the waist of some woman. The woman, a redhead, is looking at him with the same bright eyes my mother looks at him. I keep crossing the street, getting closer to them, but he's not looking my way at all. He says something in her ear, and she laughs. Then he kisses her, pats her on the butt, and turns and walks away.

If I tell my mother, she'll think I am just trying to break them up, and get mad at me. I need her to love me right now.

The receptionist says my mother is in a meeting. Would I care to wait?

"Sure," I say. I sit on a dark leather couch held tight with leather buttons. The desk the receptionist sits behind is curved and polished. People in suits walk by and look at me, turn away, and try not to look again until they are almost out of sight. My bell-bottom jeans are torn at the bottom and soggy with melting snow. My flannel shirt is a few sizes too big. I didn't wash my hair today, or yesterday. I sit for ten minutes, which seems like an hour, but the clock says it's been only ten minutes. My teeth ache. I could just write her a note. If I went to Lannie's and did coke, I could write a long letter. I'm sure of that. And I'm getting hungry. The receptionist said it will be a long wait. I'll go to Woolworth's and eat something. I tell myself I'll come back, knowing I won't.

I get on the bus. I go to Lannie's. It's a transfer, then a walk. I'm cold and wet when I get there.

"Where were you this morning?" he asks me.

"I slept in," I say.

"I was counting on you."

I'm unlacing my boots, but I can hear the frown in his voice. "Sorry," I say.

"You're wet."

"Yeah," I say.

"You should take off those pants."

"Yeah, I guess so."

"Take them off here."

I do, right in the kitchen.

After we make love, we do coke. It works better this way. It's almost perfect.

Every day I go to Lannie's. Every day we do coke. He doesn't offer me as much as I'd like. One day he leaves a vial of coke on his dresser and seems to forget about it. I slip it in my pocket.

Friday night Lannie has something to do he can't tell me about, so I stay home. Most of my friends thought the idea of Lannie was cool—the guy in the car—but none of them want to be associated with him, so they stay away from me. Alone in my room, listening to Jefferson Airplane, I do coke by myself. This is not a good idea. I go into my sister's room. It's like having a conversation with a plant. She just ignores me. I go into my brother's room. He gives me the finger. "You're high," he says. "Get lost."

There's always my mother.

She's asleep on the couch, still wearing her yellow dress and high heels. She was supposed to have a date with Joe tonight, but he didn't show up. That happens more often now. I haven't told her about him kissing that lady. She should know what a creep he is. She's so innocent about this stuff. She probably thinks he loves her. I need to save her from herself.

"Mother," I say, shaking her shoulder. I have all this energy. "Mother!" I yell. She jerks, and her eyes open and close, as if looking at me was too much to handle. I'm getting pissed. No one in this house wants to talk to me. I'll do more coke and just fucking talk to myself. But I should eat before I do any more coke. I can't eat on coke; the food tastes dead, disgusting, like cardboard. I've lost some weight. I don't look so good in bright light.

I eat three bowls of cereal, then throw up. I'm not trying to throw up, it just happens.

Back in my room I turn up my music and just as I'm snorting my second line, I hear someone stomping up the stairs. Thinking it's the police, I jerk and spill everything; all the fine white powder flying into the air. And it's only my goddamn brother.

"Turn down your music! It's too loud!"

"Get out of my room!" I can't believe the coke has all spilled.

"You're a drug addict! You're a poor excuse for a human being! Look at you!"

I pick up the mirror that held my coke moments ago and throw it at him. "Get out of my room!" The mirror shatters at his feet.

"You're disgusting!" Peter yells. His hair is cut short. He's a stupid jock. Well, not stupid, really, but an asshole. I pick up my shoe and throw it at him. He moves to the side. I jump up and run at him, and the next thing I know I'm on the floor, my head pressed to the wood, my arm behind my back. He is going to break my arm.

"Turn your music down. Do you understand?"

"Yes," I say, because he's breaking my arm.

"Good. And listen, Betsy and I are going to a movie. When Mother wakes up, tell her I took the car."

Oh, yeah. He gets to drive, and he just turned sixteen. I'm seventeen and three months, but I'm not allowed to drive. "Let go of my arm!"

"Promise me you'll stay here and watch her." He gives my arm a little extra tug.

"Yeah. I promise. I'll stay here." What else am I going to say?

He lets go of my arm. As soon as he walks down the stairs, I jump up and get a playing card to gather up all the spilled coke. There's so little. Not enough. I can't breathe from crying. I couldn't snort it now, anyway. I climb into bed and put the pillow over my head because I can't close my eyes. I can't breathe under the pillow, so I punch it hard and throw it against the wall. Walking over to where the shards of the mirror cover my floor, I look down. I can't see myself. The pieces are too small to hold even a fraction of my image.

I do all the coke that I scraped up. It really burns my nose, and I think maybe I got some broken mirror mixed in by mistake.

I'm really edgy. Some part of me was planning on giving the coke back to Lannie. What if he finds out I took it? I feel like spiders are crawling all over me. Then I remember the two downers. Quaaludes. That's what they are. I take both of them.

In fifteen minutes I'm floating. I can hardly see straight. And I'm hot, in a sexy way. I need Lannie. What in the hell is he doing that I can't know? I decide I'll get dressed sexy and go see him anyway. None of my clothes are sexy, so I go into my mother's closet and find her little black dress. I put it on, and her stockings, and her black high heels. We have the same shoe size.

My legs are so wobbly, I can hardly walk down the stairs. My mother's still out. She'll never know I left. I'll come back before Peter and Betsy come back, so I can keep my promise to my brother, and so he won't break my arm. As I'm about to leave, the phone rings. It's Joe.

"Hi, Jenny," he says, like were old friends. "Can I talk to your mom?"

"She's not here," I say.

"Huh? I thought she would be. We were supposed to go out.

Something came up. Could you tell her how sorry I am? It was unavoidable. An emergency. Tell her—"

"I saw you, you asshole," I say. "With the redhead. Is she your emergency? Well, I told my mom all about you. She stood you up tonight. She never wants to see you again. It's over. She told me to tell you if you even look her way at work, she'll slap you, right in front of everyone. She said stay out of her life!" I know my words are slurring, but I think he gets what I'm saying.

"Look, I just—"

I hang up the phone. Pick it back up. Leave it off the hook. I grab my coat. In high heels I stumble outside, slip in the snow and fall on my butt, smacking my head against the side of the porch. It hurts like hell, but I start laughing, giggling. God, I was good on the phone. He'll be scared even to look her way. I go back inside and put on my tennis shoes that were by the back door, then walk away, toward Lannie's house, carrying my mother's shoes. The shot of adrenaline from the fall on my butt has really kicked in the quaaludes. I'm as white and fuzzy inside as it is outside. I can hardly feel the cold. My stomach's doing all sorts of waves, like I'm in the ocean. Snow is frozen water, right? I'm in the middle of a big white ocean.

Lannie's place is over a mile away. Less than halfway there, I'm weaving pretty badly and not sure where I am. I see this old one-room schoolhouse that's used to store desks and file cabinets. It's a historical building and can't be torn down. I break a window and crawl in. I pass out under a desk. In the morning I'm awakened by two policemen.

This time my mother doesn't come to pick me up right away.

. . .

It's late at night when my mother shows up at the police station, carrying a paper bag. She talks with the cops for a while, then signs some papers. I'm not talking to her. How could she wait this long to get me? It's got to be eleven o'clock at night.

She tosses the bag at me. "Go change," she says. "Right now." I'm still wearing my mother's little black cocktail dress. They must have told her. A cop points to the bathroom. I've been here a while—I know where it is. When I come back out, I hand her the dress. "Let's go," she says. I can smell alcohol on her breath. Her hands are shaking. I'm scared just to get into the car, but how far can I run from a police station?

It's sleeting and the car's covered with a thin sheet of ice. "I'll do it," my mother says, grabbing the ice scraper from the back-seat. "Just get in the car." She chips at the ice with a vengeance, and I hope it keeps sleeting and she keeps scraping until she's sober, but she quits when there's just enough space to see out, not bothering with the back window. In the dark of night, slivers of ice on the windshield are lit up like jewels and I think how pretty it is, how cold things glitter in the dark. Then my mother gets in the car and slams the door.

At first she can't even get the key into the lock to start the car. I sit with my arms folded tight across my chest, hoping the key will break. But after some fumbling, the car starts and she pulls out of the parking lot, the car slipping and sliding on the ice, almost nicking the back of a police cruiser. She drives fast and makes the first light. At the next light, where she should turn left to go to our house, she turns right. The car fishtails and I grab the handle on the door. "You went the wrong way!" I yell.

"You think so?" she says. It's not a question, it's a sneer. The car weaves across the center lane and back again.

"Jesus, you really are drunk! Be careful!"

"Be careful? You put on *my* dress, run away in a snowstorm, again, and I come to the police station to get you, and you don't say sorry or anything, just tell *me* to be careful? Who the hell do you think you are?"

"Your daughter!" I shout. "But I wish I wasn't!"

She turns onto North Park, which curves along the small man-made lakes in Shaker Heights. Ancient, thick trees line both sides of the street. On the left is the lake, frozen but not solidly—there are watery spots from the thaw last week. There's almost no traffic. People are staying in tonight, unless they have to go to the police station to get their daughters.

We're going at least fifty. The road is covered in a shine of black ice. "Where are we going?"

"Oh, who cares?"

I can't look to see if she's smiling because I can't take my eyes off the road, but I can feel her grin, I can feel it on my skin. I have goose bumps the size of molehills.

She swerves into the left lane. There's a car headed right for us, but it veers into the next lane at the last second, the horn blaring. We were inches from being killed! My mother yanks the steering wheel, and we swerve back into our lane. My heart's thumping hard. "You're scaring me."

"Oh, really?"

"Yes! We could get killed."

"I guess we could. As a matter of fact, I think that's pretty much what I'm going for." The car speeds up. "You think I don't miss him, don't you? Don't you?" she screams. "Well, I do. Want me to prove it? Will you leave me alone if I prove it? Here! I'll show you just how much I miss him."

"Stop it!"

"Hey, kid," my mother says, so calmly, so quietly, that I turn to face her. She's looking right at me, not at the road. "Let's get this over with. Just you and me." She's crying now, wet trails running down her cheeks. I want to put my hands over my eyes, but I'm holding on to the door handle with one hand and the other one is braced against the dashboard. My mother turns the steering wheel toward the lake.

Going at least sixty, the car spins on the icy road, turning in a large circle. I'm screaming so loud that I don't know if she's laughing or screaming, too. There's towering piles of snow plowed up along the side of the road, with dozens of huge trees just behind them. If we hit a tree, we're dead. If we miss a tree, we'll go into the lake. The back of the car catches a snowbank, and my head flies backward, then forward, and smashes against the dashboard.

The next thing I know, my head's killing me and my arms ache. There are no sounds, and I think I've gone deaf. My mother's head is against the steering wheel. She may be dead. I reach out to touch her arm. She sits up, slowly, and looks at me, puts a hand to her head. She shakes her head. "Oh, well," she says. "I tried. Maybe I can do better next time." Then, looking both ways, she eases the car back out onto the road and heads home.

My mother tried to kill us both in a great act of passion and rage. That night I leave my family for almost ten years.

Chapter Thirteen

After the trip to the nursing home, and our stop at Draeger's, I head home. There are no messages on the machine. It's not like Todd at all. He always calls me at noon, and it's at least one now.

In the kitchen I wipe a smudge of hot fudge off my mother's face with the tip of a wet paper towel. "There you go," I say.

"Thank you," she says, very sweetly.

How could I have ever been so mean to this woman? "Mother," I say. I'm tired of this Mrs. Morgan stuff.

"What, Jennifer?"

My breath catches. I smile like an idiot. "Hello," I say. We're going on three hours of me being me. I want to sing and shout, but I am careful of hope.

"Hello," she says, with a smirk, like I'm nuts for saying hello to her. Maybe I am.

"Would you like me to tell you about Jazz's father? About the ten years I was away?" I've never told her. I promised myself I'd never tell her because of what she said about Jazz. But tomorrow she won't even remember what I told her, and in the long run, it'll be just as if I kept my promise.

"Yes," she says. "I'd like to know."

She seems so normal right now, I think as we walk into the living room. Maybe it was never really Alzheimer's at all. Or maybe hot fudge is the cure.

She sits on the couch and I sit next to her, turning toward her, crossing my legs underneath me. I can feel a tight stretch across my knees, an ache in my thighs, but damned if I'm going to give up sitting cross-legged yet.

"Jazz's father's name is Hunter Phillips. I met him in San Francisco."

As I walk through the snow to Lannie's, I swear I will never speak to my mother again. Once again I'm freezing. I add another promise; I'll never run away again in the winter.

It's one A.M. when I get to his house.

"What the hell happened to you?" he says when he lets me in. At least he's here, I think. I'm so glad he's here.

"I fell," I say, feeling the bump on my head.

"Where have you been?"

I walk past him and sit on the plaid couch. It's filthy and makes me sad. "I ran away last night. Well, I was coming here, but I crashed in the schoolhouse and got picked up by the cops this morning, and they took me to—"

"The cops? You got picked up by the cops?" He looks paranoid, like my getting picked up by cops is a problem for him.

"It's got nothing to do with you. But then my mom wouldn't get me. When she did, I ran away again. I'm never going back." I take off my shoes and rub my feet, trying to warm them up. My toes are numb.

"Where's your stuff?" he says.

"I didn't bring anything. It's a whole new life now, Lannie. I'm not bringing anything from the past. Nothing. It's you and me now."

There's a pause before he says, "Good. Cool."

But nothing's good about it.

In less than two weeks we're fighting all the time. The coke is making us mean. We fight over whose line is thicker, who needs the last downer. The place is a mess, and when I straighten it up, he tells me I can't open certain drawers and that I'd better not touch the pot in the basement. I tell him he's an asshole, and he slaps me across the face.

The next morning I'm gone before he even wakes up. I can't find any coke to take with me—he has gotten better at hiding it—but I know where the money's stashed. I take three hundred dollars, the price of a slapped face.

I stand on Cedar Road and stick out my thumb. It's late March, the end of 1971, and the snow and ice of just two weeks ago has melted. I'm seventeen, with long brown hair. It doesn't take long to get picked up.

I'm going to San Francisco. Where I was born.

The first ride takes me as far as the highway, although the guy offers to take me to his place. He's just joking around and wishes me good luck. It takes two more rides to get to Chicago. I sleep in a motel and buy myself an atlas. I didn't study my geography and am not sure of the best way to go. I'm also edgy as shit, depressed, and keep thinking about turning around and going back. Maybe Lannie will be sorry he hit me. Maybe he'll give me more coke to make up for it.

The sheets are like sandpaper. The light too bright in the bathroom. The room too hot. I sleep on the blanket with my clothes on. My eyes feel as if there are hot pokers stuck in them. I dream I'm doing cocaine. I wake with a headache that blinds me.

It's mostly guys that give me rides. They ask me questions and I make up answers. "My name is Esca Echo," I say. "My parents are dead. I'm going to live with an aunt in California. She's in *Days of Our Lives* and she's going to get me an audition." The way they smirk makes me mad, but I learn to make up better lies. Somewhere in Wyoming, I tell one old guy the story about my mother trying to kill us in the car. It's the first time I tell the story. Later I get better at it and can tell it with all sorts of great details. It gets longer each time.

In Salt Lake City I go to a Salvation Army Thrift Store and buy clothes and a knapsack. In the motel I take a long shower and throw away the clothes I've been wearing for six days. Now there's nothing left of Cleveland and my old life. Even my bruises have healed.

But I really want some coke. I feel empty without it. On coke I'm more fun, smarter. Now I just feel tense and uneasy, stupid and not worth much. I'm sure my mother doesn't miss me at all. I almost call her once, but then I don't.

Just the other side of the mountains, I get picked up by some hippies in a Volkswagen van that has vines and flowers painted on it. I arrive in San Francisco in style and get dropped off on Haight Ashbury with $152.00 left to my name.

Just a few feet away, standing around some motorcycles, are two big guys and a woman, all wearing heavy black leather jackets. The woman laughs loudly, and I turn and walk the other way. Many of the stores are boarded up, layers of ragged posters pasted to the boards. People sit on the sidewalks, their backs against the buildings, their clothes like the posters behind them, ragged and layered. One woman's talking in a stream of monotone words even though there's no one near her. I thought San Francisco was going to be all hippies with flowers in their hair.

Now I see them. They're here, too. I see jean jackets and suede-fringed coats and guys with long hair and girls with long skirts. Music drifts out doorways. I hear a riff of Jimi Hendrix, then, from a narrow store with sandals in the window, just a line: "Help, I'm a rock." A black man with a huge Afro plays a guitar, his case open on the ground, and just as I had imagined, a girl with a baby in her lap sits against a building, handing out flowers—white carnations. I take one and thank her. She smiles wildly and gives me the peace sign.

I get to a corner and don't know where to turn. On Clayton there's a group of hippies about my age standing by a doorway. I slow down as I walk by, and someone passes me a joint. I take a toke and pass it on to someone who is now standing behind me. Now I'm in a line. The line, with people dressed like me, looks inviting. Curious, I follow them in the door and up the stairs to the second floor.

We proceed down a hallway to a large room with old furniture—chairs with the stuffing coming out, scratched tables, stained couches. There's a old plaid couch, just like Lannie's couch, and I want to sit on it. Then I see the sign. It's the Haight Ashbury Free Clinic. This is the waiting room. I stay in the line.

Maybe they can tell me where I can sleep tonight. Maybe on that couch?

The girl in front of me wants a pregnancy test, so I say I do, too, afraid they'll turn me away if I ask where I can sleep. I wait an hour before getting my history taken, and when the woman who introduces herself as Fern starts asking me questions, I am more than ready to tell her everything. That I'm homeless, from Cleveland, tired and edgy, that I don't know how I am going to support myself, and that I might be pregnant—something I've decided is true in the last hour. Fern takes my blood pressure and temperature, and tells me a woman's counselor will see me before my test. She'll give me pamphlets listing places I can stay. Fern's kind, with a soft smile, and I want her to be my mother. I don't tell her this, but I know I would if I were on cocaine. I miss the way I talked when I was high, the fluid sentences that poured out of me and seemed to mean so much. I'm beginning to suspect, though, that they didn't mean much at all.

She leads me to a bathroom and I pee in a paper cup.

I wait another half hour for a blood test, sure now that not only am I pregnant, but have some awful disease. I'm edgy again. People are staring at me. Finally the woman's counselor calls me into a small room covered with pictures of female anatomy and a poster about self breast exams. She has pudgy fingers and tiny white teeth like a baby's. Her name is Paula. She, too, is friendly and asks me questions. When I tell her I have never had a pelvic exam, she hands me a plastic model of a vagina, explaining the whole thing to me, showing me the speculum and wooden sticks the doctor will use. Then she gives me flyers for everything imaginable, including places to get organic food and free yoga classes.

"Does this place hire people?" I ask.

"Well, some," she says. "Most of the people who work here are volunteers, like me. You can be trained to take histories, or be a woman's counselor, or work the hotline. I'll give you the name of the person to talk to." She has this wonderful, melodic voice.

"Do you need a roommate?" I ask.

She laughs. "No, not really. But there's a message board in the waiting room. Check it out. I'll call you when the doctor's ready."

I sit on an old stuffed chair in the waiting room for another hour. The plaid couch is full, which is for the best. The less I'm reminded of Lannie, the better.

Finally Paula calls my name and escorts me to the exam room. She leaves me there. I put on a blue paper robe and wait.

I wait for a long time. On the walls are cutout figures from rock posters; Janis, Jim Morrison, and Bob Dylan are grinning at me. I can hear people talking about drips and sores. Someone's collecting money for pizza. Finally the doctor comes in with Paula.

The doctor tells me to spread my legs, and Paula holds my hand. It doesn't hurt much. What I feel most is curiosity. What really do I have down there? How might it work? With my eyes closed, the doctor's fingers inside me, I imagine the diagrams Paula showed me, like there is a map of *me*. I'm surprised when the doctor pulls his fingers out, tells me to sit up. It only took a minute. Aren't I more complicated than that?

"Well, you're not pregnant," he says. "If you'd like birth control, talk it over with your counselor, and I'll write you a script for a diaphragm or the pill. Let me take a look at these slides, but you seem fine to me. Other than that, you're done." He leaves the room, and Paula asks if I'd like to talk to her about birth control. I tell her not right now, but I'll be back, as a volunteer.

"That would be nice. Good luck."

When I leave the Free Clinic, it's dark outside. There are still people walking around but not as many, and the people sitting against the buildings look even dingier than before. I look around for a taxi, but after ten minutes I start walking. About five blocks farther away, I see a cab and flag it down, asking the driver to take me to the closest cheap motel. Not a good idea. The room smells of bleach and cigarettes. I curl up on the bed and shake. This is the place I have run to.

I've been without coke for almost a week now. Lannie told me the stuff was pure and when we wanted to quit, we just would, no problem. I was stupid to believe him. I'm stupid and alone, and I shake all night. By morning my whole body feels weak and sluggish. I stay in the motel room all day, get a little food from a place next door. By nighttime I don't tremble anymore, although now I'm sweating, cold sweat. I keep taking hot showers, but I have to sit in the dirty tub, I can't stand up for too long. The next day I feel better. I've kicked coke by running clear across the country. Maybe I'm not so stupid after all.

The next day I leave my suitcase at the motel and wander around the town, asking for jobs. Everyone says no, but nicely. The woman at Tracy's Donuts gives me a free doughnut. I glance at every pay phone I pass.

Somehow, I end up back at the Free Clinic. I go inside and am immediately comforted by the old furniture, the posters, the drawings on the walls. I ask a good-looking guy with long hair if I could speak to Hunter Phillips, the man in charge of volunteers. He *is* Hunter Phillips.

"I'd like to volunteer as a woman's counselor," I say.

"Great. We can always use volunteers." His has wrinkles at the corners of his eyes, but he's not old, maybe thirty. His hair's in a long braid that lays across his shoulder and over his chest, almost to his waist. "The next training session starts in three weeks. They're twice a week for two months. A lot of effort goes into the woman's counselor training. Sure that's where you want to start?"

"I'm sure," I say.

"Good. I'll get the schedule." He comes back with a piece of paper. Hands it to me.

"Do you have any jobs I could do now? Anything? Like cleaning, even?"

"New in town?"

I nod. "But I was born here." As if he wants to know that. And I only lived here for three months. "I don't have much money."

"Well, we hire mostly from the volunteers, but I know the guy that owns The Sprouted Wheat. Tony. He told me one of the dishwashers just quit. Tell him I sent you. It's just down Haight a few blocks." He leans against a wall. "So, where you from?"

"Cleveland." I say this like I'm ashamed, then blush.

"Cool. I've never been east of the Mississippi."

"You're not missing much," I say.

"Well, I hope you like it here. It's a good town. A little different than in the sixties, but it'll come back."

I don't know what he means. We just stand there, looking at each other.

"Good luck," he says.

"I'll be back, to take those classes," I say.

He nods. "Peace. I'll be seeing you."

"Yep. You will."

I work at The Sprouted Wheat for two years, eventually becoming a waitress and barely surviving on two-seventy-five an hour, tips, and all the wheat bread I can stand. I tell people that my mother tried to kill me, and they all want to take care of me. For a few months I live with one of the waiters, then with three people in an upstairs apartment on Clauge. I become a woman's counselor at the Haight Ashbury Free Clinic, and good friends with Paula, whom I eventually do move in with. I don't do cocaine anymore—I remember too vividly that awful week, and besides, it's too expensive now that I actually have to pay for it—but I do enjoy pot and a few quaaludes and occasional acid. I give myself limits. No hard stuff, no shooting anything, no first-date sex. I keep my first two promises.

I don't need a driver's licence, since I walk everywhere, or take the trolleys. I get paid under the table, so I don't pay taxes. I get my medical care at the Free Clinic. There is no paper trail, no way to find me.

I write a letter to my mother and never mail it, and one day I can't even find it. Now that I can't find it, I decide it said everything perfectly and I could never do that again. I think about calling her, and my palms sweat. I tell myself I will call her tomorrow night. What's one more night after so long? I sleep well, thinking I will call her tomorrow, knowing I won't.

What could I say? I'm sorry? Would she?

Two and a half years after I walked into the Free Clinic, they hire me as intake coordinator, but that's just a title they make up for me. I do all sorts of odd jobs, like answering the phones and cleaning the exam rooms. The plaid couch is still here, and sometimes I take naps on it, hardly thinking about Lannie at all.

One night, after counseling a girl who ran away from Indiana who thinks she has crabs, I write Peter a short letter—it feels easier to write him than my mother—telling him where I am, even giving him my phone number. I don't hear back from anyone.

The clinic is like a big incestuous family. We work together all day, party all night, celebrate birthdays, holidays, and the days the temperature goes above seventy. We fight about programs, salaries, and whose dog puked in the waiting room. Someone's always not talking to someone else, and there's much shuffling as we sit down for staff meetings, trying to figure out who to sit next to, and who not to sit next to. The Haight area is improving, businesses moving back in, less crime. George Harrison does a benefit concert to raise money for us, and he comes into Medical to meet us. We walk around in a daze for days. I pretend I have lived here my whole life.

Almost three years after running away, I call my house. Peter answers the phone. Within two minutes we're shouting at each other. "Well, she tried to kill me!" I yell. "What do you expect me to do!"

"Oh, grow up, Jenny. I don't believe you. Jesus fucking Christ, she's been nuts since you left. She said she said something she shouldn't have. Nobody tried to kill you. You're so goddamn dramatic."

I take a breath in that hurts my chest and shout, "What the

hell do you know? You're Mister Perfect, Mister Goody Two-shoes. You don't know what this world's all about!"

"Oh, yeah?" he says. "Try telling that to the draft board!"

"What do you mean?"

"Hey, Jenny, what do you care?" He hangs up on me.

I should have hung up on him first. How dare he call me a liar?

Still, I get worried. But the war's almost over, right?

I call my house a week later. Peter answers the phone again.

"Are you going to Vietnam?"

"No, I'm in college."

"Why did you say that?"

"Why did you say what you did?"

I hang up.

I call back the next week. Now that I've done it twice, it's easier.

My mother answers the phone. My hand shakes so badly, I hang up.

The next time I get Betsy. "Is Peter there?" I ask in a high girlish voice.

"Don't hang up on me," I say when he gets on the phone. "Will you just talk to me a little? God, was that really Betsy? Do you think she wants to talk to me? Betsy? Or Mother? What do you think? Would they?"

"Mother's pissed you sent that letter to me. She thought you were dead, then you write *me* a letter. She says she'll never talk to you again for scaring her so badly. Betsy's on her side."

"Who's side are you on?"

"Mine," he says, and I laugh.

"Will you call me now and then, just tell me what's happening?"

"Why should I?" he asks.

"Because I'm begging you to," then I hate that I said that. "Because you stabbed me with a pencil when I was seven and I had to have a tetanus shot. Because you nearly broke my arm. Because we lost the same father, Peter."

"Why don't you just come home?"

I can't talk. My throat closes up. I want to be asked home, but he's not the right person to do it.

"Just call me, now and then." I give him my number. "Please?" He's such a good kid. I believe he will call me if I ask nicely.

"We'll see."

"Thanks," I say, and he says goodbye.

He does call me now and then. Half the time we end up fighting. I make sure I keep my phone number, no matter where I move.

A little more than two years after starting work at the clinic, and just a few weeks after my twenty-first birthday, Hunter Phillips offers to walk me home. Halfway there, he says, "Let's walk up to the Hill." I'm so proud to be seen walking up to the Hill with this good-looking guy. McKendree Spring is playing and we sit under a tree, holding hands. I know he's married, but I try not to think about it. The next night, with hardly a word spoken, we close up the clinic and make love on the waiting room floor. Afterward, I tell him all about my father dying, and Lannie, and that my mother tried to kill us both in a mad act of passion so I ran away. He holds me, tells me it's not my fault, any of it, and I think I must have the story right now, because that's what I want to hear.

The next night we make love in my bedroom. Afterward, he tells me he still loves his wife, but he believes in free love. I've known him for years and he's never been one to cheat on his wife. This must be a new breakthrough for him—this free love. Then again, he's been married about seven years. "Does *she*?" I ask, and he just smiles. "Why now?" I ask. "Why me?"

"You're tough," he says. "I like that."

I've never thought of myself as tough, but I like the idea of being tough, so I punch him lightly on the arm, then kiss him.

We sneak around, but everyone knows it, including his wife. He's the best-looking guy I've even seen, and he's passionate; about me, the plight of endangered animals, the rain forest, pollution, and his wife. He loves her, he loves me, he loves the whole damn planet. We fight about me smoking pot, that I don't get involved in politics, that he won't leave his wife. There's a whole six months we don't talk to each other, then a whole year we sleep together on Wednesdays when his wife take French lessons. He quits the clinic because she makes him—because of me. I get his job. I see other men, I just don't fall in love with any of them. Hunter is the only man to leave me, but he always comes back. I leave the rest of them first. Sometimes I'm sure I'm in love with Hunter, but mostly I think that just after we have sex, or when we haven't been together for a long time.

Hunter is Jazz's father, but he doesn't know it. I left him, and the clinic, in the summer of 1981. One night I told Hunter that he had to leave his wife, and he said love was not something he could cancel, like a stamp. I told him that was the stupidest thing I'd ever heard. "Get out, and don't ever come back," I said. But he would have come back, and I would have let him in.

A few days later I quit the clinic—as much as I loved it, I'd been there too long already. I hugged Paula goodbye and drove off.

The drive home was a long one. I had an old green Plymouth that I bought a year before. I wonder if buying a car was like having a suitcase under my bed, an escape plan, like my mother's story about sleeping above her suitcase, waiting to leave home.

I had a lot of time to think and I came up with this: Hunter was my symptom, not my problem. I was my problem. Maybe I'd listened to too many drug counselors talking to addicts, but maybe it was just plain true. It was a very weepy ride, and I didn't pick up any hitchhikers. Most of them were going the other way.

I wasn't sure if I was going back home, or leaving it again.

I found out I was pregnant two weeks after I got back. Being a woman's counselor, I knew the signs. I got the news from a doctor at the Cleveland Free Clinic. My diaphragm had failed.

Chapter Fourteen

Filling in my lost years for my mother, I don't tell her everything. Plenty of mistakes can be made in ten years. It wasn't all
fun and games at the clinic, and saying I enjoyed a few quaaludes
now and then doesn't really say anything about the quaaludes I
didn't enjoy. There's a way to say things that shade the truth,
even from myself.

"He was married?" my mother says. She has been listening
very well, nodding at the right spots. She seems so much like her
old self. Jesus, I almost put my mother into a nursing home
when she didn't need to be there at all.

"Yes. Married. I never talked to him again."

She nods. "You're good at that."

I hold perfectly still, knowing I deserved that. But is she

really having a conversation with me? Is this possible, that we are really talking about all this?

"Mother," I say, carefully, as if the word itself might be a trap, "do you know what's going on? Who I am?"

She looks at me, very calmly. "I know who you are."

"Who?" I say. "Who do you think I am?"

Her shoulder twitches. Her hands close, fist-like. She looks to the side, to see if there's anyone listening. My stomach sinks. I have pushed her too far.

"I know who you are," she repeats.

"Good," I say, placing a hand on her thigh. I smile kindly. "Can I tell you another story?" I ask.

She nods. "You're always good at telling stories," she says. "Go right ahead."

Maybe she does know who I am.

"Once there was a woman whose real name was Mary. She had a big family, and a mother and father she loved very much, but her father left them. And then, when she was twenty-seven, she fell in love with a man named Michael and they had three lovely children. Sadly, Michael died while her children were still young. It was a hard time for everyone, but after a few years she began to date again. Unfortunately, the oldest daughter—lets call her Esca Echo—was so sad and bitter because her father died that she made it difficult for her mother to have a relationship with another man. But then something happened and the daughter left home and moved far away. She wrote a letter to her mother, but never sent it. Then one day, she came home."

Even though my salary at the Free Clinic wasn't very much, I have saved money and I find an apartment in Cleveland Heights near Coventry, the small "Greenwich Village" of Cleveland, where there are Mid-Eastern restaurants and shops that sell rock posters. Sometimes I walk to the store to get milk or bread, and the flatness of this place makes me feel off balance. Buses look dirty and boxed in, and I keep wondering what happened to the trolleys. I miss the people I care about; I can't afford long-distance phone calls, so I write a lot of long letters. I don't write to Hunter.

I decide I won't contact my mother until I have a job. This plan is only a way to put it off. I'm terrified. She's moved out of the house we lived in and bought a bungalow covered in ivy, fifteen minutes from where I live. I looked her up in the phone book. Sometimes I drive by the house and my heart beats too fast. I get clammy and afraid. Really afraid. The simple thought of my mother makes me panic. I am living in a place in between what happened to us and facing her again. It is quieter where I am now, safer. If I don't see my family, I can stay here, in the Eye of Regret, where the only one blaming me is me.

After a month back in Cleveland, I call my brother Peter. He lives in Lakewood, on the other side of town. He's a successful chemical engineer, although I never understand exactly what he does. We agree to meet at a park. He brings his wife, Emily, and their four-year-old son, Dylan.

The first thing I notice is that Peter has a neatly trimmed mustache, and then I just stop walking. His face is slim, not a trace of baby fat. He's handsome and fit, a man with a wife and son. He looks like someone who earns good money and owns a house, and even though I knew that, I didn't believe a word of it till right now. The last time I saw him, he had just turned sixteen and had pinned me to the floor, making me swear I would stay home and watch my mother. I had promised him I'd stay home, and then I didn't see him again for ten years.

"So, you're back," he says, grinning, as if my coming back will provide him with some added amusement in his life. He comes up to me and gives me a hug. It's a warm, strong hug that makes me feels guilty as hell, and I bet he knows it.

His wife is tall and pleasant looking and I feel her studying me. Do I look like the sister my brother has described? How has he described me? Dylan's adorable, with my mother's curly brown hair and fat little boy cheeks, just like my brother used to have. There's a playground a little way off, with children climbing wooden jungle gyms. I touch my stomach and think of teeter-totters and merry-go-rounds.

"I'll take Dylan to the playground," Emily says. "So you two can talk."

"You don't have to do that," Peter and I say at the same time. But she does, anyway.

"Are you going to see Mother?" he asks.

"Yeah. I am." I stick my hands in the pockets of my jacket, take them out, stick them back in. I'm so nervous. I have a few Valium I've been saving for the right moment, but I figure that will be later, when I really do see my mother.

"When?"

"When I'm ready. Does she hate me?"

"She might, Jenny. Jesus, you left for ten years."

"I know. I know. That's why I'm back. I just want to get on my feet, first. I want to have a nice place to invite her to. I want to show her I did okay."

"Do you think she cares if you have a nice place? That's not what she wants to hear. She wants to know why you left and never talked to her again. Hell, you should get down on your knees and beg her to—"

The blame is beginning, just like when we fought on the phone. "Don't start telling me what to do, Peter. I'm not getting down on my knees. This is my life. Don't tell me what I should and should not—"

"Yeah, *your* life. That's all it's about. Just do what *you* want, Jenny. Whatever the fuck you want to do. Why start now thinking about anyone else?"

I'm glad now the wife and son are gone. Maybe she knew exactly what would happen. Some kids playing volleyball look our way. It's a Saturday in early September and I'm not showing yet. There's not a cloud in the sky. Everything could be just fine, if you were looking at us from far way.

"Look, Peter, I don't want to argue. Really. Maybe she never wants to see me again. I'm scared."

"Well, you don't have a child. You don't know. If Dylan did something like that . . ." He pauses, looks around. When he finds his kid, his whole face relaxes. "Well, I'd want to see him. I'd want to know what happened. I'd want to make it better."

I nod. What can I say to that? That she knows what happened? That some things you can't make better, even with a kiss and a really big Band-Aid.

"Thanks for coming to see me," I say, touching his arm. "Your wife and son are just beautiful. You must be so happy." I'm getting emotional. It's the hormones. I've started having these thoughts that I'm actually excited to be pregnant. I could have had an abortion—I talked to hundreds of girls about their right to decide—but I didn't. I imagine myself holding a baby in my arms like an award I won, my mother so proud of me. These are surely a pregnant woman's fancy, because I'm not that dumb.

"Thanks," Peter says. "I am happy. I just wish you were around to see Dylan when he was a baby. We're trying for another."

"Good luck," I say. I take my hands out of my pockets, give him a hug. It's not as good as the first one. "Don't tell Mother I'm back, yet. You have to promise me. I'll call her soon. I have an interview at the hospital for a job. Then I'll call her. Please don't tell."

He looks pissed again, but then nods. "It's your life, Jenny. But remember, her dad did the same thing to her. It stinks. She misses you. I missed you. I think even Betsy missed you."

We both laugh. He's taken it too far, now. I wrote Betsy twice and she never answered me.

"She got married a year ago," he says.

"Yeah, you told me." I turn away, shake my head a little. Turn back. The kids play volleyball, ignoring us. A woman walks a golden retriever. Peter's wife looks this way. I wave. They don't come any closer.

"Tell your wife I said goodbye. Love you." And I walk off. God, I'm so fucking good at this part.

I get a job at University Hospitals as a receptionist. It's not the job I want, but they don't seem to think my years as volunteer coordinator are equivalent to anything they do there. The only reason I get a job at all—being a high school dropout—is because I get two great recommendations from well-known doctors in San Francisco who volunteered at the Free Clinic there. I would have liked to work at the Cleveland Free Clinic, but I'm going to have a child and will need to make more money than they could afford. I have to think of my future, not my politics. And the truth is that it was never the politics that kept me at the Free Clinic; it was the people—the hundreds of volunteers, the staff, and the people who came in for help. It never felt like working, just hard play. Now it's time to get a real job, with benefits, which is just what I get. I answer phones, fill out forms, and file. That's pretty much it. Except I throw up every day at eleven, like clockwork.

I don't call my mother.

One night in November, the trees black, bare skeletons outside my third-floor window, I feel the baby move. I've just smoked half of the second-to-last joint that I own.

At first I don't know what it *is* that I feel. It's like a bump from inside, a nudge, and then nothing. As I hold up my top, staring at the round swelling of my stomach, something rises up under my skin, moves a little to the right, then disappears. Amazement mixes with pot paranoia, and I'm so terrified I can't move. What have I done? I'm smoking pot and there is a tiny person inside me. I watch my stomach for another ten minutes, and it never moves again. Please move, I think. *Please move.* I'm suddenly afraid the pot has gotten into the baby's bloodstream and made it stop breathing. I know better, but knowing the pot won't do that doesn't mean a thing to me because I'm high, paranoid, single, and pregnant, and the branches of the trees outside scrape against the windows like bones. I don't normally get this wacked out on pot, but it's good pot and I don't smoke that much anymore. *Please move again*, I whisper to my stomach. The branches hiss.

I place my palm against my belly. "I promise on your life I will never smoke pot again," I say. I say it loud enough that the walls that hold out those dark, bare branches can hear me. And then I know what I've done wrong. It's not the swearing on my baby's life that's wrong, it's the wording; I have made the promise so specific that it leaves the door open for all sorts of other things. Palm still on my belly, I say, "I swear I will never do any drugs that are not prescribed to me by a doctor, and that I won't talk a doctor into prescribing me anything just because I want it." I know there are doctors who will do that, so I am closing that door, too. "I promise."

Something moves. A foot or a fist, just a quick jab; a small thing that will change me for the rest of my life.

Just before Christmas I phone Peter. It's been three months since I met him in the park. "I'm ready," I say. "I just don't know how. Help me."

"Come to my house for Christmas Eve. Bring a present for everyone." He reminds me of his wife's name, his son's name, and Betsy's husband's name, as if I might not know them. I write Betsy and Jasper down on a piece of paper, underline Jasper three times.

"Will you tell her I'm coming?" I ask.

"Yeah, Jenny. I think it's only fair to warn her."

"Okay," I say. "Thanks. Really. Jesus, I'm scared."

"You better show up."

"Hey, Peter," I say. "I'm glad you're my brother. I could use someone who doesn't pull punches."

"Well, to tell the truth, sometimes I wish we we're kids again, so I could just beat you up."

I laugh. "I'm coming back, Peter. Ready or not. And thank you. I missed you. I can't remember why, but I did."

"Dinner will be at six. Don't be late."

"Can I bring something?"

"Oh, I think you'll be bringing quite enough as it is. No, really, there will be tons of food. Emily's become quite a gourmet cook. Just come with a good attitude."

He doesn't know I will be coming with something more than that.

Peter answers the door. I have on a heavy winter coat and am carrying three paper bags with Christmas presents. He takes the bags and puts them down, steps behind me to help me take off my coat.

I turn around, and his smile fades. "Oh, my God! You're pregnant."

Fresh pine wreaths wander up the banister. Dozens of green and red candles dapple the living room. A fire burns hotly in the fireplace. The house is neat as a pin. My protruding stomach and the future it holds is out of place in this well-planned home. I look down, almost expecting my stomach to have flattened out in embarrassment. "Yep," I say. "I sure am."

"Shit, Jen," he says. "You haven't changed at all."

I look at him, robust and innocent. A guy with a house and gourmet wife. I want him to understand something that I'm trying hard to believe myself. "No, Peter, I have. I *have* changed." I put my hand on my stomach.

He shakes his head. Tries a smile. "Well, you're here. And on time. They're waiting in the family room. Come on."

I follow him down the hall. I tell myself that no matter what, I will remain calm and dignified.

"Hi, Jenny," Emily says. She's standing at the doorway to the family room, blocking my view, wearing a canvas apron with artist paint splotches. I say hi, and tell her the food smells so good. She steps back.

Betsy and her husband are standing by a glass table that's covered with cookies, peanuts, and swirls of shrimp around a bowl of red dip. My stomach heaves and I take a deep breath. Betsy's no longer fourteen. She's a woman in a pale lavender pantsuit, holding a drink that doesn't look like a soft drink. Her husband, a man who looks just like a college professor—thin hair, turtleneck, tweed coat, and loafers—puts an arm around Betsy's shoulder as if protecting her. Immediately I don't like him. My mother sits on a yellow couch, wearing a bright floral skirt and an orange blouse, her hair cut shorter than I've ever seen it, without a trace of gray. Her smile is so tight her lips have vanished. Next to her sits Dylan, with a book open in his lap.

"Well, hello, Jennifer," my mother says. She stands up slowly and moves toward me as everyone else holds still. "So good to see you." She gives me a hug, the kind where our bodies hardly touch, which is quite a feat, considering my stomach.

"Hi," I say, and realize something Peter must have thought of already. Since Dylan's here, and it's Christmas Eve, we'll all be kind and polite. There will be time enough for recriminations later on.

I am breathing hard. Everyone's staring at my stomach.

"Hi, Betsy," I say. I can't meet her eyes.

"Hello."

She's a stranger with my sister's voice.

"This is Jasper," she says. He steps forward, offers his hand. We shake.

"Hi, there, Dylan," I say brightly, as if we are old friends. He says hi. Now what?

"Are you hungry?" Emily asks. I like her. I have this feeling she feels a bit sorry for me. I wish I were hungry. I shake my head. "Not really. Thanks, though."

"Well, let's put your presents under the tree," Peter says. "Jennifer brought three bags of presents!"

I want to die and crawl under the table, but the table is glass, and no good for hiding. I'm nervous and laugh. Everyone frowns. Oh, yeah; if Jenny laughs, she must be stoned. I want to say I'm not stoned, and I'm sorry, and please stop looking at me that way. And I want really badly to be stoned. What I want, and what I do, though, are now two different things. The night I made my promise, I threw out the Valium, the pot, and a quaalude I was saving for the right guy. Or the wrong guy. They're better used with the wrong guy, so you don't know it at the time. But I haven't met anyone who looks interesting. Like food, men don't look so good to me anymore.

"Okay." I follow my brother back down the hall, where we pick up the paper bags and carry them into the living room.

"That went well," I say. "Guess I'll go now."

"Jenny, give them some time."

I grin. "I did. Just not enough, obviously."

Under the tree is a profusion of gifts covering the floor like loud voices, bright colored paper and shining bows clamoring for attention. I bought a lot of presents—boxed apologies—and had the clever idea of wrapping them in the Sunday comics like we did when we were kids and didn't have much money. The clever idea was to remind them of our childhood together. Now

I know what these comics will say—that Jenny still doesn't have money, but everyone else does. I push them to the back. Maybe they will be forgotten.

"Okay, so do I crawl back in now?"

Peter puts a hand on my shoulder. "Stick to small talk for now. Just let them get used to you."

"Small talk?"

"Yeah. Ask them what they do. Tell them about your job."

"This is nuts," I say.

"This is your family," he says. "And they're just as nervous as you are. Take it slow."

I take a deep breath and nod. "Lead the way." We go back into the family room a second time, like a retake on an entrance. This time I sit down on a chair not too close, or too far, from anyone in particular. Once again, all talking has ceased. It's my cue.

"Okay. I'm back. I know this is really weird. I'm sorry." I look at my mother. Her eyes are steely, focused on my face. I look away, and catch my sister staring at me. I didn't know it before, but she has my mother's eyes. This is not good. "Can you fill me in a little? Tell me what you're up to? Are you working, Betsy?"

The pause waiting for her to answer is overly long. Bet she can't wait ten years. But she will be polite and answer me because she is in a lovely home where the turkey smells delicious, and the glass table holds shrimp, and almost everyone is wearing expensive shoes. These are not the kind of people who walk out of a life, even their own. I tell myself they are not my kind of people so that when they tell me I am not welcome it won't hurt so bad.

"I'm in graduate school at Case Western Reserve University," she says. "Getting my master's in paleontology. My thesis is due next spring, and then we're moving to Arizona, where Jasper's parents live. We were married last year at Westwood Country Club."

"It was a beautiful wedding," my mother says.

"It sure was," Peter says.

"Dinner's almost ready," Emily says. "Could someone mash the potatoes? Then everyone should wash their hands and sit down."

I will write her the best thank-you note I have ever written. The only thank-you note I have ever written.

Betsy offers to mash the potatoes. I fill the glasses with water and ice. My mother carries out the cranberry sauce. Dylan carries the rolls. I think he's taking all this in—that I am like the bogeyman invited to dinner. As I sit down at the beautifully set table, I imagine us a year from now, a high chair next to me, the conversation lively, my coming home just old news. Everyone loves babies, right?

But all through dinner no one mentions my stomach. Maybe they think I'm just fat. A skinny woman with a round fat stomach.

We talk turkey. How golden it is. How ingenious to have stuffed herbs under the skin, to have filled the inside with vegetables. Carving it is a feat all its own, which we watch with intense focus, asking carving questions as my brother sharpens the knife with a long metal rod, and cuts the turkey as if he is a famous turkey surgeon. When my mother looks at me, her eyes don't linger on my face for long; they lower to the area of my stomach. She sees through the white lace tablecloth and the hard walnut wood, holding bitterness in her heart that sours every bite she takes. She doesn't have to say a word about me being pregnant. My pregnancy has been declared an abhorrence as we eat turkey and mashed potatoes, discussing Natalie Wood's death and the Davis Cup.

I vow to do what I must on my own, never ask for help.

"And what are you doing, now?" Emily asks me. Mouths stop in mid-bite. Eyes turn my way.

"I have a job at University Hospitals. I'm a receptionist in pediatrics." This seems to be a good way into the discussion about babies, but no one picks up on it.

"So you're staying in town?" Betsy says. She wipes her mouth with the linen napkin. Places it back in her lap.

"Yeah. I'm going to stay here. I worked at a free clinic in California for the last seven years. I guess I got burnt out. It happens to people who work in that field. It was time to move on." There are several nods, as if they know what I am talking about, and as if they don't believe a word I'm saying. All that in a nod.

"I got a place in Cleveland Heights, an apartment near Coventry. Nice neighborhood. I have a cat named Solar, because she's orange. I'd love for you to come visit." I say this last part to Dylan. He nods but looks at his dad. He wants to see where the bogeyman—lady—lives, but he's not coming without his dad.

No one says anything. I blunder on. "I hear you moved, Mother. Do you like it?"

"Yes, I do," she says.

"When did you move?"

"While you were gone."

Touché. Peter's eyes smile, although he's trying to keep a straight face. He's getting both his entertainment and a chance to see me get my comeuppance.

"Oh," I say. "I see. Well, maybe you and I can talk about that some other time."

"Oh, maybe." She's calm and collected, holding quite still, with her back straight, hands in her lap. I want to shout *Boo!* I want to knock the table over.

Lovely Emily breaks the now deadly silence to tell us a story about Dylan learning to swim at the YMCA, and how quickly he's catching on. Peter tells a story about a mountain he's going to go climb in May. Jasper actually joins in the fun and tells us that he's going to a meeting in Wisconsin in a few weeks. I'm going to have a baby in April, I don't say. I was often accused of trying to get the limelight. Not this time.

Pumpkin pie and ice cream are served. Then it's time to clean up and open presents. We all clear the table and scrape dishes, handing them to Emily to put in the dishwasher. My mother walks all the way around the other side of the table with a plate to avoid me. Betsy won't speak to me. Peter jabs me in the side with his elbow. "Having fun?" he whispers.

"Go climb a mountain," I say. I wonder if I had stayed in Cleveland, if it would have all turned out this way, anyway. It feels so familiar.

I pull my brother aside. "Does she still drink?" I ask.

"Sometimes. Not like before," he says.

"AA?" I ask.

"Well, for a while, but she quit before she had to do those steps. Said they were stupid."

"What made her go? To AA?"

"Betsy," he says, tilting his head toward the kitchen.

I walked away and let them deal with her. Betsy was not quite fifteen when I left, and here I am, with a child inside me. She must hate me so much.

"God, I'm sorry," I say.

"There were a lot of good times you missed, too. You just never saw the good times, even before you left."

"The good times?" I ask. "Like what?"

"Euclid Beach. Going to the museums. The snow fort we built. Every kid in the neighborhood was jealous of that fort. Mother even let us put that rug inside and bring in pillows. No other mom would have done that."

"Peter, she had no clue we took the rug and pillows into the fort. Daddy just died. We could have painted the house pink. And who the hell went to Euclid Beach?"

"We did, Jenny."

"Not me. I never went to Euclid Beach."

He shrugs. "Yeah, maybe you didn't. That's just my point."

"The dishes are done. Let's open presents," Emily says. She ushers us into the living room. Somehow I end up sitting on the couch with Jasper and my sister. Jasper sits between us. We open presents.

Emily comments on my wrapping paper, what a clever idea it is. She says the toolbox with real tools I got for Dylan—at Peter's suggestion—is just the very best gift. Dylan does seem to like it; his eyes widen as he hefts the hammer. I have wrapped each tool separately, so it looks like I've gotten him dozens of gifts. "We're going to make a go-cart," Peter announces.

I get a Christmas candle and woven place mats from Betsy and Jasper. A soft green shawl from my mother, which I really like and tell her so. She nods. Peter, Emily, and Dylan give me a set of pots (my suggestion). I have gotten all the women wind chimes, and all the men carved wooden boxes. For an extra gift for my mother, I give her a handcrafted cedar picture frame. I was going to tell her it's for a picture of her grandchild, my child, but now I don't. She thanks me.

By the time we're done opening gifts, it's past ten and Dylan rubs his face and lays his head down in his mother's lap. Betsy says they have to leave—they need to wake up early tomorrow on Christmas Day to fly back to Arizona and have Christmas dinner with his parents.

I say I have to go, too, but I don't say why and no one asks. They all walk me to the front door, maybe to make sure I'm really leaving.

"Can I call you? Get together to talk?" I ask my mother, who stands with her arms folded across her chest.

"You know what," she says, then pauses. Looks at my stomach. "I'm not so sure about that. Why don't I call you."

"Okay," I say, my eyes hot. I pick up the bags filled with my gifts. It's awkward, these pots and things, my belly. "Well, you can get my number from Peter. Goodbye."

Peter steps forward, holding Dylan in his arms. "Go ahead," he says to Dylan, nudging him.

"Goodbye, Aunt Jenny," Dylan says.

I burst into tears. I try to kiss Dylan on the forehead, but he ducks his head into Peter's chest. I catch the back of his curly hair with my lips. Tears are streaming down my cheeks like big fat traitors. I turn, but can't open the door with all the packages in my arms. Emily opens it for me.

"Thank you so much," I whisper to her, my voice catching. "Merry Christmas."

Driving home in my old car, wearing my thrift-shop coat, I pretend I would have been like Emily, if my father hadn't died, if my mother hadn't drunk so much, if I had stuck around to face my fate—and family—ten years ago. But it's all a lie. I am simply who I am, and I did okay. I had a great job at a wonderful free clinic, which grows more wonderful as I think about it. And I have a baby inside me. A wonderful baby, which I will raise all by myself. I won't bother these people anymore. I will do it all on my own. I'll show them. I'll even send the shawl back.

My mother never calls. I keep the shawl. I don't see her again until I am in the hospital, holding my daughter in my arms. And then things are said so that we don't see each other again for a long time.

Chapter Fifteen

By the time I'm done telling this story, my mother's asleep, her head drooped forward onto her chest. I don't know how much she heard, or understood.

The idea of keeping my mother here, at my house, is to build her life back up, but it occurs to me now that she *has* her life; maybe what she is missing is mine. Maybe when I left, it created a hole in my mother that never got filled, that got bigger, as holes do. Maybe I am not only responsible for her being alone, but for the Alzheimer's itself.

Later in the day, when my mother wakes, we play gin rummy and watch the soaps, which she loves. No matter where you are in time, the characters are always the same. For the rest of the afternoon she has the use of most of her words and is pleasant enough, so I'm sure this is a real rebound. I feed her dinner at four, before Jazz and Todd get home, and promise her a short walk later, to look at the changing leaves. She should rest first, I say, and she agrees. She only calls me Tiffany once.

I make Chicken Kiev while my mother sleeps, Jazz and Todd's favorite meal. When Todd comes home, his eyes are red, his clothes covered in sawdust. He smells like fresh-cut pine. I tell him dinner will be ready after he showers. He looks at the table, set for three.

"How did the nursing home visit go?" he asks, standing there in his stocking feet. His boots have been left by the back door, as always. He has to take careful steps, like this. The floors are slick.

"Go take a shower," I say. Then, because he doesn't move, "She's still here."

He doesn't frown or shake his head, but I can tell he's disappointed by the way he takes a deep breath through his nose, then turns and walks away.

Jazz comes home and she, too, stops and looks at the table, but when she sees the three place mats, she looks worried, a crease on her forehead I've never noticed before. "Is Nana still here?" she asks. I say yes, and the crease disappears.

"Are you glad she's still here?" I ask, surprised.

She shrugs and drops her backpack on the floor. "I want to ask her some questions. Is she okay today?"

"What kind of questions? And yes, she's much better, actually," I say, dropping the rolled, breaded chicken into the hot oil, being careful not to get burned by splatters.

"We got an assignment to interview someone who remembers World War Two."

"Jazz, You can't count on her memory, you know that."

"Mom, you can't count on anyone's memory. God, according to you, it took your dad two years to die. But Nana says it was real quick, and it was *her* husband that died. And you tell stories differently every time. Anyway, I don't know anyone else who was around back then. I mean, you're old, but not that old, right?"

So much goes through my head I can't speak. First, that this is *my* daughter, with this complicated idea about false memories that she tosses off as if it's something everyone knows. She's so smart. Does she know that? I don't think she does. And is she serious, does she think I'm that old, or does she just not understand when World War II was? And finally, how long did it take for my father to die? Whom can I ask? My brother is climbing a mountain. I hardly talk to my sister. What is the truth when there aren't any photographs to prove it?

"Is she awake now?" Jazz says, going up the stairs, dismissing me and my stunned look.

"No, she's resting while we eat, and then I'm going to take her for a walk."

Jazz stops halfway up the stairs and leans over the banister. I have to look up at her. "I'll take Nana for a walk. What's for dinner?"

Jazz take my mother for a walk? Just when I thought everything was back to normal, my daughter has become someone else in the few hours she has been at school. But my heart tells me differently. She hasn't changed since this morning, she has been changing for a while now and I just haven't noticed. "Chicken Kiev," I say.

"Great!" She runs up to her bedroom and slams the door behind her, just like always. And she still likes Chicken Kiev.

. . .

Just before I serve dinner, I ask Todd to light the candles. It's been a long time since we ate a meal with the candles lit, and he looks at me warily as if I have asked him to let wild animals into the house. *It's just candles*, I think, but we both know it's not just candles. I'm trying to make this a nice dinner, but something tells me he's not in the mood for a nice dinner. For the past month he's been working twelve hours a day, but the job is almost done, and he's home for dinner at a decent time tonight.

I call Jazz. She comes skipping down the stairs and, bracing herself with one hand on the banister, jumps over the gate, landing with a thump on the hardwood floor. I see Todd wince. I know he'll go over there later and check the floor for skid marks from Jazz's dark-soled shoes. He's asked us to take our shoes off in the house, but we forget.

"Jazz, don't jump over the gate," I snap.

"Fine," she says. But that doesn't mean she'll stop jumping over the gate. She says fine because then, what's there to argue about, she agreed, didn't she?

"Candles?" Jazz asks as she sits down.

"Looks nice, doesn't it?" I say. Todd doesn't chip in with a *sure does*.

The dinner's on the table, and Jazz digs right in. Todd waits for me to pick up my fork. His hair's still damp. "How was work?" I ask.

"Not good," he says, and starts to eat.

"Why?"

"We were sanding floors in an attic. Ever carry a floor sander up two flights of stairs?"

Obviously I haven't. "No. It's heavy?" I say, just trying to make conversation.

"Yes."

Jazz watches us. She knows something's up.

"I'm sorry," I say.

"Nothing for you to be sorry about."

We're quiet for a while and I'm just about to ask Jazz how school was, when Todd clears his throat.

"So, what happened at the nursing home?"

"She wouldn't even get out of the car," I say.

"So you just drove away?"

I'm getting pretty tired of the short, sharp tone he's using. "I almost pulled her bodily from the car and onto the asphalt, if that makes you feel better, but I just wasn't strong enough."

Now he stares at me. He's stopped eating.

"The good news, though, is she's better," I say, trying to ease up on the tension. "She's going through some kind of remission."

This is apparently not the answer he's looking for. "How so?"

"She's more alert. Knows who I am. Even answers questions. We had a great talk today. Really. She's not someone who should be in a nursing home."

"Oh, really?" he says with a sneer, changing his perpetual sweet baby face into something frightening, like a cruel clown. "What *is* she, then? A woman who should be living with her daughter and her family, a daughter who has to quit her job to take care of her, so she doesn't hurt herself, doesn't hurt someone else, or tear up the house? Because, Jen, she's not going to be able to live on her own. You know that. And this seems to be her only other option, and it's not an option anymore." He balls up his napkin, tosses it sideways across his lap and onto the floor. It's a small thing, a napkin, but it's a big thing, his disdain.

I take a breath, try to speak. "I'm not saying she should live here indefinitely, just that it's too soon to ship her off to—"

"Yeah, right," Todd says. "Just last week she turned on the hot water in the shower and let it run for hours before you noticed. I still don't know how you couldn't have noticed that, if you're watching her so carefully. If you're taking such good care of her. And just the day before that, she wandered out of the house because Jazz forgot to lock the door. Thank God I saw her walking down the street. And, Babe, she goddamn hit me when I tried to get her into the car. I didn't tell you that part, because I'm Mister Fucking Nice Guy, but don't try to tell me she shouldn't be in a nursing home because you had a lovely talk with her today."

Before I can say anything, Todd picks up his plate and starts for the kitchen. "I'm going up to the computer room. Just leave me alone for a while, all right? Leave me alone." I nod dumbly, my stomach getting tight. He walks back out of the kitchen and goes upstairs. He doesn't say thanks for dinner.

Jazz and I look at each other. In the silence I feel a special connection between the two of us, like the way it used to be before I married Todd. We could say so much with a look, a nod, a smile. I'm afraid of what she sees in my face right now. She knows me too well. I blush.

I wonder how she will explain me to her children some day. What she will exaggerate, what she will leave out.

"He's right, I didn't lock the door," Jazz says.

"That's not the point," I say. I lean on the table, resting my forehead in my hands, my eyes closed and cupped in my own warm flesh. I want to go back to San Francisco. It was a cocoon to me—not only a place that held me safely from myself, but where I emerged new again, and that's what I want now. To get through Todd's anger, my mother's illness, and to come out of it on the other side.

"It's hard, Jazz. I don't know what to do. She's my mother. What would you do, if it were *me* with Alzheimer's?"

Jazz lets loose a huff, and with my eyes closed, she sounds just like my mother. I look up.

"Jesus, Mom, you always ask me questions like this! You asked me if you should marry Todd, and I said sure, go ahead. What was I supposed to say? He's okay, I mean, I like him now, but what the hell did I know?—just that he was tons better than most the guys you dated. If you and Todd break up now, are you going to blame me?" She shakes her head, her left eye squinted like it does when she gets really angry. "How the hell am I supposed to know what I'd do if you got Alzheimer's? We could all be dead by then!"

I straighten up, startled by her anger, and worried. When I was her age, wars were in other countries, far away. I never felt threatened by Vietnam, even if I should have. "I'm sorry. You're right. Unfair question." I cut a piece of chicken, turn it around on my fork, put it back down. "Still, I want to know if having Nana stay here is bothering you. Is it really a problem?"

"Well, yeah, sometimes. But I guess it's mostly your problem."

I laugh. "God, I wish I'd been as smart as you when I was your age. I mean, do you know how stupid I was to just stick out my thumb and go to San Francisco with three hundred dollars?"

"You didn't starve or anything," Jazz says.

"No. I was very lucky. The Free Clinic had good people. I was lucky I walked in there that day, that I didn't end up on the streets. Who knows, maybe if I had, I would have come back home. But then I wouldn't have had you. Believe me, that's my best luck. You. Having you."

"So, who's my dad?"

I freeze. It's not an offhand question that she doesn't expect to get answered, like it usually is. The stillness in her face says she really needs an answer now. Today. Has seeing Todd get so angry made her want her own father? All along, I thought Jazz had gotten used to me saying it didn't matter, and finally it didn't, but maybe she was just waiting until the right time. Which is now. She's right. It is important she know who her father is. She has his genes, too. And it's part of the story of me, that she may have to remind me of, someday.

"Come on, Mom. It would be good to get over the fantasy that it's Mick Jagger or some rock star you met in San Francisco. It's time you told me."

"Okay," I say.

Her eyes get huge, and she drops her fork. Now we're both not eating our favorite dinner.

"He was a man I met at the Free Clinic. He worked there." I pause, but then tell the truth. "He was married. I was ashamed he was married, that's why I didn't tell you. He doesn't even know about you. I'm sorry."

I see Jazz's eyes fill with tears, so of course, I get weepy, too.

"What's his name?"

"Hunter Phillips."

"Hunter Phillips," she repeats after me. I nod.

"Would you tell him about me? See if he wants to meet me?"

"Do you want me to?"

"I don't know! It's just a maybe. But would you?"

"Yes. I would. If we can find him."

Jazz starts crying. She doesn't even bother to wipe her face. "I thought he knew about me but didn't care. God, Mom, it's . . . it's like if he doesn't know about me, it's like I'm . . . less. Like I don't exist. I've been waiting all this time for you to tell me. This is too weird. I don't know how I feel." I get up and walk over to Jazz, coming behind her chair. I wrap my arms around her shoulders and hug her, my cheek against her forehead. "Shhh, honey," I say. "It's okay. I know it's not easy, but you're okay. You're a great kid."

"What did he look like?" Jazz asks.

I still see him sometimes, in dreams. He has come back to me and we fall madly in love. They are the saddest dreams I have. "He worked at the clinic. He had long brown hair, the same color as yours, even longer than yours, and he wore it in a braid most of the time. He was very handsome, a strong jaw, brown eyes. Everyone liked him. He didn't have any kids. He had really big toes." I laugh, but my tears are falling on her cheek. "He was healthy. No heart problems, except for liking me, I guess."

"Did you love him?"

I don't say anything, just squeeze Jazz more tightly. Then, after a minute, "I thought I did, sometimes. I don't know. I didn't love him like I love you. It wasn't that kind of love, where I'd step in front of a truck to save his life. He made me cry, sometimes. I thought that was love."

"Do you love Todd?"

I nod. "Yeah. I do. I love him very much."

"Enough to step in front of a truck?" Jazz asks very quietly.

I wait a minute, thinking about it, then shake my head no. A little shake. "I don't know if I can love like that. A man, I mean. I love you that way."

I move back a bit, so we're not touching cheek to cheek anymore. I look at her. God, I love her. "I want to love Todd that way. He's the only man I want to love that way. There's no one else comes close. I just keep stepping back, somehow." Now I think I've told her too much.

Jazz looks thoughtful, and I wait to hear what she has to say. It feels so good, to talk to her this way. I am so lucky to have her, and I believe at this minute she knows we will make it, she and I, no matter what. No matter what happens in the world.

"Maybe if adults were always sacrificing themselves for love, it wouldn't be so good," Jazz says. "It's like the survival of the fittest thing. There wouldn't be kids."

"Yeah." I laugh. She is smart. "But it would be nice, just once." I kiss her on the forehead and stand up.

"I guess," Jazz says.

"Anything else?" I ask. "Anything else you want to know about him?"

She shrugs. "Do you have a picture of him?'

I shake my head no. "Sorry."

"Was he smart?"

She wants to know if she got smart genes. What might become of her because of him. "Pretty smart. Street smart."

She nods. Here eyes are beginning to look a little distant. I wait a beat, and when she doesn't ask anything else, I put my hand by her plate. "Are you done eating?"

"Yeah."

"Okay. I probably ought to go talk to Todd, huh?" I glance up at the ceiling. A piece of plaster is missing about the size of saucer. What makes them fall down like that?

She nods slowly, probably thinking about something else entirely.

"Were you really going to take Nana for a walk?"

"I guess."

"Could you do that now? If I get her ready?"

"Okay."

"I'll do the dishes later," I tell her. "And, Jazz. Thank you. I know how hard this is. Think about it. If you want, we'll find him."

"Thanks."

As we walk up the steps, Jazz stops, and I look back to see why.

"Did Nana love you that way? The step-in-front-of-a-truck way? Sorry, but she doesn't seem the type."

"I think I didn't let her. I think I wouldn't let anyone, after my dad died. I think she might have, if I let her."

It's the first time I've ever said this, even thought it out, and it makes me quiet inside, as if I found something that I didn't know I was looking for.

"Oh," Jazz says, then she starts up the stairs, and I have to move on, to get out of her way.

I watch Jazz and my mother walk slowly down the drive to the sidewalk. It's starting to get dark. Everything takes longer than I expected.

I stand outside the computer room, listening to the harsh, quick clicking of the keyboard through the closed door, remembering his face when he told me to leave him alone. Todd hardly ever shuts the door. He doesn't like being in closed rooms. He doesn't like snakes, either, and he hates country music. He hasn't talked to me in a while about things he likes, or doesn't like. I should ask him who he has been talking to on-line, but I'm afraid of his answer.

My heart starts to race. That same panicky feel I used to get when I thought about my mother now comes when I think about Todd. I turn and walk away from the door.

The house is so quiet that even downstairs I can still hear him typing. I didn't even know he could type so fast.

I should call Betsy, I think, now that she might really be home. It's something I should do, and I need something I should do right now, something besides go and face Todd. It's time Betsy and I talked, if it's not too late already. I look for the portable phone. It's in Jazz's bedroom, of course.

Rose walks with Tiffany along a sidewalk in the dusk. She's not sure where they're going, but she's not going to put up a fuss. What god ugly shoes she's wearing, though. She doesn't remember buying them. Maybe Tiffany did—her shoes are just as ugly as Rose's, and the bottom of her pants are baggy and torn. Tiffany reminds Rose of her daughter Jennifer, who used to wear bell-bottom jeans that dragged on the ground. She can't remember the last time she saw Jennifer, or what she was wearing. It hurts her head to think about it, so she doesn't.

"Hey, Nana," Tiffany says, stopping to pick something up. "A feather."

"Starling," Rose says, the word slipping out all on its own. And it's the right word. It comes with a knowledge of its rightness. Her shoulders straighten. She likes this word, this feeling. "Starling," she says again.

"You know about birds? Mom says you do."

Rose doesn't answer. She doesn't want to take any chances with the one word she has. She puts out her hand, palm up. Tiffany gives her the feather. "Starling," Rose says with a sharp nod, clutching the feather. If she never speaks again, at least the last word she has said was right.

They continue walking. Tiffany shuffles her feet, kicks at a stone. "I don't know much about birds," she says. "Cardinals and blue jays. That's all. I want to study sharks. I'm thinking about going into oceanography." They turn the corner. Rose looks back over her shoulder, then ahead. Nothing looks familiar. She holds the feather tighter. Where are they going?

"Can I ask you some questions, Nana?" Tiffany asks her. "About World War Two?"

Something in her heart flutters sharply. Her hand moves to her chest, a fist with a feather hitting her, as if it moved all on its own. She looks down at herself, and it's not her body. "Oh!" she says, and stumbles. Tiffany takes hold of her arm so she doesn't fall.

"Are you okay, Nana?"

Rose looks at this girl calling her Nana. It's not Tiffany, not at all. How could she think that? "Oh, no." Then, "Starling."

"No, you're not okay?"

There's a bright light flickering in her right eye. She closes her eyes, but it doesn't go away. "Don't tell," she says to the girl. "Don't tell about the light." They'll do something to her. She remembers this light from before.

The girl looks around and points to a ledge by some steps. "Let's sit down."

Rose nods. Legs that are not hers take her to the steps. They bend. She sits.

"Jasmine," she says to the girl, knowing this is her granddaughter. She has a granddaughter, and a starling feather, and someone else's legs.

"Yes, Nana?"

"I'm tired."

"Okay, Nana," Jasmine says.

But Rose is no longer there, on that step, which is her future. She's in the hospital. For a moment, she thinks she's in the hospital because she's had a stroke, but no, that hasn't happened yet, either. She is in the hospital to meet her granddaughter.

Rose didn't call Jennifer after that Christmas Eve dinner at Peter's. She had been so sure she could handle seeing Jennifer with some grace and poise, but had been dead wrong about that. It wasn't the sight of Jennifer pregnant that froze every muscle in her body, including her face, which could not have smiled if she'd paid it, it was just Jennifer herself, ten years older. It was absolutely frightening and infuriating, the same damned emotions that took over Rose's life when Jennifer left ten years ago. How dare she just walk in carrying bags of Christmas presents? Was Rose to forgive her daughter for all that pain because she bought them wind chimes? Did she think it would be that simple?

No one had any idea what Rose had gone through. Three years, believing Jennifer had been picked up by some crazy man and murdered, left in some shallow grave on the side of the road. That's what she believed, because that was her punishment—to believe the worst. She woke up each morning as if out of a nightmare, just to find she was living the nightmare. When Peter told her that he'd gotten a letter from Jennifer, that she was in San Francisco, Rose couldn't breathe it hurt so bad. Her legs gave out and she had sat on the floor with a thump. Peter helped her up, then asked if she wanted to read the letter. Rose said no. It wasn't addressed to her.

Apparently, it did include Jennifer's return address; if anyone wanted to write back, they could. It may have been Jennifer's way of testing the water, but it was not what Rose was waiting for. Yes, things had happened in that car that night, and Rose had blamed herself for three long years; still she believed with all her heart that if she found her daughter, they would hug and cry and forgive each other. But this letter, to her son, made her furious. What had she done, really, to deserve this? Nightmares every night, two thousand dollars paid to a detective who turned up squat, that look of pity from people she knew—three years putting her life on hold in hell, and then a *letter*, to *Peter*? No, she was not going to write back.

Jennifer had punished Rose with her absence, now Rose would do the same. It had been a game with no winners. She was smart enough to know exactly what she was doing.

And now Peter has dragged her down here to the hospital because the baby has been born. A girl. Here Rose is, riding in the elevator to the eighth floor while Peter waits downstairs in the lobby because he says she has to do this on her own. Why the hell does she have to do anything? Jennifer comes for Christmas bearing gifts, and now it's Rose's move? Well, damned if she's going to be carrying anything. Still, she does—she carries hope so deep inside that she hardly knows it's there. She can remember loving Jennifer. She is sure she does. Maybe she can, again.

A nurse tells her which room Jennifer is in, and Rose runs her hands through her hair. Smooths her skirt. Would kill for a cigarette. She steps around the corner and into the room.

Jennifer lies on the hospital bed, the baby in her arms, unaware Rose is standing in the doorway. But this cannot be her daughter. This is a woman holding a baby. A woman who gave her a wind chime for Christmas.

Maybe that would be the best way to go about this. This is just a woman she's met recently, who is not the same person who hurt her so badly. If she thinks this way, maybe she can trick her heart.

She clears her throat.

Jennifer turns and sees Rose, her look changing to surprise and shock. Good, Rose thinks. *Good*. Then the baby mews, little soft wet cries. Without a word Jennifer lifts up her loose nightshirt and exposes her breast, holding it from underneath, adjusting it so her nipple is closer to the baby's mouth. She shifts the baby now, and the two meet. There is a moment when both the baby and Jennifer close their eyes, and Rose is no longer here, could be dead, but then Jennifer opens her eyes. "Hello, Mother," she says.

It's not enough. Nothing would be. Even this child, her granddaughter. Rose is suddenly furious with herself, because she doesn't want to hold this baby, and that will make her look bad.

"What's her name?" she says, still standing only a foot inside the door.

"Jasmine," Jennifer says. "But I'm going to call her Jazz."

Her daughter has said this just to be ornery. Certainly no one is going to call their daughter Jazz. Rose rolls her eyes, then unable to pull back a gesture, she becomes ashamed at herself and gets angry at Jennifer for making her feel ashamed. "And does the baby have a father? A last name?"

"Mine," Jennifer says.

"My God, Jennifer. How are you going to raise a child without a father? Seriously, what is the man's last name, if I may ask?"

"You may not," Jennifer says.

They stare at each other for a minute as the baby nurses.

Rose swears she's not going to talk first, but she does. She just can't hold it in anymore. "If you can't answer a simple question with a little kindness, I'll have nothing to do with either of you. You shouldn't have had a child, if she can't have a father you can name."

Before Jennifer can say anything, Rose turns and leaves the room. Her hands are shaking again, quite badly. She can hardly catch her breath. She is alone in the elevator going down.

Chapter Sixteen

"Nana? Are you okay?"

Rose lifts her head. She must have fallen asleep. On a step? Her bottom aches from the hard concrete. A girl who looks familiar sits next to her. Rose pats the girl's thigh, comfortable with this child, whoever she is. On the ground is a feather, black and glossy like a wet night. "Starling," she says, and bends down slowly to pick it up. Holding the feather to her chest, she grins. She loves birds, and cats. A funny combination. Like me and this young girl here, both in god ugly shoes. She laughs and pats the girl's leg again. "Let's get going," she says, the words slipping from her so easily. And why shouldn't they?

. . .

I pick up the phone, call my sister, Betsy. Her husband, Jasper, answers. I hear alarm in his voice. He must think I'm calling with bad news. Why else would I call? It's not that I never talk to Betsy, but the times I do are always the times I must.

"Mother's okay," I say. "I'm just calling to talk to Betsy. Is she there?" Holding the black portable phone in one hand, I close the door. I've never been in Jazz's room alone with the door shut. It feels strange, like I'm doing something wrong.

"I'll get her." Jasper doesn't bother with the *how are you's*, or the *how's the weather* stuff. We have never been a how's-the-weather kind of family. When we want to avoid something, we avoid each other.

"Hello?" Betsy says.

"Hi," I say. "Mother's okay. She's out on a walk with Jazz. I think she's doing better, like a remission. We had a long talk today."

"That's nice," Betsy says. She's not dumb. She's very, very smart, it turns out; has a master's from Case Western, a Ph.D. from the University of Arizona. She knows I didn't call her to say I had a nice talk with Mother.

"That nursing home called. I left you that message. Did you get it?"

"Yes. I called you back, remember?"

Yeah, she did. We played phone tag. Now I'm It. "I think I'd like to keep her here for another month or so, but I keep going back and forth. What do you think, should I keep her here?"

There's a pause. "I can't tell you what to do. You'll have to figure that one out on your own."

"God, I wish I could. Actually, I wish I took her in a year ago, so sending her to a nursing home now would be okay. Two months isn't that long."

Another pause. I haven't asked a question. She might just wait till I do. I skip over all the worries I have about keeping Mother, and cut through whatever Betsy's thinking in silence. "I know you're mad at me. I know you don't like me much. I know I never gave you any reason to." Which is probably exactly what she *is* thinking. I stumble on. "Look, I've been doing a lot of soul-searching. I missed so much. I left you and Peter, and I'm really sorry. I know I never said that to you, except in a perfunctory way, but you always look at me like you hate me, which you might, I don't blame you. I'm really sorry I left you behind. You don't have to forgive me, but I've got to say it, okay?"

"Is this some kind of AA thing?" she asks. "For some addiction you have? Because I don't want any part of that."

"No. No, it's not. I don't do drugs anymore." I sit on the edge of Jazz's bed, try to relax. She has stuffed animals on her bed, even at the age of sixteen. I missed knowing Betsy at this age. She went from fourteen to twenty-four in a leap I took.

"I just want to say I'm sorry because I want to. It's all my own idea. Really. I know I can't make up for everything. I just want to talk to you. I want to know about you, and Mother, while I was gone."

"Oh, I'm supposed to give you a synopsis? You want footnotes?"

Shit. I stand up, pace. This is not going to be easy. "No. Jesus, Betsy. Just talk to me. Okay?"

There's a pause. "All right. What do you want to know?"

The first thing I think of is, "How long did it take Daddy to die?"

"What do you mean?"

"From the time he got sick, till he died. Wasn't it a few years?"

"No, six months. Why?"

I swallow. "It seemed longer. Did she tell you why I left?"

"No. Why did you leave?"

"Can I tell you that later?"

"Whatever."

I smile. The professor saying *whatever*. "Did she try to find me?"

"Yeah. Of course she did. She called the police a hundred times, your friends, she went and hung out by the school. Do you know how embarrassing that was for me? She talked to everyone until she got the name of some guy you hung out with. She confronted him in the parking lot, screaming at him. That was my school, too, Jenny. Not that you cared. He said you were gone. He didn't know where. I don't know what else she did, except she always asked if you called. You didn't."

"Sorry," I say.

"Tell her," she says.

I'm walking in circles like a dog trying to figure out where to lie down. I sit on the floor. "Did she drink more because I left?"

"What do you think, Jenny? The shock of your leaving drove her to sobriety? Yeah, she got worse. Peter joined the football team, the track team, the baseball team. I stayed home. She lost her job, but they took her back. She filed a claim for disability. She thought of that all by herself, when no one did stuff like that yet. She was smart, smart enough to write you off. But, hell, she didn't. She just pretended to. She cried a whole lot. Is that what you want to know? Does that make you feel better?"

"It's not about feeling better," I say, knowing it is. This won't do it, that's for sure. "So how did she stop drinking? Peter says it was because of you."

A pause again. I wait, slipping off my shoes and socks. I rub my feet.

"I came home for Thanksgiving, from college, and she was a mess, just lost her job. I transferred back to Cleveland, dragged her to AA. She hated it, but she went, because she knew if she went to AA she could prove she had a disability. But she faked half the steps. She's cagey. She knew how to pretend she wasn't drinking. She cut back. She didn't stop. She never did."

"Jesus, Betsy. I'm so sorry."

"You said that already."

I hear the downstairs door open and close. Jazz and my mother are back from their walk. I'm sitting on the floor, my upper body moving back and forth, like those Jewish men saying their prayers. If Jazz walks in here, she's going to think I'm having a seizure or something. I want to hang up the phone so bad my hand sweats trying to loosen my grip on it.

"But Peter says she stopped drinking. I didn't see her drink after I got back."

"Yeah, well, Peter was in college, playing football, riding his bike across America," Betsy says. "And exactly how often did you see her after you got back? She drank when she was alone, and with people she felt might understand. Like me. She was a functioning alcoholic. I got that term from my trips with her to AA. I learned a lot while you were out in San Francisco, wearing flowers in your hair."

"Mom! I'm back!" Jazz yells. I hear footsteps on the stairs.

"But she's forgotten about alcohol now," I say.

"You want to bet?" Betsy says.

"Mom? Where are you?"

Betsy must hear Jazz shouting. "You probably have to go,"

she says. "That's okay, because I'm done with this now. Nice talking to you."

"Betsy, I just want to be friends. I'll do whatever it takes."

"Next time you call, try asking how my kids are." She hangs up.

"Mom! Where are you?"

"What are you doing in my room?" Jazz says, looking at me sitting on her floor like it's some crime.

"Talking to my sister." I shrug. "Well, I was. I'm not anymore. How was the walk?"

"Okay." But her face doesn't say okay.

"What? Did something happen?"

"Well, I didn't get to ask her anything about World War Two, that's for sure. She kind of got into this feather I found. She kept saying *starling*. We had to sit down on the Shermans' steps. She was twitching. I guess she was a little weirder than usual, but that doesn't mean I'm telling you she should go to a home."

"I understand. Thank you for taking her. Where is she?"

"In her room."

"Okay." Then, "Jazz?"

"What?"

"Do you still like stuffed animals?"

She squints at me, like I'm asking a trick question. "Sometimes," she says. "Why?"

"Nothing." But I smile, a big smile.

"Jesus," Jazz says. "You're just as nuts as Nana." She doesn't say this meanly, she's just trying to make a joke.

· · ·

I check on my mother. She's watching TV with the sound off. I ask if she wants to be left alone and she nods. Sometimes I do ask the right questions. I turn the sound up, close her door. Jazz is in her room, with her door closed. All the doors are closed. It's time to talk to Todd.

He turns and looks at me as I enter the computer room, his hands poised above the keyboard. He types with just two fingers, so now it looks like he's waiting to direct a little orchestra. "Ready to talk?" I ask. He shakes his head no, then yes. He types a few words, signs off.

There are clothes all over the place, heaped on the high-backed chair, the guest bed, the ironing board, spilling out of the plastic laundry basket. The basement is locked to keep my mother away from Todd's tools. It also makes doing the laundry more of a pain in the ass than it already is. I take the stuff off the chair, throw it on top of the basket. Todd swivels his chair toward me. We are Three Ages of Woman apart.

"I'm sorry about dinner," he says. He always apologizes first, and suddenly I see it not as a kindness but as a manipulation. If he's apologized, what's there to talk about?

"I'm sorry, too," I say, automatically, although all I did was make a nice dinner and say my mother was doing better. "Who were you talking to?"

He looks at his hands. There are dark stains under his broken fingernails, and his knuckles are large—a workingman's hands, the kind I like. He's wearing his wedding ring; the double rings were his idea. The whole marriage thing was his idea, but I took it seriously. *Take* it seriously.

"Friends," he says.

"What friends?"

"Why is this important?"

"You know it is."

He nods. We're speaking slowly, carefully. My stomach's churning.

"So?"

Todd cocks his head to the side, thinking, his eyes looking up and right. I read once that your eyes look up and right when you're remembering something or imagining things, and you look left when you're lying, or doing math in your head. I wonder who he's remembering, or imagining. I'm comforted only by the idea that he's not about to lie.

"There's a Web site for my high school, an alumni chat room. I found some old friends there. We talk sometimes." He shrugs, as if it's really nothing at all.

"Any women?"

"Two."

"Two? Have you seen them? Did you meet up?"

"Not yet," he says. How can the right answer sound so wrong?

"You want to?"

"Jen, there's men in this group, too. Old friends I haven't talked to for years. Most of them live out-of-state. We're thinking about a reunion. There's an old friend, Lue Levin, lives in Montana, he carves trees stumps into art. We used to hang out, drink. We've had some good talks, on-line. It's good to have someone to talk to, sometime."

"And the women?"

"One's in town, the other's in Columbus. One was a girl-friend, the other just a friend."

"The ex-girlfriend lives . . ."

"In Columbus. I'm just talking to them, Jen. I'm not having an affair."

At least he doesn't say *yet* this time.

"Because I don't talk to you enough?"

He nods.

The both of us sitting in chairs, facing each other, makes me feel as if we're having an interview. I get up, start folding clothes. "I'm sorry. It's temporary. I'm a bit overwhelmed with my mother—"

"Jen, it's like you have this little goddamn club going. First it was the Jen and Jazz Club, and now it's the Jen and Rose Club, and I'm not supposed to understand the secret hand signs. Well, I'm making my own." He shoves the sliding shelf with the keyboard so hard it bangs closed under the desk with a *thunk*. "Look what I'm fucking doing, Jen. I'm using a goddamn computer to talk to people. That's not how it's supposed to be. I thought we had something special. I'm living in this house full of women, and I'm completely left out. Don't tell me I'm imagining it."

"Okay. I won't." We stare at each other. "I know I've been distant recently—"

He laughs, a harsh laugh. "Babe, you can be the queen of distant, it's not something recent. But I accept that, sometimes. Hey, it intrigued me when we met. You were like this mystery. When you'd tell me stuff, when you said you'd marry me, I felt special, like I had done something no one else could—"

"You did." I sit on the corner of the bed. I'm within touching distance of him now, but we don't touch.

"Let me ask you something," he says.

"What?" There's a bit of nastiness in his voice. He's not going to ask me to sit in his lap, give him a kiss.

"Why did you marry me?"

I hold perfectly still. I know where he's going with this. "Because I love you."

"Not *in* love, though, right? You never say it that way."

He's right. I married him because I was afraid of being alone. For a long time Jazz was all the love I could stand. She was always with me, like my arm, or my heart, even when she was at school. And then she turned thirteen just as I started dating Todd. Casually dating; I didn't need a man. I could take care of myself. But my daughter's hips grew wider, her breasts swelled like rising bread, and I knew she would leave me soon. But I did feel more for Todd than other men. I loved him in moments. We were good together.

Looking at him now, mad, hurt, wanting something from me, I love him. I *am* in love with him. It stuns me, this thought. It's so strong; a sinking, swelling feeling all at the same time, and I don't know what to do with it. Telling him right now, he's not going to believe it. It's too damn convenient. I've finally fallen in love with my husband and how the hell do I say that?

"Why did you marry me? You had other boyfriends. Why didn't you marry them?" He's asking for the truth, knowing it might hurt him. I want to protect him. But how can I love him, and not be honest?

I tell him part of the truth.

"Because I wasn't in love with them."

"But you weren't in love with me."

"Not all the way," I say. Then I tell him, because it's building inside me, because I know it's true and it's wonderful, even though I know he won't believe me. "I am in love with you now. I really am."

"And when the hell did that happen?"

"Right now," I say. I try to smile. "I think it started a while ago and I didn't even know it, but right now, I feel it. I know it." My face and eyes are hot. My heart feels like it's stuck in my throat. This is so goddamn unfair. No wonder I've been afraid of falling in love.

He rolls his eyes.

"I mean it. I know what I'm feeling now."

"Do you?" he asks. "Come on. Why did you marry me, if you weren't *in* love with me then?"

I don't want to say this. Why is he making me? "Because I thought we were good together. Not just the sex, which is good, but the way we get along, like we've been good friends for a long time. I like how you treat Jazz, how you take pride in what you do." This is all going in the wrong direction. "I do love you. It's in these bright flashes, and then we get on with our regular life. I didn't know that that was being in love. I didn't know it till now."

He doesn't say anything.

"I didn't believe in a great overpowering love, and I didn't want to lie to you."

He raises his chin. I can see the anger in his jawline. "Bullshit. All I've ever heard about is this great love your parents had. You believe in it. But you settled for less, because you got tired of trying. Plain and simple. And now I'm supposed to be overjoyed that you're in love with me? Hey, Jen, maybe this is just a fucking flash. You'll get over it."

"No, I won't," I say.

He has his hands braced against the desk, like he's ready to push away his chair, get up. I put my hand on his. He doesn't jerk away, but he's sure as hell not smiling. "So you don't love me anymore?" I ask.

"Sure I do. I wasn't lying about anything. That doesn't mean I'm not . . ." He closes his eyes, breathes. It's his way of calming himself down. When he opens his eyes, he looks right at me. "Hey, it's nice you're in love with me now. Thanks, but I'll think about it." He stands up. Brushes his hands on his pants as if he's got something dirty on them.

What have I done by telling him I'm in love with him? Has it ruined everything?

"I'm sorry," I say. Everything inside me hurts and turns and shifts. "Let's just go to bed. I'll love you tomorrow." Shit, that sounded wrong. "I mean, I'll still be in love with you tomorrow."

"Maybe even Wednesday, huh?" he says.

"Yeah," I say firmly. "Wednesday and forever."

He just nods.

We brush our teeth, do all the ordinary things we do every night to go to bed.

Lying next to Todd, his back to me, I understand something; being in love with Todd is a great thing for me. It's like a gift for myself. For Todd, it's something he thought he already had, and I just took it away. My love's not something he trusts anymore, or understands.

Still, *I* know what it is. It's like stepping out in front of a truck.

And just when I have found the strength in love, it hurts the man I love.

Chapter Seventeen

I am up and dressed when Todd comes downstairs in the morning, just as I used to be, when I, too, went to work, except I'm in jeans now. The coffee's brewed, and the newspaper sectioned. I popped raisin bread into the toaster oven when I heard footsteps on the stairs. We look at each other silently until the toaster dings, making me flinch.

He nods a thanks, fills his car cup with coffee, picks up the toast, and leaves. If it's time he needs, I can give him that; I want to give him all the time I have.

Jazz gets picked up for school. I have never wondered if she plays hooky. It has never crossed my mind.

After I dress, feed my mother, and make sure she swallows every pill, I ask if she would like to go for a walk.

"Out to get . . . cream ice?" she asks.

"No, not for ice cream," I say. "Just a walk, for fresh air." It's a lovely day outside, the October air is cool and clear. I grab my mother's wool cap and place it on her head. Hold out her coat.

"Well . . ." she says, looking around as if for help—someone who will save her from this woman who wants to walk to nowhere.

"Good," I say quickly. "I'm so glad you want to come with me. Thank you."

Another trick that works with Alzheimer's patients, one I discovered all by myself. Act as if they have agreed with you, maybe they won't remember they didn't.

I take my mother's elbow and spur her down the drive and onto the sidewalk, where we turn left, and already I know where we're going. The high school's a half mile from our house, and Jazz is a third-generation student there. My mother went there, I went there—for a while—and now Jazz.

My mother and I walk slowly, lost in our own thoughts. It will probably take us a long time at this pace, and I wonder if this is not such a good idea. What if I get my mother there and she can't walk back? I imagine setting her in a bus shelter while I go back for the car. I imagine her getting on a bus, going God knows where. I imagine her face on the news. "This woman was found wandering alone with no identification. If you know who she is, please contact . . ." I've told myself a million times to get one of those ID bracelets, but I haven't done it yet.

The neighborhood we walk through is familiar. I kissed a boy inside that white colonial with the eagle above the front door. He had a small face like a doll's, and I can't remember his name. We pass a brick house where the Coopers lived. They had five sons, and the youngest, Rob, was my brother's best friend, until they moved away.

"Do you remember Mrs. Cooper?" I ask, pointing to the house. Since it's brick, it hasn't been painted another color, and she may recognize it. Small things, like the change of a color, upset her memory. One of the very first signs of her Alzheimer's was while she was staying with Peter and his family. Emily, whose natural hair color is a dirty blond, dyed her hair red, and my mother didn't know who she was. Really didn't know.

"Yes," my mother says. "Of course I do."

I pause, look at her. Her eyes are bright and clear as the day. She looks at me, and squints.

"What?" she says.

"Mrs. Cooper," I say. "You remember her?"

"Didn't I just say I did?"

"What did she look like?"

"Jesus, Jennifer, what is this, a quiz?"

Standing on the sidewalk in front of a stranger's house, I take my name into me on a deep breath of air. I hold on to her hand. Her skin is cold, and so thin, hardly attached to her anymore. I cover her hand with my own. She looks at me like I'm crazy, and I laugh.

"Hi, Mother," I say. "You need gloves." There are some in my coat pocket, and I take them out, put them on her. It's really not that cold. It must be almost fifty-five.

She rolls her eyes, and I grin. Suddenly I believe in miracles, just like a kid. I believe in a greater being, not God, but something that unites us all. I believe in ghosts. I believe my mother knows exactly who I am. This is the opportunity I have been waiting for. Because I have made her a promise that I have to break, and she needs to know that. I can't hide behind her Alzheimer's.

"Mother, I'm sorry, but this isn't working. You have good

days, like this . . ." I motion to her, and then the day around us, as if she, the blue sky, the late blooming mums, the fall leaves at our feet, are all part and parcel of the same thing: the good days. "But I can't do this anymore, because it requires all of me to take care of you, and I have a daughter and a husband who need me, too. Jazz and Todd. Remember?"

She nods.

"I wanted to do this, take care of you, to make up for everything, but I can't." I thought I had more to say, but I don't. That's it.

She tilts her head and looks at me. Then she looks away, points down the street. "Where are we going?"

Does she think I'm walking her to the nursing home, so I don't have to drag her out of the car?

"Just for a walk, Mother. Just for a walk around the neighborhood. Do you understand what I'm saying? That I have to break my promise? That you do have to go someplace where they can take better care of you? I'll come visit every day. Do you understand what I'm saying? That I'm sorry?"

"No. I won't go." She walks around me, continues on the way we were going. I feel a deep sadness invade me, the inevitability of hurting her once again. I follow her, catching up quickly because she moves slowly. I take her arm, and we walk.

I said what I had to, and she heard me. That will have to do.

We actually make it all the way to Heights High, walking by the beauty school, where we might have turned in, past Wendy's, where we could have stopped, crossing the street and coming right up to the front steps of the school. I drive by this place often enough, but walking up to it is a different experience. I belong in a car driving by. I do not belong standing here, and the kids who hang out in the parking lot stare at us. Too much of me has been stuck back then, when I was seventeen. It's time to move on.

I had to come here, to my old school, to say goodbye to who I was.

I remember a science teacher, a thin woman wearing drab, utilitarian clothes, who reached her hand into a bottle of fat leeches, smirking when the class groaned and covered their eyes. But I watched. This is what I wanted from school. Something startling. She asked if anyone would come up, hold leeches in their hand. I wanted to say I would, but I didn't. I was afraid of those slimy things that would attach themselves to me. The teacher became disgusted with our weakness. I could see her shoulders sag. "Sissies," she said. I think she wanted to find the one student she could teach that year, and standing here on the front steps of the school that I walked out of so long ago, I wish I had been that student, for her and for me. I tell myself that if I had put my hand in that jar, I would have loved school, and gone on to be a scientist, someone important.

I want to be someone my mother would love.

"Let's go into Wendy's," I say to my mother. I think she needs to sit down.

"For ice cream?" she says.

"Sure," I say, even though I know they don't have ice cream. A Frosty will have to do.

"Well, good." She adjusts her wool hat so it sits back on her head, then she pinches her cheeks. "Let's go!"

As we walk across the street, I'm thinking about reaching my hand into a jar of leeches, knowing I would do it now.

. . .

I order coffee for me and a Frosty for my mother. She doesn't complain. It's not strawberry.

"You know," I say, looking around to make sure no one can hear us, "I'm sorry I was so difficult when I was a kid." I shrug. "I was pretty bad." I've waited for so long to say I'm sorry, and now I'm doing it in a fast-food restaurant. But I've been waiting for a moment when she seems to be doing okay, and this is it. "I was awful. I'm sorry."

My mother nods like all get out. She can't even get the spoon to her mouth. I don't know how much more I can say while she nods like that. She's supposed to say I wasn't that bad. This is when she's supposed to apologize, too.

I let her eat, and I drink my coffee. An elderly man and woman sit on the other side of the room. There aren't talking, either. The quiet and the warmth remind me of church. Only when my mother is done do I whisper, "Did you ever come back that night?"

She opens her mouth, and nothing comes out. Her eyes widen, and she starts breathing in quick shallow breaths, and then her arm shoots out, knocking the pepper shaker to the floor. She looks at her arm, and then at me, and now she's badly frightened. I can see it in her eyes.

"Mother?" There's impatience in my voice. I can't help being angry. I was so close. She was going to answer me. I know she was.

"Ah . . ." she says. "Ah . . ."

Damn it, there is something wrong. "Let's get back to the house." I stand up, go behind her, and pull out her chair so she can get up. She doesn't.

I help her up, get her into her coat and wool hat, lead her out of Wendy's. I have to hold her elbow tightly as we walk. She's wobbly. I can feel her arm twitch hard, then it stops.

Just as we get outside, she shouts, "Damn you!"

There are so many kids out here. Why aren't they in school? "What?" I say, not loudly.

Pulling her arm out of my hand, she turns. I reach out to grab her. She trips and falls to the ground. She cries out in pain. I think I heard something snap.

"Oh, my God!" I bend over her; she's moaning loudly. I look up for help. We're in front of the beauty salon, where women sit under huge hair dryers, the windows fogged from the heat. Behind me, I hear loud music. I turn as a young black kid hops out of a large silver car.

"Hey. You need me to call 911? Looks like she hurt bad."

"Please," I say. "Please." I squat down next to my mother. "Are you okay?"

She whimpers, and I want to die.

The boy reaches in his jacket and takes out a cell phone so small it looks like a toy. His pants hang down around his ankles, and his head is covered with a tight black stocking. His car's still running. It throbs with music, the bass loud enough to feel in my chest. Cars are piled up behind his. Someone honks their horn. He gives them the finger, then speaks into the phone. "A lady here is hurt. Bad. We at the high school." He listens for a second. "Cleveland Heights High School. Front of the beauty salon. Better get here quick." Another pause. "Don't want to give no one my name, thanks." He closes his phone. "They coming."

"Thanks."

"She your mom?"

"Yeah."

Kids are crossing the street, pointing. A hairdresser comes out of the salon and asks me if she needs to call an ambulance. I shake my head no. People surround us, talking to each other.

"Don't move her," someone says. I nod. I'm sitting down, and my mother's head is on my lap, but I don't remember doing this. The sidewalk is so cold. Her head is warm. Her hat is missing.

"Her hat," I say. The black kid moves away, then comes back.

"Here." He hands me her wool hat.

"Thank you," I say. This kid is so wonderful. I get teary thinking that if he walked up behind me quickly, I would have been scared. I start to cry. I can't help it. "What's your name?" I ask.

"Hey, don't be needing to give you no name."

"Please," I say. "I want to thank you."

"You did," he says. "Hope she be okay." He nods and goes back to his car. Just before he gets in, he looks at one of the kids standing around. "Don't you be saying nothing, you hear. I wasn't here, you got me?"

"Yeah, Darnel. It's cool."

Darnel gets in his car and drives off. I'm left with a dozen strangers and my mother. The blare of the siren sounds like a loud accusation.

We go to University Hospitals, where I work. I've been here only once in the last two months, to check in with my boss and the woman replacing me on my leave of absence, which is supposed to be over. I feel embarrassed being here, bringing in my mother. I'm on the wrong side of the stage and don't know my lines. The bustle and hurry bothers me. Can't they slow down?

My mother is wheeled into a room and transferred from the gurney to the table with a careful thump. She's frightened and confused and won't talk. I have to answer all the questions. Even when the doctor asks her if this or that hurts, she just looks at me, still breathing shallowly like she can't catch her breath. The doctor says she needs X rays; she has broken her wrist, and maybe a rib or two. Jeanne Sonville, a nurse I know, asks me if I'm all right.

"I've been better," I say.

She gives me a hug. "She'll be okay."

"Thanks." It's hard to say more, and she seems to understand. I feel as if Jeanne is a dear friend, even though we have seldom done anything together. I promise myself I will make plans with her when this is all over.

I go down to X ray with my mother. We have to wait. Two kids were in a car accident. Minor injuries. I close my eyes and give thanks to whoever, whatever, might be listening.

Finally we find out that she does have a broken wrist. Her ribs are only bruised. She might have a slight concussion. She didn't fall that far, I think. She just tripped.

But what I'm not expecting is that they think she's had a small stroke, and want to keep her here overnight for observation. Meanwhile, they'll set her wrist. There's nothing they can do for her ribs but medicate the pain with codeine. They ask her if she understands, but she doesn't answer. The doctor motions to me to step away, so we can talk in private.

"I don't believe there's been much damage from the stroke. We can only hope that whatever abilities she had before will return in the next forty-eight hours. Her body's in shock at the moment. Let's just give her some time."

I call Todd, but no one's home. I leave a simple message. *My mother tripped outside Wendy's and hurt herself. We're at the hospital. Don't worry. I'll call back later.* I didn't push her, I think, and then wonder why I even thought that.

It's almost four o'clock by the time she gets moved into a room. She's sleeping heavily—a combination of the medicine and the trauma. I pull up a chair and sit by her bed. This is so familiar, my sitting by her bed, and even though she's hurt, I feel relief flood me—because I don't have to do it all. There are doctors and nurses just down the hall. I sit in the chair, fold my hands in my lap, and breathe. I would say I've held my breath since she fell, but who would believe me?

Todd and Jazz find me, just as a nurse rouses my mother to make sure her sleep is not too deep. I let her do her job, even though I know I could rouse my mother easily. She mumbles something, and the nurse seems satisfied.

Todd's still in his work clothes, still wearing the bandanna. There's melon-colored paint on his hands and a smear on his forehead. Melon's popular for bathrooms. Sometimes I can tell what room he painted just by the colors on his clothes. I stand up, kiss him, give Jazz a hug. She looks at her nana in the hospital bed and sits down in the chair I was sitting in. She puts her hand on my mother's arm. "It's okay, Nana," she says, and my eyes well with tears. I am so blessed with this child, and I don't know why.

"What happened?" Todd asks. His words are said so kindly that I understand that we are putting last night behind us. My mother's fall has saved us, for now. I don't know how to feel about this. I'm afraid to think about it. I didn't push her. Not physically. Does that count?

I tell him about the walk to school, Wendy's, how my mother

shouted something at me and turned to walk away, that she tripped, about the boy who stopped to help. That her wrist is broken, her rib bruised.

"You walked to my school?" Jazz says, turning to look up at me. She has brown specks in her green eyes, just like my mother. "Why did you walk to my school?"

"It was a nice day," I say.

"Were you checking on me or something?" Jazz asks.

"No, I just wanted to walk her to the school. Show it to her."

"Who would want to see my school?"

I smile at Jazz, then notice she has on a skirt that's way too short.

"You wore that to school?" I ask her.

She rolls her big green eyes with the brown speckles. "Yeah, and I've worn it plenty times before. You just noticing now?"

"I guess so," I admit. "It's too short."

"Whatever."

"Did you eat, Jen?" Todd asks.

"No." It never occurred to me to eat. "Did you?"

He shakes his head no.

"Let's go to the cafeteria. I'll tell the nurse where we'll be." My mother's sleeping soundly. I tell myself it will be fine if I go get something to eat.

In the cafeteria there's the familiar clatter of silverware and chairs being moved. I've spent too much of my life in this building. I've had four different jobs here, slow steps up the secretarial ladder because I was a high school dropout. But I proved I could work hard, and have had my job in the Department of

Emergency Medicine for five years now. They gave me family medical leave without blinking.

"This is where Nana came when she had her first stroke, and where you were born," I tell Jazz.

"Yeah, Mom, I know." She's gotten two scoops of mashed potatoes and gravy, just that, for her dinner. I don't nag her to get some protein and vegetables. Why bother? Will she really jump up and go get them? I doubt it. My fish and peas aren't looking so good to me. I slide the plate to the side, rest my elbows on the table. Todd slides in beside me. He couldn't decide between the meat loaf and the roast beef, and seems to have decided to get both, along with a double helping of mashed potatoes. They're beginning to look pretty good to me.

"I'm telling Jazz about the time my mother had her first stroke. They brought her here. I still had the job in pediatrics. Jazz had to be around five. My mother was working downtown, and she had Betsy's phone number in her purse, so someone called Betsy in Arizona, who called Peter in Colorado, who called me. We hadn't spoken for a while." I look at Jazz, thinking how my mother had stormed out of this very hospital when Jazz was born, just because I wouldn't tell her the name of Jazz's father. God, how stubborn we both were.

"Was she glad you came at least?" Todd asks.

I shrug. "She was in intensive care with oxygen and a drip, attached to a heart monitor. I don't think she knew I was even there. Peter and Betsy came into town the next morning. They thought I should stay at her place with her after she got out, but I told them if she needed help, she had to stay with me. I thought you needed to sleep in your own bed," I tell Jazz.

Jazz gives me that warning look. She used to wet her bed, and she doesn't want me to add that part. Why does she even think I would? "You know what?" I say, picking up my fork and helping myself to some of Todd's mashed potatoes. "Right before Peter went back to Colorado, he told me something funny. He said Mother said that the first thing she remembered after the stroke was opening her eyes and seeing an angel by her bed, come to take her away. When she figured out it was just me, she was so relieved she was ecstatic. I wasn't an angel, but she was glad." I laugh. "She was glad I wasn't an angel. Things work out funny, sometimes."

Chapter Eighteen

On the seventh floor of the hospital Rose drifts in and out of consciousness. She's unsure of what has happened to her. She aches all over. Oh, yes. She's had a stroke. Jennifer was just here. She must have gone to get the car, to take her home. No, not home yet. She has to stay with Jennifer first. Just for a few weeks.

Rose fumes as Jennifer drives them to her apartment. Her thigh is killing her where they took out a vein to replace a clogged carotenoid artery in her neck. They say it clogged because of smoking cigarettes, but she doesn't believe that. They just want her to quit because that's the thing to say these days. She would kill for a cigarette right now, but knows her daughter would have a hissy fit.

"I'm going back to work, you know that," Rose says. "I won't be dependent on anyone. I'm a damned good secretary, and they'll want me back."

Jennifer nods. "I know, Mother, you told me. I perfectly agree."

Well, that's a first. This stroke must have scared Jennifer, too.

They pull into a parking lot next to a small brick apartment building. She'll be a captive in this place for three weeks. Peter moved to Colorado; otherwise she would have stayed with him.

It takes forever to get up to the third floor, and she's near to tears by the time Jennifer says, "Welcome to my humble abode." They step into her daughter's apartment.

The first thing that strikes Rose is that it reminds her of the apartment she and Michael lived in when she found out she was pregnant with Peter. Her legs get weak and she wobbles. *Michael.*

"Let's get you sitting down," Jennifer says, helping her over to a gray, tightly upholstered couch, very forties, very much like the couch they had when Rose was a child. The years wave hello from the couch, from the shape of the room. Rose's legs collapse beneath her as she tries to sit down, and she lands with a painful thud. "Ow!"

"I'm sorry," Jennifer says. "I'm sorry it's so many floors up. Are you okay?"

"Fine. Where's your baby?" She only sees Jennifer and the baby at Thanksgiving and Christmas.

"Jazz, Mother. Her name is Jazz. And she's not a baby, she's five, almost six. Harriet has her, so I could pick you up at the hospital. Can I get you something?'

"A gin and tonic."

"I don't drink," Jennifer says. Rose hates the way her daughter says that. She's sick to death of being judged by her own daughter—who has a child out of wedlock and is living in an old brick apartment building on the third floor.

"Well, something wet, then," she says. "How about a Coke?"

"I don't keep pop. It's not good for Jazz."

"Jesus, Jennifer, what the hell do you have, then?"

"Orange juice, apple juice, and papaya juice. And milk and water."

"Oh, hell. Apple juice. Are you a vegetarian, too?"

"Sure am," Jennifer says with a nod. Then, "Just kidding. I'm making you pork chops and mashed potatoes for dinner."

Thank God for small favors, Rose thinks, then corrects herself. She's not thanking God for diddly-squat. She's still ashamed that she thought she saw an angel. Jennifer leaves the room, and a cat comes around the corner, an adorable black and white. "Hi, sweetie, what's your name?"

"That's Terra, Mother," Jennifer says, handing her a glass. The apple juice reminds her of the hospital, but at least it's cold.

"What happened to that other one you had? Orange, right?" She remembers Jennifer telling her about an orange cat.

"She got out of the apartment and got hit by a car. It was awful."

"I'm sorry," Rose says. She shudders at the thought of hitting a cat.

"Do you have a cat now?" Jennifer asks.

"No. I haven't had one since last year, when Lovely died."

"You had that cat for so long. How old was she?"

"Eighteen years old. I'm thinking about getting another one when I get back home. Here, Terra, here pretty kitty."

"At least you use the cat's name," Jennifer says.

"Excuse me?"

"You know what I mean. Just try and be nice to my daughter, will you? She's old enough to understand if someone doesn't like her."

Rose is about to say something, can feel it in her mouth like spit, but she stops herself. She feels her anger shift, throw her off balance with the idea that Jennifer is right. The stroke has changed the way she thinks—she's quite aware of it. Some things don't seem so important anymore, like holding grudges. Other things seem more important. "I *will* be nice to her. When will she get home?"

"Not for a few more hours."

"Then, I'll take a nap now, if that's all right."

Jennifer insists Rose sleep in her room. She falls asleep quickly. She dreams that her wrist is broken. *No, I had a stroke,* she tells her sleeping self. *Right?*

"I remember when Nana stayed with us," Jazz says. All around us people eat, chat, laugh. It feels comforting.

"Out of nowhere there was this weird lady who could hardly move, who sat on our couch all day. I didn't know who she was. When Mom said Uncle Peter was her brother, or Aunt Betsy was her sister, I thought she was making it up. I thought brothers and sisters were only kids. When Nana stayed with us, I thought that was her name. Nana. My mom called her Mother, but I didn't get it that *Mom* and *Mother* were the same thing." Jazz looks at me. "The way you said Mother sounded so formal, it didn't sound anything like the way I said Mom."

I nod. I know exactly what she means.

"I stayed in my room a lot, peeking out around the corner to see if the Nana lady was still there. One day Nana told me to bring over a deck of cards. She taught me how to play War. I bet I could recognize Nana just by her hands. Her ring finger is as long as her middle finger."

"I've noticed that," Todd says. I try to remember if I've ever noticed that, but I haven't.

"Oh!" Jazz says, smiling. "I remember you made her walk around the apartment for exercise. You stuck cartoons on the walls, so it wouldn't be so boring!"

"Gahan Wilson," I say. "I always liked his cartoons. They were so sick."

"And you set the table with a tablecloth, then we kept doing that for a while after she left, 'cause I liked it. It made me feel important."

"So, it worked out okay?" Todd asks. "Her staying with you?"

I nod. "Yeah. It did. Her stroke was the best thing that happened to us. I guess there's a Gahan Wilson cartoon in there somewhere."

"But we didn't see her a whole lot after she left," Jazz tells Todd. "We went to the museums a few times and had pizza at her house once, but then she moved away, and when she came back, she was different."

"Because of the Alzheimer's," I say, trying to explain my mother. But we didn't know it was Alzheimer's for a long time. We just thought it was her.

Today's her last morning at Jennifer's apartment. The din of street sounds hasn't started yet. At first Rose couldn't get used to so much clatter and activity—her own home is on a street without much traffic—but now Rose lies in bed, waiting for the world to wake up around her. She's gotten used to living here, enjoyed it even.

The feeling of familiarity that washed over her that first day has grown stronger. Living with Jennifer has brought Michael back to her. Jennifer's so much like her father. Sensitive and bull-headed, self-confident and a hard worker. Michael would have been proud of her. He loved the kids so much. She was too busy taking care of them, making sure one of them didn't touch the hot stove while another one didn't run into the street. She remembers Jennifer six, Peter five, Betsy four, she wishing she could just tie them together with a rope and keep them in one place. She's seen those halter things that some parents use now, like leashes, and she understands very well those mothers who choose to use them.

Rose misses her past. She wants to travel again. The idea creeps in and tugs at her. She doesn't really want to go home, go back to work. She wants to see new places, and old ones.

She could do this. She's saved enough money, and if she rents out her house . . . Yes, she's sure she can do this. She has a mind for money. Funny, she didn't know that until Michael died. She's made some good investments, and her house is almost paid for. And her old friend Betsy is still living in Florida. Maybe she'll want to travel with her for a while. That would be fun

A door slams somewhere, and a bus squeals to a halt. Rose gets out of bed, puts on the silly satin robe Peter bought her, and tiptoes out of her room. Jennifer sleeps with her door open, on the mattress with Jasmine. Rose watches her daughter and granddaughter sleep, knowing she will miss them.

She and Jennifer have never brought up all that mess, so long ago. They pretend it never happened, which is for the best.

Quietly walking about the apartment, Rose touches some of the odds and ends that Jennifer collects: little porcelain children which are really vases, Christmas ornaments hung from strings in the window even though it's March, green Depression glass cups and saucers. Picking up one of the vases, the glaze thin and perfect, she wonders about the life of this woman who goes to house sales, who supports her child all by herself, who likes little vases. Rose doesn't know her very well, but at least now, finally, she has laid to rest the image she has had of her daughter for all these years; that teenage girl with so much anger and bad will. She grew up, and became a mother. And Rose knows how hard that can be.

She puts the vase back on the shelf. She'll look for such things, in her travels, to send back to Jennifer. Rose imagines herself traveling all over America, going into thrift shops and to outside markets where people sell the things they no longer need. She has so many dishes and linens. Maybe she'll box them up, sell them. Why not? Life is short. It is time to do what she wants.

Rose rents out her house, and against the protests of all her children, she packs up and drives off. For the next seven years she travels all over America, visiting the places where she and Michael lived, finding new places she wishes they had seen together. The small park in San Antonio, Texas, is still there, although the playground is now covered with interlocking rubber mats and the jungle gym and slide are one big contraption of bright plastic. Kid-safe stuff. Was allowing her children to climb up metal jungle gyms really so dangerous?

She stays with her daughter Betsy and her family for six weeks each year, and for a month in the winter with Peter and his family. She loves travel guides. There's a great pleasure in the planning; where to go, where to stay, what to see, how to get there, how much she can spend. She keeps notebooks of different colors—one for finances, one for postcards, one for the places she has seen, one for the places she still wants to go.

Sometimes, in quaint, floral-wallpapered rooming houses, Rose pretends Michael's still alive, that he's just at work. Sometimes she's lonely. Sometimes she's the most lonely when she stays with her children.

Still, she's satisfied with her life now. She's found new interests. Birds, for one. She buys binoculars and a bird book and keeps a list of all the birds she sees. The two bald eagles in Wyoming, flying high above the pines, that was a moment she will never forget. And there was a flock of cedar waxwing that descended on the very tree she sat quietly beneath on the edge of a lake in Wisconsin. Those glorious birds, all about her, brought her a peace, and comfort in her self, in her aloneness, that contented her for a long time. Yet, she meets people easily. At the Grand Canyon, standing a good deal back from the edge of the cliff, she and another woman joke about what sissies they are. The woman, Holly, is taking a year off from her job as a social worker to travel the country in a small RV. Rose stores her car at a gas station and travels with Holly for the next few months, then takes a bus back to her car. In Montana she meets a Native American woman, Rain Tree, who makes jewelry and sells it at a roadside stand, and after chatting for an hour about everything under the sun, Rain Tree says she's looking for a roommate, and Rose moves in. She finds a job as a temp in a real-estate office, where she works for the next seven months, making enough money to keep her traveling.

She is no longer the girl she used to be, or the wife, or the mother, or the widow, or the secretary. Oddly, she feels as if she is finally just herself. Sometimes driving down a road she has never been on, she finds she's grinning so hard her mouth aches. She'll roll down the window and hold her hand out, just to feel the wind against her skin.

It is not the life she imagined, ever, and that's why it's so much fun. It is not what anyone expected of her.

While my mother is off seeing America, I date men, sleep with some, but never stay with anyone long enough to make it to a one-year anniversary. Then one morning, on my way to work, I get a flat tire. I pull over to the side of the road and get out of the car. I've never changed a flat tire. I don't even know where the spare is. A guy in a truck pulls up behind me. It's August, and hot and humid already, and he's got on a black tank top. I notice his arms first, then his face, and I know this is a guy who will change my tire for me, not ask if I need to use his cell phone. I like the look of him. We're both smiling. His smile says he's more than happy to change my tire. He does it easily, has me hold the lug nuts. When he's done, I thank him. We just stand there, cars pulling around us. I've already seen him looking at my hand, to see if I'm wearing a wedding ring. "Doing anything later tonight?" he asks.

"No. Want to do something?"

"Would you meet me for dinner at Winking Lizard?" he asks. "Six-thirty?"

I nod. I'm grinning so hard I'm embarrassed.

Two weeks later I sleep with him. A year and a half later he asks me to marry him, and I say yes. My mother dances with him at the wedding, a small affair in his backyard, catered by a friend. Jazz is my maid of honor. My brother and sister come, and Todd's whole family drive in from P.A. At moments I am overwhelmed by the emotion that everything is too perfect, but then one of Todd's brothers gets drunk, and my mother wanders off. Betsy and Peter drive off looking for her. It starts to rain. Now I feel okay. I can deal with this.

Jazz sleeps at a friend's, and after the wedding Todd and I make love in his bed. Jazz and I moved in a month before, but it's still his bed. I'm just happy to be here.

Chapter Nineteen

After Todd and Jazz eat, we go back up to my mother's room. She's awake.

"How are you?" I ask.

She looks at me, then at Todd and Jazz, her lips pressed together, her forehead creased. She doesn't know who we are.

"It's Jennifer," I say. "Your daughter." Her eyes open a little and she puts out a hand covered in age spots. I hold it, asking again how she is. She doesn't answer.

"She's very worn out," says the nurse, my mother's new interpreter. "She'll be better in the morning. Why don't you come back then?"

But I can't leave.

"I want to stay here," I tell Todd, Jazz, and the nurse. They all nod, as if they understand. The nurse leaves the room.

"I'll take Jazz home so she can do her homework," Todd says. "Then I'll come back and sit with you."

"Thanks."

"Bye, Nana." Jazz kisses my mother's cheek. "See you tomorrow." Standing back up, she whispers to me, "Will she be coming home?"

"For a little," I say. "Just for a few days."

Todd looks at me and our eyes meet. He nods, and I smile tightly. It's how we say that I have to do this. Put her in a home.

They leave, and I'm alone with my mother. Her eyes are closed again.

I have to call my sister and brother. I tell the nurse at the desk where I'm going. That I'll be right back.

I walk through the long halls of the hospital to the office that I share with two other people. There's a framed photo of three children on my desk. The photo, and the children, belong to Shelly, the woman who has temporarily replaced me. Unfamiliar paperwork covers the desk. I place a palm on a stack of paper, feel the thickness of work.

I sit in the chair, and the seat is not at the same height anymore. My feet don't quite touch the floor. Shelly is taller than I am. I don't adjust the chair. That wouldn't be right.

I get out my phone card, pick up the phone, and for the second time in less than twenty-four hours, I call my sister. Should I tell her about Mother's fall, the broken wrist, the stroke, or ask her how her kids are.

"Hello?" It's Betsy. I'm glad I didn't get her husband again.

"Betsy," I say. "It's me. Your sister, Jenny."

"What is it?" There's no anger in her voice. Somehow she knows that I wouldn't call again unless it was important. She understands that this call is not about us.

"I'm at University Hospitals. Mother fell down and broke her wrist, and bruised a few ribs. They think she had a minor stroke."

Betsy doesn't gasp. She's not the type to gasp. But wheels are turning. I can hear her thinking. "How bad is it?"

"Not so bad," I say. "They think she'll be fine in a few days. She's confused now, but no one knows if it's the Alzheimer's or the stroke. But I can't keep her anymore. Just before she fell, I told her I had to put her in the nursing home. I think that's what caused the stroke." I haven't told anyone else this. I want to tell someone who will blame me. If I tell Todd, he will just try to make me feel better.

"I think that's a wise decision. I'll fly in and help you. How about Friday? Can you call the Sheraton? Get me a room? Oh, get two. I'll call Peter and tell him to come, too." She doesn't mention staying with me. She also doesn't blame me. Did she hear me? Should I repeat it?

"Sure," I say. "But I thought Peter was off climbing a mountain."

"He's been back for two weeks." The way she says this lets me know I should have known, but she's not surprised I didn't.

"Did he get to the top?"

"Not this time."

"But he's okay?" God, don't let him be hurt.

"He's fine. I'll call him. I'm sure you have enough to do."

I can't think of a thing. "Thanks. Tell Peter I'm glad he's okay."

"We'll come help you move her. Hang in there."

"I will," I say, appreciating that she's trying to comfort me. "Remember when she danced at my wedding?" I ask.

"Did she?"

"Yes, she did. Really," I say.

"That's nice. Well, I'll let you get back to her. I'll call Peter. Tell her we're coming."

"I will."

I hang up. My brother and sister are coming.

On the way back the nurse stops me in the hallway. The doctor's examining my mother. "He'll come out and talk to you when he's done with her," she says.

"Thanks." I stand in the hallway and wait.

The nurse's words bother me. *Done with her*. I thought *I* was done with her, once, and then the other way around, she was done with me, and then we came back together, for a brief time after her stroke, during the six months it took her to pack up and rent the house. Then she left, and I hardly saw her again, until three years ago, when Peter called me and said she was acting strange and needed to see a doctor. I worked at a hospital. Would I take care of it? Tell the people who were renting her house that she was coming back, see that she got settled in? Make sure she had some furniture? Get her to a doctor, watch her carefully? I said yes. What else could I say?

She moved back into her house, but she wouldn't go to the doctor. Then one night, at two in the morning, she was found wandering around outside, calling for a cat who had died long ago. Still, even after she was diagnosed, we both refused to believe it. Some days it was easy to deny, other days, not so easy. Slowly, and then in leaps and bounds, the Alzheimer's took over. The Alzheimer's became its own person and pushed her into the background, so that at times, all that was left was her face.

I have lost so much of my life in the last two months, and even before, when I spent so much time dealing with the home-care people who kept leaving, getting the house ready to sell, moving out the rest of her furniture. I miss my job, going to lunch with my friend Harriet, playing loud music; I miss Pat Benatar and Sheryl Crow as if they were old friends who have moved away. And I have lost part of *myself* in my memory of my mother's life; the ordinary events I didn't bother to recall— playing Putt-Putt with my family, the crisp, sweet taste of the cold orange pop we drank there; my brother and I throwing stones at telephone wires to hear that zipping sound that traveled along them; watching fireworks burst above Lake Erie on the forth of July, my sister Betsy with her head on my lap. I have dwelled on what I have done wrong as an explanation for what became of my mother and me, trying to convince myself that all I have to do now is be good, and she will love me.

When the doctor comes out of my mother's room, he doesn't tell me anything I don't already know.

Todd comes back to the hospital and we sit by my mother's bed. Each time she opens her eyes, I explain to her why she's in the hospital. While her eyes are closed, Todd and I talk of simple things. He paid the house insurance late, but it shouldn't be a problem. The truck needs new tires. Did I know I left chicken on the counter? He threw it away.

I don't remember leaving chicken on the counter.

Our words grow quiet and slow. My eyelids close, and he says we should go home. It's almost eleven. We say goodbye to my mother, who is sound asleep and snoring ever so slightly.

On the ride home I tell Todd to turn right, onto North Park.

"But that's the wrong way," he says, kindly, as if I am just too tired to have known that.

"I know," I say. He's treating me nicely because of my mother getting hurt. I want him to treat me nicely because he loves me, knows I love him. Understands I do love him. Last night was bad. I want to make us good before we go home. "There's a place over there, next to the lake, where joggers park. Could we stop there for a little bit?" I point to a small parking lot near the north end of Shaker Lake. He pulls in and leaves the truck running, the heater on, but I'm still cold.

"I blew it," I say, looking down at my hands. It looks like I'm holding hands with myself. "I waited too long. I never got a chance to have a good relationship with my mother. We never really talked. I'm not going to let that happen to us." I look at him. "Let's talk."

He takes a minute before answering. I know he's tired. "About what?" he asks.

And then it hits me, why I've made him come here. "I know what it's like to think someone doesn't love you. I don't want you to feel that way."

He pulls back a little, leans against the inside door of the truck. There's not a lot of room in here, but enough to move slightly away. We're up higher than if we were in my car, farther from the ground. It feels safe in here, relatively speaking. But I've brought up a subject we could have kept closed for a while, while my mother gets better. We could brush this under the rug until we trip on it later.

"Jen—"

"Remember I told you my mother tried to kill us both? On North Park? In the winter?"

"I remember, Jen. You've told me that story a few times, you know."

"Yeah. Well, I lied."

He looks surprised and I'm oddly pleased that he ever believed me in the first place. The first person I told, the old guy who picked me up outside of Chicago, believed me. Hunter believed me, I know he did. Everyone in San Francisco believed me. I don't think Peter ever did, but most everyone else has because I tell it with such fervor. My mother tried to kill us both in an act of great rage and passion. But it's not even close to the truth.

His face squints up. That little slash of melon paint wrinkles on his forehead. "What do you mean? Why did you lie?" There's a touch of disgust in his tone, and I don't blame him.

"Because it was a better story. It got me the right reaction. I didn't like the real one."

"Go on." He pulls the bandanna off his head, lays it on his thigh like a napkin. It seems like such a gentlemanly thing to do, take off his hat, so to speak. I bring my knees up, turn, and lean against the other door. Wrap my arms around my legs to keep my hands from shaking.

"Remember I told you about the night I took those pills and tried walking to Lannie's and fell asleep in the old schoolhouse?"

"Yeah."

"Well, that part was true, but the rest wasn't."

When my mother finally comes to get me at the police station, it's late at night. The policeman tells her they aren't going to charge me with breaking and entering. They're going to use me as an example of their kindness and understanding. She has to sign papers and promise she'll get me help. She hasn't said anything to me except *get dressed* and handed me the bag of my clothes. As we walk down the steps outside, I swear I smell liquor on her breath.

It's sleeting outside, the freezing rain coating the windshield. It's dark and cold, and as I get in the car my mother jerks open the back door and grabs the scraper. "Guess I'll do this," she says, and scraps at the windshield. It makes a sound like birds screaming. Then she gets in the car and slams the door. She's not wearing gloves and her hands are shaking. She can hardly get the key in the lock.

"You're drunk," I say, and she turns at me with her face contorted. Her eyes are squinted, her jaw bones grinding, her face turning red.

"How dare you?" she says. She turns on the car and backs out. The tires slip, and we weave backward, nearly hitting a parked cop car. I almost laugh.

On Lee she tries to stop at a red light, but the car keeps going and swerves to the right. "Damn it," she says.

"Watch out!" I shout. "Can't you drive?"

She shakes her head. "My God, you looked like a fool in my dress. What the hell were you thinking?" She's looking at me as she drives. A car horn blares. We're in the middle of the road.

"Jesus, look where you're going," I say loudly, my voice reverberating inside the closed car. "I can't believe you drank before you picked me up!"

My mother keeps driving. No one says anything for a full minute until she says, very quietly and calmly, "I didn't."

"Yes, you did!"

She shakes her head.

"Jesus, you make me crazy!" I'm shouting now, sure of myself.

"You just won't give me a break, will you? Ever? It doesn't matter what I do, how hard I try. . . . You don't understand. . . . If it was me that died, I'd be perfect, I'd be the one you loved."

I don't want to hear this. She makes me so mad. "That's not true! I'd never think you were perfect, even if you died! You don't care about me, either! Admit it. You know what, why don't you just marry any old guy? I don't care anymore. Sleeze-ball Joe. The next guy that asks you out. Drink and be merry. Drive drunk. What do I care? I don't. Don't pretend I do."

"Oh, Jesus, Jennifer. It's really hopeless, isn't it?"

"Yes!" I shout. "It is! We are! I'm going to keep running away until you figure it out. Every night you go to bed, think about that. I might be gone in the morning!" I got her now. Tears are running down her cheeks. I don't know why I want to make her cry, but I do. I want us to get to the worst place possible, so it's all over, all the bad things are said and all the tears cried. I want to break down and weep inside this dark car with my mother, but I can't. When I get scared, I get angry.

She turns the car right, onto North Park. The wrong way home. "You're going the wrong way! Don't you even know the way home?"

She pulls into the parking area at the head of the lake, where kids park to make out. She leaves the car running. The heater's turned on too high.

"All right. If you are going to run away, do it right."

"What? What do you mean, *do it right*?" I don't tell her I wasn't trying to run away. I was just trying to go to Lannie's house.

"Try leaving the state this time. Get out."

I stare at her. She can't mean it. It's freezing out. She nods her head in the direction of my door.

"Do it right, this time," she says, deadpan. It's the lack of passion that makes me open the car door. It's the thought that maybe she isn't drunk that makes me start to cry, but only with my back turned.

Before I'm a few yards from the car, she drives off. I'm standing near a pile of snow and I sit down on it. It's stopped sleeting and it's so silent, as if there is nothing left alive. The streetlight circles me like a spotlight, and I stay here, so she can find me, when she comes back.

My eyes ache and I rub them hard, tell myself to stop crying. She'll be back soon.

I wait, but waiting makes me angry. In the silence I hear our whole fight all over again. My mother looked right at me and said, *Run away right this time*, and she meant it. She wasn't drunk. I was wrong about that. I won't wait till she comes back. I'll leave. I'll never come back. She'll never know what happened to me.

I walk away, leaving the circle of the streetlight. I stay in the dark so that when she does come back for me, she won't find me, and she'll feel so bad. Only twice do I look behind me, but I never see our car.

I never really meant to leave for so long. Things just happened. I told myself a thousand times I would call her tomorrow.

And then it was just too late. Tomorrow had become ten years too late.

Chapter Twenty

The heater's still blasting, but I'm trembling all over, just like that night. Todd's waiting to see if I'm done talking. His face is neutral, as if he's not sure what to think. Even if he's mad at me, I'm not getting out of this car. No more running away.

"I just wanted you to know," I say.

"I don't get it," he says. "Is this like those recovered memories? Something you forgot but just remembered?"

"No. It's not like that at all. Trying to kill us . . . It's just the story I told everyone. Sometimes I didn't even know what parts I was making up. I told it so many times, I made it seem true, even to me."

"But why?"

"Don't you see? If I said I ran away because my mother told me to, people would wonder what I did to make her say that.

Wouldn't you? So I kept telling this story, this great passionate story, when the truth was there was no passion at all. No great rage. She may not have been drunk at all. Sober. I think about that a lot. Sober, she told me to run away right this time."

He looks at me like he's listening to what I say, might just understand what I'm trying to understand myself.

"I stayed in San Francisco because no one there knew the truth. Everything I did was to get away from being hurt, starting when my father died. I moved away from pain in the wrong direction, one step at a time until I was so far away I never knew how I got there. I spent years trying to figure out what it was I *wanted* to believe about my mother. Would it be easier to forgive her if she were drunk, or not? Did I hate her more for being straight that night?

"All along I wanted redemption, forgiveness, and for her to say she was sorry, too. Here I am now, asking this old woman who's too sick to remember. . . . I have to forgive myself, and her, for both of us. Then I've got to move on."

Todd nods thoughtfully, but he's not jumping in with any words of wisdom. I lean my head back against the cool window. There are a few stray stars in the sky. The heater makes a constant shushing noise. I want to curl up and go to sleep. It would be nice if he held me. I wonder if my mother came back that night, just a few minutes after I walked off. I never got to ask her. I'll believe she did. That's what I will tell myself.

"I want to be a family, Todd, it just took me a long time to figure out how."

"I was thinking of moving to Montana," he says.

I freeze. "What do you mean?"

"In the Kesslers' attic yesterday. I had to open the windows because of the wood dust. It's one of those big houses, you know, along Lake Erie."

I nod.

"I leaned out the window and stared at the lake a long time. It's big. You know what? I've never gone swimming in it. Not once. What the hell's wrong with me?" He stops, shrugs. "I had this thought. Montana sounded nice. See my friend Lou Levin. Build a log cabin."

"Without me?" I ask. I don't know if I want to hear his answer.

"I didn't think you'd come, Jen. Did I ever tell you what that psychiatrist said?"

"No." I know he had to see a psychiatrist, after he burned the mattress.

"The psychiatrist said . . ." He stops, laughs to himself. "He said, 'Your wife treated you like shit, but you're okay, just get on with being you.' I didn't know if he really thought she treated me like shit, or if he was just saying that to be nice. I took his advice. Bought the bike, then the house, started fixing it up. In the Kesslers' attic, looking at the lake, I just started thinking about what he said. Montana sounded pretty damn good."

"And now?"

"It still sounds good. But that doesn't mean I'm going." He puts the truck in gear. Looks at me. "You want to be a family? It's not that hard. You just got to let it happen. And your story? I can see how that could happen, and it could fuck you up. It's sad and kind of pitiful, but it doesn't excuse you for lying to me. About loving me or not."

"I didn't lie," I say. That was the whole problem. Telling him that I fell in love with him three years after I married him—that was the problem.

He backs the truck up, turns it around. I was here once before, I think, but I'm never coming back.

I put my hand over his on the wheel. Somebody's got to touch somebody before we pull out of here. It's going to be me.

"I want us to work," I say. "I want to have fun again. Go dancing."

"We never went dancing before," he says.

"So we should, right?"

He smiles. It's not a great smile, but it's there, on his lips like a kiss.

He drives us home, and we turn down our street. Our house is the fifth on the left. The light in Jazz's window is still on. My mother isn't here, but it's my home. I've been trying to return home now for thirty years, and now Todd wants to move to Montana.

"Let's both go to Montana, for a visit," I say.

He turns off the truck. "Look, Jen, I'm still confused why you made up that story, but—"

"Hey," I say. "I really don't want to go over it all again. I just need to forget it. Let's just think about the future now, okay? We'll never mention it again."

"Okay," he says. "If that's what you want."

I do. I open the truck's door, get out. "Peter and Betsy are coming," I say as we walk to the house. "Did I tell you? They're going to help us move her into Kethley. I'd really like to have a good time, as sick as that sounds. I'd like to have a party, for my mother. Is that nuts?"

"No more than anything else."

We go inside. Jazz is waiting up. I tell her my mother was

doing fine when we left, but it's time to put her in a home. Jazz glares at me like I'm going to put my mother into prison and torture her. Good. I hope she still feels that way when I get old.

Todd and I sit at the kitchen table and drink tea with honey, discussing the next couple of days. We're both trying to hard to be kind to each other. Maybe that will last a while.

Chapter Twenty-one

My mother comes home the next day with a whole new set of pills. She's not talking much, and she thinks she's just come back from her first stroke, and that Todd is Peter. Her chest hurts from the bruised rib and she moves so slowly it hurts me to watch. I called the nursing home and they still have a room for her. The broken wrist won't be a problem. They say Friday will be fine. Two days from now.

I call my office and tell Shelly that I'll be back next Monday, a few days later than what I promised them last time. She says don't worry, they're just glad I'm coming back.

On Thursday night I tell my mother about the nursing home.

"Tomorrow we're moving you into a place where they can take very good care of you," I say. "It's just lovely. So many plants! Do you remember it? The place with the ice-cream shop?

Peter and Betsy are coming. They want to see you and the pretty place we're moving you to. It'll be fun. Really." She nods. Still, I pack her stuff while she sleeps.

In the morning Jazz says goodbye to my mother, then gives me a dirty look as she goes off to school. Todd stays home. He wants to help, even though there will be almost more people than boxes. He's just as nervous about seeing my brother and sister as I am. They're both so successful it radiates off them like bright sunshine.

I bring my mother downstairs to the family room. Her wrist is in a cast and her arm in a sling. I turn on the TV, and the three of us watch a special about meerkats. They're so goofy, and I laugh out loud as they stand on their hind feet and turn their little heads back and forth in unison. I wonder what other strange combinations of people are sitting around on a Friday morning watching meerkats? God, I need my job back.

Betsy has arranged it so that she and Peter land at the airport within a half hour of each other. I would have picked them up, but she insisted they rent a car. The last time we were all together was at my wedding, three years ago.

As I open the door, everyone says hello all at once so that our voices become a big muddle of noise. Todd's standing right behind me, and with his hand on my arm, he pulls me backward, so they can come in the house.

Betsy's much taller than I am, with dark brown hair cut close-cropped to her head. She's wearing a pantsuit of silky black material, the kind I've never worn, and shoes that have thick, square heels. Next to her, I look like an idiot in my blue jean overalls.

Peter's graying at the temples and extremely tan, with wrinkles etched around the corners of his eyes as if he's constantly squinting into a windy day. He's exudes such good health that just looking at him makes me want to join a health club. I show them into the family room.

"Mother, how are you?" Betsy says, and sits on the couch, giving Mother a gentle hug. She stiffens, and I wonder if it's from the pain in her ribs or being hugged by a stranger.

As Peter walks over to Mother, I speak up. "Watch her ribs."

He leans down and gives her a kiss. "You're looking good, Mother. Emily and Dylan say hello. They'll come visit after you get settled in."

"So, how's your wrist?" Betsy asks. My mother looks down at her bandaged wrist, touching it with her right hand as if she's not sure what it is. "Does it hurt?"

"Yes. When I . . ." She puts a hand to her chest and breathes, then winces from the pain.

"Her ribs hurt when she coughs," I say.

Betsy puts a hand to her own chest. "Oh, right."

"Can I get anyone anything?" Todd asks. "Coffee? Something to eat? Jen's got lunch meats, and potato salad, and some fruit . . ."

"No, no," Peter says. "We're all ready to help out. Get her moved in. We'd better get going. It could take a while."

"Not really," I say. "There's not much to take. The place is furnished. I thought we'd take her bedside table, the one that used to be in her room on Canterbury. It should make her feel a little more at home. Other than that, there's about six boxes."

"I'd like a . . ." my mother says, stretching out her right hand as if she were holding a glass. I always think of her as *my* mother, even when Peter and Betsy are around.

"A soda? Would you like a soda, Rose?" Todd sounds thrilled to have something to do, to get out of this room. We're are all strangers—my mother isn't the only one who thinks so.

"Please," my mother says.

"Anyone else?" Todd asks. They all shake their heads.

"Excuse me just a minute," I say, and follow Todd into the kitchen. As soon as I get there, we hug. A wordless hug that says *help*, and *thanks*, and *everything will be okay soon*.

In the kitchen is a picnic basket with a bottle of nonalcoholic champagne, crackers, and the tiny triangular packs of cow cheese my mother loves. There's also a canvas bag with plastic champagne glasses and presents, for a party at the home. Then we're all to go out to dinner, with Jazz, but not my mother, at a Mexican restaurant.

"You okay?" Todd asks.

"Yeah. You?"

"Fine."

"I'll get her soda," Todd says.

I go back into the family room. Betsy's telling Mother that her sons love high school.

When Todd hands my mother the soda in a plastic cup, Peter and Betsy stop talking to watch her lift the cup to her mouth, waiting to rush to her side when she spills it. She doesn't spill a drop. Who do they think they are, worrying if she's going to spill her soda?

"Hey, Todd," Peter says. "Should I carry some boxes to the car?"

"Sure, lets do that."

Then it's just Betsy, my mother, and me.

Betsy and I are sitting on each side of my mother. She can't see us both at once, and I think this must make her nervous. I should move over to another chair, but I'm unwilling to give up this place next to my mother. She's nervous around strangers, and I need to protect her from Betsy.

"You really do look good, Mother," Betsy says. "I like your haircut."

I've gotten my mother dressed up nicely in her plaid wool skirt and her favorite white blouse that has tiny mother-of pearl buttons. I have even gotten stockings on her, and some stylish, but flat, shoes. I know she will want to look nice when she goes to the nursing home. At least she would, if she understood what she was doing. She doesn't answer Betsy. She doesn't even say thanks to a compliment.

"She does look nice," I say. "You really do, Mother. And Betsy, I like your pantsuit. What's that material?"

"Acrylic," Betsy says. "It doesn't wrinkle. It's good for traveling."

My mother turns her head to look at Betsy.

"I'm going to get dressed up later," I say, pulling at the material on my blue jean overalls. "I just thought I'd wear these for now."

Mother turns back to look at me. She looks so confused, and I can understand. This is just about the dumbest conversation I've ever had. I want to scream and shout at Betsy. *If you lived nearby, we could do this together, keep her out of a nursing home. It's not my fault, I just can't do it by myself! We can't afford my not having a job. I can't watch her all the time. She got out once and Todd found her, and she hit him! She hit my husband. I just can't do this. I'm sorry.*

"Overalls are a good idea for today," Betsy says. "Good choice."

"Thanks," I say.

"Two of them," my mother says with a roll of her eyes.

"What?" both Betsy and I say at the same time. This really confuses my mother, and she turns her head back and forth a few times.

"Two," she says firmly.

We wait for her to say more, but she doesn't.

"Two people?" Betsy asks.

"Two sisters?" I say.

"Never mind," my mother says.

"But we'd like to hear what you think, Mother," Betsy says. "Two what?"

My mother faces forward, puts her free hand in her lap and purses her lips. She looks so prim and proper. She's not going to bother talking with these two fools. And then I get it. She thinks us two fools. I know her so well.

Todd and Peter come back. I've never been so glad to see Todd in my whole life.

We take Todd's truck. My mother rides with Betsy and Peter in their rented car, and I'm glad. When Solar got hit by a car and I had to take her to the vet to put her sleep, I laid her on the seat next to me on a towel. She couldn't move, so I knew she wouldn't get up and wander around the car. She just lay there, looking at me. For years I saw her there every time I got in my car.

When we pull into the parking lot at the nursing home, I stall before I get out of the truck. Let Betsy and Peter drag her out of the car. I'll just wait here. But when Peter opens her door, she gets right out.

Todd carries the picnic basket, and I carry the canvas bag.

"Are you okay?" Peter asks me.

I get teary, that he asked. "Fine," I say. "Let's go."

Everyone in the nursing home is kind, friendly, and knows exactly what they're doing. They offer us tea, they smile, they chat in a calm, reassuring way that doesn't seem to overpower my mother. They give us a plant for her room with a pink bow. My mother sits in the high-backed chair in the corner near her bed while we arrange her room. It takes less than half an hour.

"Party time," I say, and pull out the plastic wineglasses. I put the food on her small table, the one we brought, and fill the glasses with the sparkling grape juice. My mother eats at least ten crackers with cow cheese. I'll have to remember to bring some each visit.

"Oh, and there's presents!" I say. All of us have this light cheerful voice thing going here, the way my mother always talked to cats. I hand her the presents, each wrapped carefully with layers of tissue because they're fragile, and because it will take up more time to open them. I really don't want to be standing around in this room with nothing to do.

The presents are photos framed in thin black frames, pictures of Peter, Betsy, and me as kids, Jazz's school pictures, Todd and me at our wedding, Betsy's boys and Peter's son Dylan, all scavenged from my albums, and my mother's albums, which I didn't bring to the nursing home. I guess they're mine now.

Finally one of the friendly people who work here taps on the door. "May I talk to you for a moment?" she says to me. I go out in the hallway. "I think it would be wise not to wear her out on the first day. We'd like her rested before she comes into the community room for dinner. We eat early, at four-thirty. One of you is welcome back for dinner, if you like. Will this cause a problem?"

"Ahhh . . . we have reservations for dinner at six," I say. "But I could come back here first. . . ."

"Please," the nurse says. "Go out to your dinner. Come back tomorrow, one or two at a time. We'll take very good care of her. I promise. You have my word."

I swallow back the tears that rise into my throat. "Okay," I say, so glad to have her to tell me what to do. "Thank you. Thank you very much."

"You're welcome."

Back in my mother's room I explain that we should be going, let Mother rest. Betsy and I straighten up the place in about two minutes, and then we all say goodbye to my mother. When we start to leave, she stands up and follows us.

"No, Mother," Peter says. "You have to stay here. It's your room now. We'll all be back tomorrow."

She just stands there.

"Do you understand?" Betsy asks, and I want to scream, *Of course she doesn't understand.*

"Yes," my mother says.

We say goodbye again. As we walk into the hallway, she follows us out. She has been so good at following us today; how can I get mad at her now? But the sweet nurse is ready for this. She takes my mother's hand.

"Oh, are those pictures in your room, Mrs. Morgan? Will you show them to me, please?" She moves my mother back into her room. "Your family's leaving now, but they'll be back. I'll stay with you now." She turns to us. "Goodbye. We'll see you tomorrow. Everything will be fine." She motions us to leave, and we do.

· · ·

I decided we should eat out, and chose Mi Pueblo for the cheer-ful colors; the walls have bright murals of Mexico and striped sombreros hang from the ceiling like painted clouds. We sit at a round table, Jazz between Betsy and Peter, Todd next to me, Betsy on my left. Jazz and I have ginger ale, everyone else orders margaritas. I've never gotten used to being around people who drink. I've seen Todd drunk only twice. He didn't do anything but slur a few words, but I felt as if I was standing at the edge of a cliff. My mother and I are both afraid of heights.

Peter tells Jazz about his mountain climbing, and Jazz tells him she's decided to become a stunt double. She asks him how you train to be a stunt double, and he laughs loudly. I wish I could laugh, but the idea of Jazz as a stunt double just doesn't do it for me.

Betsy and Todd talk across me about spring bulbs. I'm con-tent to just sit and listen to the sounds of their voices. I want to fit into this family around the table, I just don't want to talk, or tell any more stories.

While we eat, Peter shares funny anecdotes about our child-hood and Betsy nods, adding a detail here and there. Jazz gig-gles when he describes the time my father entered us into a singing contest. We must have been all under five years old, and I don't know how Peter remembers a single thing about it because I'm older than he is, and I don't. He starts singing "Row, row, row your boat," out of tune, imitating the voice of a four-year-old child, and even the people sitting next to us laugh. They're drinking margaritas, too.

Betsy leans over and talks to me quietly. "It was good of you to take Mother in for a while. Thanks. I think the home is just beautiful. I didn't expect that."

"Thanks," I say. "I'm glad I could take care of her for a little while, anyway."

"Your daughter's beautiful."

I smile. "Thanks. I think so, too." I wait a minute, then since she doesn't say anything else, I do. "I hope we can start getting together. How about Christmas this year, at my house? I'd love to see your boys. And we can all visit Mother."

"Yes. Let's do that," Betsy says, as if she means it. "Hey, Peter, how about Christmas here this year? Do you think you can make it?"

"Think so," he says. "I'll have to ask Emily."

"You could stay at my house," I say. Both Jazz and Todd turn and stare at me.

"Yeah, we'll make it work," Todd says.

After dinner we divvy up the times to visit Mother tomorrow so there will always be someone there. Peter and Betsy are staying in a hotel, and will be visiting friends tomorrow when they're not at the nursing home. They won't be coming back to the house, just the home.

Outside the restaurant we hug goodbye, even though we'll see each other tomorrow.

When we go to bed, Todd holds me while I cry a little. "It's a really nice place," I say. "She'll like it."

On Monday, Shelly welcomes me back with a big hug. I have been hugged by so many people in the last few days that I feel well hugged, like being well fed, or well rested.

Shelly shows me what's been going on, what I need to work on right away, what can wait. Only when she leaves the room do I readjust the chair. I spend lunch in the bathroom, crying on a toilet.

After work I go directly to the nursing home. As I walk in the front doors, I stop and look around at the beautiful atrium, the hundreds of plants, the chairs that are so inviting. There are clusters of people, each with an old person in the center.

My mother's door is open. She's sitting in a chair, watching the news with the sound off.

On the bureau are the photos I brought, and I look at them. Jazz is the only granddaughter. The one to carry on the female genes. I'm going to have to talk her out of the stunt double idea.

"Hello, Mother." No more of this Mrs. Morgan stuff. I am her daughter. So be it.

She nods, puts a finger to her lips, nods at the TV. I don't know if she means I should be quiet so she can hear the TV, or if she means I should be quiet, like the TV.

"Hello," I whisper. "How are you?"

She rolls her eyes and shrugs.

"Did you like your dinner tonight?"

"No."

She doesn't talk much, but give her a reason to say no, and she will.

"Too bland?"

"No."

"Too spicy?"

She shrugs.

"Miss my cooking?"

She shrugs, missing a good opportunity to say no. I smile.

"Tomorrow I'll bring cookies. And Sunday, Todd and I are

going to come and pick you up, bring you to my house for dinner. Would you like that?"

"They don't go there," she says.

"Where? Who doesn't go?"

"Them."

"Who? Go where?"

"Oh, you know!"

I don't, but I have a feeling this could go on forever. "Okay," I say.

"Fine!" she says. "Good."

I tell her about going back to work, and she smiles. She always liked working. After an hour of this, I ask her if she'd like me to help her get ready for bed.

"No. They do."

"But I could," I say.

"Don't bother."

"It's no bother. I'd be happy to."

"No."

"Are you sure?"

She nods, a big, solid nod, and then says, "Oh!" clutching her chest. The nod must have hurt her bruised ribs. Good thing she doesn't agree with me much.

"Can I help you do anything before I go?"

"No."

"Okay, then, goodbye. I'll be back tomorrow." I see a bit of relief in her eyes. I think it's because I'll be back tomorrow, not because I'm leaving.

"Love you," I say. And I mean it.

. . .

At least twice a week Jazz or Todd comes with me. We take her out of the building for walks and car rides, trips to the mall, home for dinner on Sundays, but as time passes, she starts to insist on staying there, not leaving. She loses more words, grows more confused. She needs the comfort of a familiar room. One day I get her coat on and we walk outside. In less than a minute she wants to go back in. It is the last time she ever wears her coat.

Peter's family can't come for Christmas. He invites us there, but we decline. Betsy has a vacation coming up in March, and the whole family is going to the Bahamas, so they can't afford to fly in for Christmas. Still, she comes in for two days in January and stays with us. It's both uncomfortable and a great comfort that she comes. Someday we'll talk about the bad stuff. For now, we talk about kids and nursing homes.

A little more than a year after she moves into the nursing home, my mother stops talking altogether. She and Jazz play cards but without any rules I can see. Jazz doesn't seem to mind at all. I've smelled pot on her clothes twice now. I'm waiting for the third time to confront her, only because I don't know how to confront her on this. I can vividly remember telling my mother that she was nuts when she said that she smelled marijuana on my clothes. "Yeah? How do *you* know?" I said, then, "It's just my perfume, Mother," then, "My friends smoke cigarettes, that's all you smell." Then, "Prove it." I'm not ready to prove it.

The comfort of the atrium only depresses me now, and green plants remind me of old age. My mother shrinks, getting smaller. Four people have died whose names I memorized, and their names stay with me. I bring homemade cookies to the floor twice a month, and can't eat them, can't stand the smell of cookies. Once, I don't visit my mother for three days in a row.

One day, when I pick Jazz up from Turtle's, I smell pot on her again. I tell Todd, and he thinks this is pretty serious. We have a family talk and Jazz says she does smoke sometimes, but not much. We make rules about grades, behavior, and driving. Todd thinks we've had a really good talk, and bets she'll stop now.

Jazz applies to four colleges, and Todd offers to go along with her when she visits them. They drive off in his truck discussing which is the best route to take and who gets to play their disc first. She's accepted by all four, and chooses Miami of Ohio. Now she's decided to be a movie director.

My daughter goes off to college, driving a used Honda we buy her as a gift. She says we can't come with her to help her move in. "You'll just cry, Mom," she says, and that makes me cry. I'm becoming a sap in my old age. I clean her room after she leaves, washing the woodwork, polishing the bureaus and bookshelves, making the bed. I like the way it looks for about two days, and then it bothers me so much I close her door and pretend it's a mess.

I try, once again, to like going for rides on the motorcycle, but I still hate it. When Todd rides off alone, I play my discs loudly and pretend I'm having fun in the house all by myself.

Two and a half years after we moved my mother into the nursing home, she dies of an aneurism in the middle of the night.

Jazz comes home from Miami University for her nana's funeral.

Chapter Twenty-two

Everyone stands on one side of the coffin so the wind's at their backs, but it still feels cold and Jazz shivers. She's surprised people can think about things like which side of the coffin to stand on so the wind is at their backs when someone is dead right in front of them. If it were her own mom, she'd be crying so hard she couldn't think at all.

They don't even know if any of Nana's brothers or sisters are alive, but her mom thinks they're not, since they were so much older. Her mom says that the one sister Nana did talk to died of lung cancer years ago. Jazz figures she must have a lot of relatives somewhere because they're Catholic and probably had big families, but she wouldn't know them if she bumped into them on the street. She's going to try make a family tree. They have places on the Web that'll help you. She wishes she'd asked Nana about her family before she died. She'd better start asking her mom about stuff now.

Aunt Betsy and Uncle Peter have come, with Uncle Jasper and Aunt Emily, but only one cousin, Lenny, who's seventeen and a nerd. All her other cousins couldn't come because they had tests or important jobs. Jazz wants to write them e-mails and get in touch, get their help in this family-tree thing. Maybe they could get together sometime when someone isn't dead.

She doesn't mean to be putting people down, especially at a funeral, but, God, it's not like they've got a whole lot of grand-parents they can just pick and choose which funeral they can get to. She didn't even like Nana much, till recently, but she knows she has to be here. It's just the right thing to do.

Uncle Peter thinks they should all say something, in no special order, just as it comes to them, but no one wants to start. They've been standing here quietly staring at the casket, and it's giving her the willies. Todd clears his throat.

"You know, I didn't know Rose all that well. I met her too late in life—she wasn't really herself most of the time. She seemed like a pretty tough lady, to me. In a good way, I mean. I really would like to hear what you guys have to say." Todd looks embarrassed now, and looks down at the ground. Jazz gives him a little bump with her elbow and smiles at him. She's proud he spoke up. He may look pretty stupid in a suit, but he's okay.

Todd built Jazz a cabinet for her dorm room, to hold her stereo system in the small space between her bed and the wall. He rides down on his bike sometimes, just to bring her some of her mom's cookies, and even went and visited Uncle Peter last fall, so they could go climb a little mountain. Uncle Peter sent photos afterward, with a letter saying, *Here's pictures of the little mountain we climbed, let me know when you're ready for something bigger.* But this summer Jazz, Todd, and her mom are going to drive to San Francisco to meet Hunter Phillips. Her mom's been saving all her vacation time so they can go for a whole month. It was real easy to find him. He still lives in San Francisco, and works as the marketing director for Haight Ashbury Publications. Her mom wrote him a letter and he wrote right back, and then Jazz wrote him and sent him a photo, and he sent a photo back. It's a picture of him sitting on the limb of a tree, and he's got a ponytail, which Jazz usually doesn't like on guys, but it looks all right on him, even though he's kind of old. It's really hard to believe he's her dad. She calls him Hunter, not Dad, but in her head, sometimes she thinks the word *Dad*. He doesn't have any other kids. They e-mail each other a lot. Hunter said he'd come see her if Jazz wanted him to, but she kept putting it off. It was Todd's idea they go meet him this summer, and he made all the plans. He says Jazz needs to see him just once, in case she loses her chance. They leave in three weeks, just a couple days after Jazz gets back home from Miami U. for summer break.

Oh, my God, for a minute she almost forgot she was standing in front of a dead person. She keeps spacing out like this, every time she thinks about meeting her dad. Aunt Betsy's talking so softly Jazz can hardly hear her with all the wind. She says something about when she was a kid and they went to an amusement park and Nana spent an hour on the carousel. But Aunt Betsy doesn't finish the story because she's crying too much. Jazz doesn't even know if that *was* the end of the story. Uncle Jasper puts his arm around Aunt Betsy and says, "Well, we all loved her. Our whole family did." It's kind of pitiful, and gets Lenny off the hook. Jazz thinks that she'll speak up now, but Uncle Peter starts talking first.

"When I was just three years old," he says, "Mother brought home these three enormous pumpkins for Halloween. Each one had to be at least thirty pounds. They were the biggest pumpkins in the whole wide world. Dad had to carry them in from the car. She carved them out and put them on our front porch. She said it was too hard to take all of us trick-or-treating by herself since Dad would be at the theatre, so we'd just have to stay home and hand out candy. She put each one of us in a pumpkin and gave us a basket of candy. We must have looked like idiots. Betsy fell asleep in hers."

There's silence for a minute, while everyone takes this in. Jazz doesn't believe her uncle really remembers that. She can't remember anything from when she was three, and she's a lot closer to that age than he is. The first thing she remembers, she thinks, is when she was four and was at some birthday party and spilled juice all over her white dress, and she cried until her mom came and got her. When they got home, her mom poured juice on her own pants, just to show that it wasn't so bad, and then they took a bath together. Jazz wonders if it's the story she'll tell when her mom dies. It's a really sad thought, but you can't help thinking stuff like that at the cemetery, while your nana's in a coffin a few feet away.

Jazz thinks she'll talk now, she really wants to get this over with, but Uncle Peter starts again. "Then, when I was seven," he says, and she rolls her eyes, right there in the cemetery. Uncle Peter could go on for a long time if he's going to tell stories starting when he was three and seven. But he only tells two more stories, and then he starts to cry, which gets Aunt Betsy crying louder. Jazz's mom's not crying at all. Her eyes are wet and red, but she isn't sobbing or making noises. When Uncle Peter's done, he turns to his wife, as if it's her turn. Jazz thought they were just supposed to speak up.

Aunt Emily says she knows Rose wasn't very religious in her later years, but she'd like to say a little prayer for her anyway. It's a short prayer, and both she and Uncle Peter say amen. So does Aunt Betsy and her family. Todd, her mom, and Jazz are quiet, although Jazz says *amen* in her head, just in case.

Finally Jazz steps forward. Every one looks at her. "I'm really sorry my nana died, and I want to say something about her." She's been thinking about what to say ever since last night when Uncle Peter made his announcement that they should all share a memory at her grave.

"I remember when my mom and Nana and I went to the Natural History Museum." She stops for a second. It isn't easy to talk out loud in front of all these people, which isn't all that many people really, but they're all staring at her. She decides to make her story shorter than she'd planned. "I got scared when we went into the room with the dinosaurs, and I was holding my mom's hand and didn't want to go in. Nana asked me what I was scared of, and I pointed to a big dinosaur with an open mouth full of sharp teeth. She said, 'You think *he* might hurt you?' and then she went right over to the dinosaur and made a fist and waved it in the dinosaur's face and said, 'Okay, you big bag of bones. Put 'em up. Come on, loose lips. Lets see what you can do.' Then she stuck out her tongue at the dinosaur and made that noise with her tongue. You know." Jazz is not going to make that noise at a cemetery, but they know what she means. "She shook her head and turned to me and said, 'Well, I think he's dead all right, or just a big sissy. Come on.'"

Everyone smiles at her, but telling it didn't make her as happy as thinking about it. She steps back from the grave.

Now it's her mom's turn to say something.

Todd holds my hand, keeping me here, in place, at the end of my mother's lifetime and the beginning of her existence as a memory. And once again there is no order to her life. She moves between us as a young mother, a widow, a grandmother, an in-law. I know she will come back to me in whispers and tugs forever.

I have my mother's eyes. They're sea-green, and slant down at the end, not up, as I would like. I have her toughness, her bone structure, her small feet, and some of her furniture. I have a daughter, who is my mother's grandchild.

Jazz's words have triggered a memory I had forgotten. The few times we came to Cleveland when I was a kid, my mother would take Peter, Betsy, and me to the museums. She would read the plaques to us in a reverent tone, and I thought the information fine and glorious, worthy of the shiny brass stands. I trusted those words.

The Natural History Museum was my favorite. The dinosaurs stood before us, enormous, ugly, yet graceful. Behind them were drawings of the world millions of years ago, the dry, flat tundra, the spiky green ferns, the endless blue sky. I was so used to sets and backdrops that part of me believed these scenes were really a rehearsal, that given months of practice, the dinosaurs would put on their skins and the play would begin. A backward way of looking at the dinosaurs invaded me; I thought they were something yet to come, not something long dead. I never mentioned this to my mother, who would have patiently explained how silly it was. I did tell my father, who said he knew just what I meant.

I don't remember our coaxing Jazz into the dinosaur room when she was little, but what I do remember about that day was the new plaque in front of a dinosaur that I had visited with my mother when I was little. It said the creature wasn't a brontosaurus at all. The paleontologists had made a mistake. They had mixed two dinosaurs together and made one that had never existed at all. It was part apatosaurus, part camarasaurus, and part plaster. They were going to dismantle it sometime in the near future. I thought they were brave to admit their mistake. Who would know?

I have tried to build my mother's life again, filling in the holes as best I can, using plaster and bones, but every time I think I see her, I see a reflection of myself; she is a relationship: *my mother*. Although she would argue with me, tell me I make much of it up, I am not afraid to remember her wrong, only afraid I may not remember at all.

It's my turn to say something. I thought I had so much to say, but maybe I've said too much. Maybe the simple truth is all I need. "She hated strawberry ice cream," I say, speaking up because it has begun to rain. "I loved her. I'll miss her." I feel Todd's hand in mine, and it's warm despite the cold weather. I take Jazz's hand, and we three are the family I have, and I am so proud.

As my mother is lowered into the ground, the rain turns into a gale, a hard rain blowing sideways, edging its way under the canopy; not a gentle rain but one that will knock branches from trees and tear shingles off well-kept homes. I imagine my father directing this scene, waving his large hands, shouting, "More wind! Get that lightning going! Thunder!" But my mother is no longer here. She sits somewhere, on a patchwork quilt in the sunlight, watching us, waiting for my father to finish the show.

Acknowledgments

For being the best writers' group in the whole wide world, and for all their thoughtful suggestions, I'd like to thank Neal Chandler, Pat Brubaker, Jim Garrett, Maureen McHugh, Erin Nowjack, Charles Oberndorf, Amy Bracken Sparks, Lori Weber, and Charlotte Van Stolk; with a special thanks to our absent Paul Ita for his two-hour phone call. I want to also thank my brother, Roger Willis, for his information on oil wells; Rick Seymour for his help with the San Francisco section; my parents, for everything; and Karen Joy Fowler for, once again, her encouragement when I needed it most (and more than a few good suggestions). For their belief in me (and hard work), I thank Christy Fletcher, Judy Piatkus, Susan Allison, and Leslie Gelbman. And finally, a huge thanks to Ron Antonucci, for his love and support.

Some Things That Stay
Sarah Willis

'If Brenda passes her maths test, it will definitely be a miracle. On the scale of one to ten, I'll give it an eight. I'm going to add them all up. When they hit a hundred, I'll believe in God. But I'm going to deduct some points for making my mom sick. I figure if there is a god, He'll prove himself, even if I stack the deck'.

Tamara Anderson's father is a landscape artist who quickly tires of the scenery, so every year her family seeks out new locations for his inspiration. But when the Andersons move to a farmhouse in Mayville, New York, in the spring of 1954, it begins to work a strange magic on fifteen-year-old Tamara. And while the girl-next-door tries to introduce the Anderson children to religion, the boy-next-door is equally keen to introduce Tamara to sex.

But then her mother is diagnosed with tuberculosis. Tamara has to struggle with her fear of losing her and her anger at being left in charge of two younger siblings, while her father becomes increasingly distant, escaping into the world of his art.

A deeply moving story, with a profound understanding of family dynamics and adolescent anguish.

Praise for Sarah Willis:
'Convincing, memorable ... quietly defiant'
   New York Times Book Review
'Brilliantly told' *OK Magazine*
'A first novel of quiet distinction that lingers in the mind'
   Yorkshire Post
'A luminous, impressive debut' *Publishers Weekly*

The Rehearsal
Sarah Willis

In the spring of 1971 Will Bartlett, ambitious director of a small resident theatre company decides to invite the cast of Steinbeck's *Of Mice and Men* to his farm for a month, giving them the opportunity to 'become' their characters. But he could not have predicted that his wife and daughter would be drawn into the ensemble, threatening fragile family ties.

When one of the actresses fails to turn up, Will's wife, Myra, takes the role, although she has not been on stage since their daughter Beth was born. Sixteen-year-old Beth is furious, having decided the part should be hers. While Will remains oblivious to the tension in his family, as well as the increasing distance between himself and his wife, the other actors find themselves drawn into a complex tangle of relationships, leading them to question not only how well they know one another, but also how well they know themselves.

'Quirky and believable ... consistently compelling'
  Los Angeles Times

The Midwife's Tale
Gretchen Moran Laskas

*'I come from a long line of midwives. I was expected to follow
Mama, follow Granny, follow Great-granny. In the end, I didn't
disappoint them. Or perhaps I did. After all, there were no more
midwives after me.'*

For generations, the women in Elizabeth's family have brought
life to Kettle Valley, West Virginia, heeding a destiny to tend its
women with herbs, experience, and wisdom. All the births and
dates are recorded in tall black ledgers kept by Elizabeth's
mother, but there is also a smaller, red ledger. Elizabeth does not
always feel comfortable with her fate as a midwife and when she
discovers the true purpose of the red book, to record fatal,
unnatural and difficult births, she is shocked and disturbed by
the contents.

As Elizabeth loses faith in her vocation, she also loses her heart,
to the one man who will never return her love, even when she
moves into his home to share his bed and raise his child. She
finds solace in mothering Lauren, her lover's child, but Elizabeth, who has brought so many lives into the world, must also
come to terms with the fact that she herself is barren ...

A SELECTION OF NOVELS AVAILABLE FROM PIATKUS BOOKS LIMITED

THE PRICES BELOW WERE CORRECT AT THE TIME OF GOING TO PRESS. HOWEVER JUDY PIATKUS (PUBLISHERS) LIMITED RESERVE THE RIGHT TO SHOW NEW RETAIL PRICES ON COVERS WHICH MAY DIFFER FROM THOSE PREVIOUSLY ADVERTISED IN THE TEXT OR ELSEWHERE.

0 7499 3257 0	Some Things That Stay	Sarah Willis	£6.99
0 7499 3299 6	The Rehearsal	Sarah Willis	£6.99
0 7499 3455 7	The Midwife's Tale	Gretchen Moran Laskas	£6.99
0 7499 3432 8	Girls in Trouble	Caroline Leavitt	£6.99
0 7499 3403 4	Olivia's Sister	Claire LaZebnick	£6.99
0 7499 3433 6	The Mango Season	Amulya Malladi	£6.99

All Piatkus titles are available from:

www.piatkus.co.uk

or by contacting our sales department on

0800 454816